W9-COL-052

BUTTERMILK SKY

This Large Print Book carries the
Seal of Approval of N.A.V.H.

BUTTERMILK SKY

JAN WATSON

THORNDIKE PRESS
A part of Gale, Cengage Learning

GALE
CENGAGE Learning·

Farmington Hills, Mich • San Francisco • New York • Waterville, Maine
Meriden, Conn • Mason, Ohio • Chicago

GALE
CENGAGE Learning

Copyright © 2014 by Jan Watson.
Scripture quotations are taken from the Holy Bible, King James Version.
Thorndike Press, a part of Gale, Cengage Learning.

ALL RIGHTS RESERVED
Buttermilk Sky is a work of fiction. Where real people, events, establishments, organizations, or locales appear, they are used fictitiously. All other elements of the novel are drawn from the author's imagination.
Thorndike Press® Large Print Christian Historical Fiction.
The text of this Large Print edition is unabridged.
Other aspects of the book may vary from the original edition.
Set in 16 pt. Plantin.

LIBRARY OF CONGRESS CATALOGING-IN-PUBLICATION DATA

Watson, Jan.
   Buttermilk sky / by Jan Watson. — Large print edition.
      pages ; cm. — (Thorndike Press large print Christian historical fiction)
    ISBN 978-1-4104-7582-4 (hardcover) — ISBN 1-4104-7582-4 (hardcover)
    1. Single women—Fiction. 2. Large type books. I. Title.
PS3623.A8724B88 2015
813'.6—dc23   2014041099

Published in 2015 by arrangement with Tyndale House Publishers, Inc.

Printed in Mexico
1 2 3 4 5 6 7 19 18 17 16 15

Dedicated to the memory of my sister,
Julia Taylor Ashcraft

PROLOGUE

Cinnamon Spicer ducked when the tin can sailed her way. The jagged lid just missed her ear. "You oughtn't do that," she said. "A body can get lockjaw off them old cans."

The old lady who'd pitched it brandished a hoe as if it were a weapon. A thin stream of tobacco juice leaked from the corner of her mouth and disappeared among the wrinkles of her chin. "You go somewhere else. I staked this spot this morning."

"You never did anything of the sort, Santy. I was here before the rooster crowed and you weren't anywhere about." Cinnamon pointed at a sturdy stick protruding from the rubble. The stick sported a stained white flag. "That's my marker, and you know it. That gives me eight feet in any direction."

The woman spit her chaw at Cinnamon's feet. "Hog," she said before stumping away, her steps as slow as Christmas. Her sack bumped along behind her like Santa Claus's pack full of coal.

A warm summer sun beat down on the garbage dump. Small fires dotted the landscape, releasing fusty-smelling ribbons of smoke.

Cinnamon blotted sweat from her forehead with the crook of her elbow. "You have to obey the rules just like ever'body else, Santy."

"Heifer!"

"Don't be cross. There's more than enough for all."

The old woman called her animal names. The other pickers called her Little Bit. Nobody shared their real names here. Cinnamon didn't know why. It wasn't like they were doing anything shameful by earning a living — such as it was. Besides, everybody here knew most everybody else. It was a small kingdom.

For as long as she could remember, Cinnamon had been picking. When just a child, she'd followed behind her father, searching for play pretties: cracked saucers, cups without handles, lids with no pots, and the like. "Mind the broken glass, girl," he would say. "You don't want to be stepping over there."

One time she'd found a string of pearls lacking only a clasp. Pap had tied the pearls around her neck and let her wear them for the rest of the day. She had fancied herself a proper princess. She didn't get to keep the necklace, but she didn't mind. She wore her father's praise instead. Those pearls fed her family for weeks.

She flicked the chaw to one side with the blade of the hoe and began to grub around. Just one time she'd tried tobacco. Pap said chewing it would cut the smell of rotting garbage and the decomposing bodies of the poor dead animals cast off here. He'd cut her a nugget from the twist he carried in his pocket. But she couldn't stomach the pungent taste or the way the brown juice backed up in her mouth like thin vomit. Besides, Ma said it would rot her teeth, and Cinnamon had nice teeth. Pap said her smile put him in mind of corn on the cob, the way her teeth were so square and even.

It was lonesome working without Pap. She would like to pray for him like the preacher said to do, but she didn't think the Lord would appreciate being called on from here in the smelly dump. Prayer was for Saturday mornings after she'd finished cleaning the sanctuary. That was the easiest job ever. Way easier than picking trash — though maybe not as interesting.

She liked when the church smelled of soft

soap and Old English furniture polish. She even liked the momentary discomfort of the kneeling bench because it kept her mind from wandering instead of praying. It took a lot of concentration to pray a good prayer.

Cinnamon leaned on the hoe. Lately she'd been thinking about the girls who lived at Mrs. Pearl's while they attended secretarial school. One of her favorite things to do was to watch the girls as they went about town. They traveled in a flock like birds. She liked how they seemed so happy and industrious, and she liked their clothes, especially that one girl with the golden hair.

She had been picking since early this morning, earlier than all the others by a good fifteen minutes. The trashmen collected on Mondays and Thursdays and dumped their loads before sunrise. Cinnamon had slept lightly last night and sprung from her cot at the first sound of the garbage wagons rumbling toward the dump. Her youth gave her a drop on the others. She could run faster, and she had a knack for selecting good sites. She knew which wagon picked up from the posh houses along North Broadway and which banged the bins in the narrow alleys behind the pricey downtown hotels. Her favorite, though, was wagon number three, which carried its load from the saloons dotting Easy Street. She was allowed to stake three sites, and that was what she'd done this morning. She dubbed her sites Park, Broadway, and Easy. Right now she was working Broadway.

She laid her hoe aside and picked up the rake, which she ran lightly over the mound of refuse, careful not to nick or scratch what she expected to find. She scraped away layer after layer of newspapers, kitchen refuse, and receipts of all kinds, then bent to pinch one bill of sale out of the muck. The printed letters and numbers darted like minnows in and out of her vision. She blotted sweat from her forehead. The print lined up. Mrs. Harry Hopewell had paid $3.50 for a velvet cloche at Suzanne Millinery. Imagine that — $3.50 for a hat!

Tossing the receipt, she watched it sail away on the swell of a welcome breeze, then returned to her work. The dry rattle of newsprint and the squish of vegetable waste gave way to the *clink, clink* of shifting glass. Pay dirt! Two cobalt bottles, stoppers intact, nestled like bluebirds in a scoop of potato peels. They would fetch a pretty penny at the druggist.

She moved on to Easy, which turned out to be a gold mine. Soon she had a gunnysack full of beer, pop, and whiskey bottles, which

11

she'd cushioned with newspaper. One more whisk of the rake and she'd call it a day.

Park had been a disappointment. Usually she found at least half a dollar in change in the trash picked up from the hotels, and often perfectly fine dry goods — linens with a tear or a cigarette burn, shirts missing a button, shoelaces, and once a pair of gold cuff links. But no such luck this time. All she'd come up with worth haggling over was a box of poker chips.

After pulling up her stakes, Cinnamon organized her carryalls — dirty stuff in one, middling stuff in another, fragile stuff in the third, wrapped and separated with squares of cardboard. The day was wasting; she needed to get on home, sort her goods, and start peddling. June's rent was on her head. Pap hadn't been able to pick since the middle of May. Thankfully she had a little more time before it was officially due. Their landlord had said, "No more leeway." One more late payment and he'd have the sheriff put their stuff out on the street. Then what would she do?

Pulling the red metal wagon that Pap had fitted with slatted wooden sides, she skirted the dump. Santy shook her fist as Cinnamon's wagon rolled past.

Cinnamon smiled to herself. Santy was

like a tired old bulldog: she still had the desire to snap and bite but didn't have the wherewithal to carry it off.

Chapter 1

1913

The blast hit Sheriff Chanis Clay square in the chest. He lost his balance, tumbled down the cellar steps, and landed hard against a rough rock wall. His head bounced twice before he slumped forward, his chin planted on his collarbone.

His last conscious thoughts were of his father. The badge on Chanis's chest was the one handed to him at his father's funeral, then proudly pinned there by his mother after the general election made it official. As darkness swirled, he wondered if his fate would be the same as his father's — killed in the line of duty. Dead before he could even serve out his term. Dead and leaving too much undone.

His own strangled breath awoke him. How long he'd been out, he didn't know. Probably not long, for a thin shaft of daylight filtered from the half-open door at the top

15

of the stairs. What in the world had happened up there? Last he remembered, he'd eased open the door to check the cellar, but he hadn't drawn his gun. Who would have thought he needed it? Obviously he was wrong about that.

Wincing, he leaned his head back. It felt like there was a pumpknot big as a goose egg on the back of his skull. His hands and feet tingled like a cracked crazy bone — circulation kick-starting. And his shirt stuck to his chest — with blood? His face and chest stung, but they seemed to be peppered with glass, not buckshot. Looked like it wasn't his time after all, and he was thankful. What would happen to his mother and the kids if he died at twenty-three?

Not to mention Mazy. They'd never even had a real kiss yet. He was decidedly unwilling to leave Mazy and all their plans behind. Well, maybe they were more his plans than hers right now, but she'd come around. He just needed to get the house he'd bought readied up. He wouldn't chance a proposal until he had a home ready for her, a home fit for a girl like Mazy Pelfrey. Just this morning he'd stopped by the general store to look at wallpaper samples. His throbbing head spun with images of cabbage roses, lilacs in bloom, ivy climbing trellises, and men on horseback chasing foxes.

Chanis rubbed the sore spot on his head, trying to put together what had happened. He'd come up here to check on Oney, who nobody had seen for days. It was known about town that Oney Evers had been ill for some time, ever since getting the sugar. The sugar was making him waste away. In six months' time he was half the man he used to be. The doc brought Oney to Chanis's attention when the old man missed an appointment with her. He was more than glad to come up here this morning to check on Oney. Now here he was blown against the cellar wall, about as useless as the sack of withered seed potatoes his elbow rested on.

Everybody who knew the Everses said Oney's wife was crazy as a jar of crickets, but he never figured she'd shoot him. But maybe she didn't — maybe Oney did. That would be out of character for him, but really, what did he know about Ina Evers? Whenever there was violence of any sort, folks were quick to blame whoever was most different. Now he'd done the same.

The door at the top of the stairs swung all the way open. Miz Evers waved a long-barreled six-shooter in front of her like a divining rod. Chanis scrabbled out of the line of fire, huddling behind the wooden steps.

"Who's down there?"

"Miz Evers? It's Chanis Clay — the sheriff."

He heard the gun cock.

"I'll blow you all to pieces," she said with a voice high and reedy.

"Where's Oney? I just came to check on Oney."

"And you figured to help yourself to some canned goods whilst you were looking around? Likely story."

Blam! The gun fired. A row of glass jars went up in pieces. Vegetables rained down. He tasted green beans.

"Did I get you? Good enough for you, you scoundrel! Your daddy will be turning over in his grave. Now there was a good man."

"I swear I meant no harm. Miz Evers? Where is Oney?"

"That's for me to know. Now get over where I can see you! I ain't wasting the one bullet I've got left."

Feeling around in the dusky dark, Chanis found a bushel basket. "All right, I'm coming out. Don't shoot!" He pitched the basket toward the bottom of the steps.

A shot drowned out her laugh. The basket was done for. Chanis thought of drawing his own pistol, but he couldn't see shooting a woman. His daddy always said, "Don't take your weapon out if you don't aim to use it." Besides, her gun was no threat without bullets. She was just confused. He'd talk sense into her.

Chanis eased out from under the stairs, brushing cobwebs from his clothes. Raising his hands above his head, he looked up at Miz Evers. She was a tall, gaunt woman with a jutting jaw and long, bony arms. She put Chanis in mind of a praying mantis.

"I'm coming up."

With a whine like a thousand angry hornets, a bullet parted his hair. Stunned, he dropped backward to the floor.

"Huh," she said. "I guess I miscounted. Are you dead?"

Her voice echoed against the ringing in his ears. Chanis lay still, playing possum. He could feel blood trickling down his face, but he couldn't be hurt too bad. He could still think and sort of hear.

She sighed — like he had really put her out. "How am I supposed to get a dead body outen the cellar?" She took the steps slowly like a toddler, bringing both feet together on each one before tackling the next.

Chanis held his breath until she prodded

his chest with the business end of the gun. With one quick motion he grabbed the barrel and rolled away from her, taking the firearm with him.

"La," she yelled, collapsing on the bottom step and clutching her chest. "You just about scared me to death."

He pointed the gun at her. "Get back upstairs."

"What? Are you aiming to shoot me now? Scaring an old lady out of her wits wasn't enough for you?"

"Miz Evers, I'm arresting you. You tried to kill me."

"Well, you was stealing my canned goods. Was I supposed to help you carry them to your vehicle?"

"I wasn't taking anything. Like I said, I was looking for Oney."

"Then how come you smell like sauerkraut?"

"Sauerkraut?" That's what smelled so bad; he was dripping in fermented cabbage.

Miz Evers lumbered up the steps, pausing by a set of narrow shelves just this side of the doorway. "Yep, there's a jar missing. Reckon it exploded on you."

Chanis felt twice the fool. He could see the headline in the *Skip Rock Tattler:* "Exploding Sauerkraut Fells Sheriff Clay. See

20

details page 2."

"Well, come on. I ain't got all day," Miz Evers said.

He hurried past the remaining jars of cabbage, glad to put the root cellar behind him. Miz Evers was waiting at the kitchen table with a jar of iodine and a pair of tweezers. "Take off your shirt," she said.

Chanis eyed the outside door. He could leave . . . but instead he spun the revolver's cylinder, assuring himself there were no bullets in the chamber, and put it on the table. He'd play along with her for a minute. Maybe she'd tell him what he needed to know about Oney if he got on her good side. Unbuttoning the top three buttons of his shirt, he pulled it and his undershirt over his head. It hurt more than he would have imagined each time she fished another piece of glass from his chest. And it was even worse when she started on his face. He couldn't help but wince when she prodded the new part in his hair and poured on the iodine.

"Too bad I ain't got a bullet for you to bite on," she said.

"Miz Evers, don't you want me to check on Oney? He might be ill."

"It doesn't matter no more," she said, sniffling as she stuck the cork back in the iodine bottle. One fat tear formed in the corner of her eye. "We don't need nobody's help."

The shirt he'd ironed just that morning was ruined, so Chanis eased his undershirt back on to cover himself. Tucking his chin, he secured his badge to the proper spot directly over his heart. There. Now he was the sheriff again.

"Miz Evers, you might just as well save me some time and tell me where your husband is," he said through gritted teeth.

Something in the old woman gave way. Her hand trembled when she raised her arm and pointed in the direction of the barn. "He's yonder — just a-laying there with his toes turned up."

CHAPTER 2

Mazy Pelfrey admired her reflection in the plate-glass window of the Fashion Shop, the city's finest ladies' store. It had taken a year, but her hair had finally grown out after the disastrous straightening treatment she'd had summer before last. As much as she hated her Goldilocks curls, she'd never try that again.

"Oh, do stop primping, Mazy. There's nothing you can do that will make these uniforms look better."

Mazy studied her friend Eva. Everything looked good on Eva — even the middy blouse and navy serge skirt that made up their daily costume. For one thing, Eva was tall, at least five feet seven, so her skirt was the fashionable ankle length while Mazy's dragged the ground. Of course, she could take needle and thread and hem them, but sewing was so tedious. Tedious and dull, as were the classes she was taking at the

Lexington Academy of Fine Arts for Young Ladies.

Fine arts indeed: master typewriting, telephone etiquette, office machines, business math, stenography — oh, she fairly despised shorthand with all those ant-track squiggles confusing her brain. A familiar twinge of dread fluttered in her chest. Tomorrow was test day. She was sure to flunk dictation. But maybe Eva's tutoring would save her again.

Mazy straightened the sailor collar on her blouse before hurrying to catch up with Eva and the rest of the girls in her study group. In her usual take-charge way, Eva pushed open the door to the tea shop and indicated a table in front of the window. Mazy sighed happily as she plopped down in a chair. She loved the tearoom. It made her feel cultured to choose her lunch from the handwritten menu, which changed daily.

With her index finger she traced the elegantly looped *S* of the *Salad du Jour.* She didn't care for lettuce — lettuce was like eating a heaping helping of air — but she might order it anyway just to find out what *du jour* meant. Eva would know; Eva was a city girl and knew everything, but Mazy wasn't going to show her ignorance by asking. Besides being smart, Eva was fickle. If she knew how unsophisticated Mazy was, she might cut her from her circle of friends, and that friendship was important to Mazy. She still wasn't exactly sure why Eva had chosen her along with three other girls — Polly, Clara, and Ernestine — to be in her social circle. But she was thankful. Lexington would be lonely indeed without her friends.

When she'd first come to the city last September, she had thought she'd died and gone to heaven. Bombarded by the city sights and sounds — screeching brakes and honking horns, jostling elbows and hurrying feet, shops with beckoning window displays, street vendors hawking hot buttered popcorn and newspapers so freshly printed the ink stung your nose — she wanted to throw her hat in the air, she was so excited. Her sisters, Lilly and Molly, had made the train trip down from the mountains with her, Lilly to interview the dean of women at the secretarial school and to inspect Mazy's room, and Molly to share in the fulfillment of her dreams.

The romance had lasted until Mazy saw her sisters back to the depot and watched the train thunder away, up the tracks. The walk to her room at the boardinghouse was the loneliest she'd ever made. When the door clicked closed behind her, she'd sat on the edge of the freshly made bed and listened to the silence. She'd never been alone before, never. Born a twin, she'd even shared her mother's womb. It seemed she'd been cutting the apron strings when she moved to live with her older sister the year before, but Lilly was as meddling as Mama. And pushy; Lilly was pushy, insisting that Mazy needed a plan and an education to put that plan in place. So Mazy had dreamed a dream and made a plan, but the dream was as elusive as a buttermilk sky — dashing away with the puff of a breeze.

"Mazy, do change places," Eva said, brushing the fronds of a low-hanging fern from her face.

They switched chairs. There was plenty of room between Mazy's head and the fern.

The waitress slid a plate of strawberries and clotted cream in front of Mazy. So *du jour* meant strawberries? Someday Mazy would like to learn French; then it would be easy to read menus.

"Excuse me?" Eva said in her ice-queen voice. "What is this?"

"Pardon," the waitress said, switching Mazy's strawberries with Eva's everyday potato salad.

Mazy fixed her eyes on the server's frilly

white cap. It looked like an upside-down paper cone, like the drinking cups on a train. Mazy wondered how many hairpins it took to keep it perched atop her head like that.

The potato salad was delicious, with half a deviled egg on the side and bacon bits scattered throughout.

Eva nibbled the end of a ripe red strawberry and delicately pointed her fork toward Mazy. "You'll never keep your figure eating that way, Mazy. I wouldn't dare. Besides, potatoes are so pedestrian."

Pedestrian potatoes? Mazy wondered if the brazen Idahos would wait patiently at crosswalks or if they might trample the timid sweet potatoes as they rushed to cross the street. With effort Mazy pulled her wandering mind back to the task at hand; finished with lunch, Eva had taken a stenographer's pad from her book bag. Good, they were going to practice.

"Ladies," Eva said, "take a letter."

With the industrious scratch of nib against paper, the other girls dashed to keep up with Eva's dictation. "Someone read back," she said once she finished. "Mazy?"

Mazy felt a blush creep across her cheeks. " 'Dear Mr. Jones.' " She enunciated each word carefully. " 'Regarding the business at hand, Bumble Brothers will ship five hundred cases of our world-renowned Bumble Brothers Finest Shave Cream Mugs posthaste.' "

"Very good," Eva said. "Polly?"

Mazy's hands grew damp with perspiration as she listened to the other girls take turns reading the dictated business letter. She had easily recited the first sentence because she had memorized it — as well as the rest of the letter. She looked down at her pad. She had used the same symbol for all the *B*s, even though she was well aware that *business* and *Bumble* and *Brothers* had differing shorthand symbols. Eva had gone too fast for her as usual, but no faster than Mrs. Carpenter, their teacher, would do tomorrow. If only Mazy could transcribe from memory instead of using the scribbling marks that gave her the jitters.

Oh, why had she thought secretarial school was a good idea? Just because she'd enjoyed the short time she worked in her sister's medical office? Just because she'd been going on nineteen and it was time to grow up? Just because her twin, Molly, was off to teacher's college? Even her brothers were above reproach. Jack was teaching at the one-room school on Troublesome Creek, and the youngest, Aaron, was already apprenticed to a farrier. Mazy felt like the runt of the litter.

After doodling a heart and arrow, Mazy penned *C. C. + M. P.* in flowing script. She'd always won the penmanship award in grade school — maybe she could be a calligrapher. Or maybe she should have stayed in the mountains and become a sheriff's wife.

Chanis Clay was undoubtedly the sweetest man who'd ever packed a pistol. And he was sweet on her; that was easy to tell. He hung around her sister's house in Skip Rock like an old hound dog waiting for supper. It wasn't that Mazy didn't like him. She must like him, for every time he came around, she had to fight the urge to plant just the tiniest kiss on his cheek. Her heart trilled to think of it. And there was something about that star on his chest — something commanding. She encompassed the doodled heart with a six-pointed lawman's badge and added a drooping loves-me, loves-me-not daisy to her drawing.

Chanis was tall and good-looking and always impeccably dressed; he ironed his own clothes, or so he said. Mazy would believe that if she saw it. Her father certainly didn't know how to iron a handkerchief, let alone a shirt, nor did Lilly's husband, Tern.

They were the only men Mazy knew — except for Chanis, of course.

Could she ever be content just caring for a man? What with all that laundry and cooking and baby tending? But if she'd stayed in the mountains and married Chanis, she wouldn't be suffering from the anxiety that gnawed at her belly like a worm in a bruised apple. She wouldn't even know about the test tomorrow.

Ink gushed from her pen, leaving an ugly blob when she wrote, *Mrs. Chanis Clay.* She blotted the ink with her napkin. The napkin sported a dime-sized purplish splotch, so she stuck it into her water glass, then watched in horror as water wicked up the linen cloth. Good grief, now the stain was big as a silver dollar. She squeezed the water from the napkin and tucked it under the rim of her plate, praying she wouldn't need it again. Mrs. Carpenter would be appalled at the mess. It would be easier if they could use pencils, but pencils weren't allowed — ink only. Mrs. Carpenter couldn't abide erasers.

Looking up, Mazy saw that all eyes were on her. Evidently it was her turn again.

"Mazy," Eva said, "Mrs. Carpenter is sure to ask for a brief history of stenography."

Mazy straightened in her chair. This was

easy. "Stenography, from the Greek word meaning 'narrow,' is a system of rapid writing using symbols or shortcuts that can be made quickly to represent letters of the alphabet, words, or phrases. Currently the Gregg method, invented by John Robert Gregg in 1888, is the preferred method — a phonetic writing system that features cursive strokes, which can be naturally blended with obtuse angles."

After pausing for a breath, she continued, "John Robert Gregg was originally a teacher of Duployan shorthand but found that Duployan-based systems, with their angular outlines, hindered speed."

Pens flew across pads as the other girls took notes in light-line semi-script shorthand.

Eva narrowed her eyes. "Are you quite finished?"

Mazy knew she should stop. It wasn't good to show off, but she'd found all this information in the encyclopedia, and she could recite it verbatim. "Stenography, or narrow writing, was used to write down the memoirs of Socrates."

"And who exactly is Socrates?" Polly asked. "Is he local?"

"Socrates was one of the founders of Western philosophy. One of his famous sayings is 'I only know that I know nothing.' He was tried in court for his teachings and put to death by drinking poison hemlock — isn't that just horrible to think about?"

Eva snapped her pad closed and capped her pen. "That's not something Mrs. Carpenter will ask."

"Eww," Polly said, nodding toward the window, where a girl looked in through cupped hands. "Who is that?"

Leaning across Mazy, Eva tapped on the window, then made a shooing motion with her hand. "Somebody needs to wash her face," Eva said, drawing back when the girl jumped. "Dreadful. There's no excuse for being dirty."

The other girls giggled and held their noses while, like ducklings waddling after their mother, they followed Eva through the door and down the street. The girl at the window was gone, but Mazy caught a scent reminiscent of stale candle wax and something else — something slightly tainted. In her heart she fretted that the girl might be hungry and regretted the half-eaten potato salad left on the plate, but she kept her attention on Eva and hurried along behind.

Chapter 3

Chanis trudged toward the barn. The day had turned hot while he was in the cellar. Sweat trickled down his face. His cuts stung like fire. Taking his handkerchief from his back pocket, he blotted his forehead, wondering what had become of his hat. The hat, like his badge, had belonged to his father. It was a tad too big. He had to angle it just so to keep it from sliding down his head. Thankfully, he had good-size ears.

A big red rooster strutted around the barnyard gawping at Chanis through his beady eyes. Chanis watched him back. When he was a kid, he'd been flogged by one such fowl and had the scars to prove it. He lobbed a corncob toward the bird. A dozen fat hens scattered, squawking like the sky was falling. The rooster flapped his wings, then scratched the ground like a bull getting ready to charge. Chanis rested his hand on the butt of his holstered gun. Miz

Evers might be having chicken and dumplings for supper.

"You'll play hob if you shoot Big Red," Miz Evers said from somewhere in the background.

Chanis felt like a ten-year-old caught with the last cookie from the jar. He was beginning to wish he'd stayed in town today. But responsibility trumped choice every time. "Feed him or something," he said. "I'm not looking to get spurred."

"My, you are a tender sort," Miz Evers said. "Let me get some corn from yonder bin."

"Could you hurry it up?"

"I told you it don't matter no more." She covered her face with her apron and wailed, "I should have gone looking for him last night. He ate a big old supper and a piece of blackberry pie, then went on out to the barn. I kindly missed him whenever I went to bed, but I figured he had enough sense to come in when he was ready."

Chanis had a sinking feeling. He pitched another cob at the rooster and picked up his pace. Miz Evers scurried along behind him, tossing shelled corn hither and yon; a good half of what she threw pinged off Chanis's back.

The barn defied the sun, keeping its secret

34

in shadow. A jar fly droned in the corner of a windowpane, bumping off the glass in a desperate search for freedom. A barn owl hooted softly, not threatened enough to fly away. Chanis paused to let his eyes adjust to the dearth of light. There were heaps of mismatched items all around: a saddle sat astride a plow, leather tack sprang like weeds from among a pile of burlap sacks, a wheelbarrow held three straight-back chairs that in turn held three violins, and Oney Evers's feet stuck out from under a mound of mildewed hay.

With a shout, Chanis dug through the fodder, desperate to set Oney free. It didn't take but a minute to dig his torso out, but Oney had already crossed over. His blue-tinged face was pale as whey. All Chanis could think to do was to pry the pitchfork from the dead man's clenched hands.

"He let the hay go bad. I told him last fall, I said, 'Oney, you're putting it up green.' He wouldn't ever listen to me."

Chanis looked up at the hayloft floor. The trapdoor was open. Oney must have been poking at the hay with the fork when it all released at once, falling right on him, the weight smothering him. Chances were he wasn't as strong or as quick as he'd once been — especially since he'd got the sugar.

35

What a terrible way for a farmer to go. It was like that old saw about women — how they dusted dirt and swept dirt and re-arranged dirt all their lives and then got buried under six feet of it.

"What am I supposed to feed the cows?"

Chanis fetched a burlap sack from the corner heap and covered Oney's face. He wondered if Miz Evers ever thought of anyone but herself. There her husband lay with his toes turned up, just as she'd said, and she fretted about what she would feed the cows. People were too strange to figure.

He tried his best to dredge up some sympathy for her. "Miz Evers, do you want me to take Oney into town, or would you rather I send the undertaker?"

"I reckon you'd best take him with you. I ain't having any visit from any funeral direc-tor with his moneygrubbing ways."

Chanis opened his mouth to say, *"Then what is it you expect me to do with the body?"* but snapped it shut. This was not the time. He'd let her sit on it for a while. The funeral director could figure out what to do next. He went across the barnyard to fetch his vehicle. He was rightly proud of that modi-fied Model T. The city had bought it for the sheriff's department and allowed him to take out the backseat, hack off the end, and install a wooden bed that stuck out over the rear tires. He called it a pickup truck because that's what he did with it. He picked things up and hauled them around.

He pulled off the cargo box that held various tools — crank, jack, tire pump and iron, as well as some wrenches — and slid it onto the front seat. He turned the crank to start the truck, backing it up to the barn door and on in as close to the body as he could get without being disrespectful. He knew from experience how heavy a dead person could be.

Sitting in the driver's seat, he took a minute, mulling over what he'd just seen. There was something niggling at him. Somehow this scene was different from the other unexpected deaths he'd attended to. There'd been a dozen or so of them since he'd been sheriff, but it wasn't something you could ever get used to. He looked down at his stained undershirt. Bits of hay clung to the soft fabric. The moldy scent of mildew assailed his nostrils.

His mind clicked back over what he had seen: a pile of mildewed hay, Oney's face drained of color, and his freckled, work-worn hands.

The hands! Oney's hands were a regular color. Shouldn't they be pasty white or even blue if he was dead?

He flung open the door, praying he hadn't made things worse for Oney when he'd draped the burlap sack over his face. "Oney!" he shouted, taking the man by the shoulders and giving him a good shake. "Oney!"

Oney Evers's eyes snapped up like window shades on runaway rollers, and he took a long breath in. "What?" was all he got out before Miz Evers went at him with words as biting as bloodsucking mosquitoes.

"Only a fool would stand under the trapdoor thataway, Oney. Did you never turn the hay? It wouldn't have clumped up and soured like this if you had."

Chanis had to move the cargo box back to the bed before he could hoist Oney onto the seat. He looked back once as he drove away and saw forkfuls of hay flying out of the barn door. He hoped the rooster wandered into the way.

By the time he got Oney to the clinic, it was closed. It was the doc's half day. He tore on up the road and pulled to a stop in the shade of a tree. Oney was not looking so good, but Chanis resisted the urge to toot the horn for fear Doc Still's children might be sleeping. Instead he jumped out of the car and knocked at the kitchen door.

Through the screen door he could see the doc coming, drying her hands on a kitchen towel.

"Chanis, what happened to you? My goodness, come in."

Chanis brushed his hand through his hair. Bits of glass and hay fell out. "I'm okay, Doc, but I've got Oney Evers in the truck. He's in a real bad way."

"Let me get my kit."

Chanis swung the automobile's door wide, then stood back, ever so glad to have Oney in the doc's capable hands.

"There's honey on the kitchen counter, Chanis. Fetch it."

When Chanis returned, the doc had Oney out of the truck. He was lying on the ground with his feet propped up on a lawn chair. He didn't know how she'd gotten him out of the vehicle by herself. She was strong — he'd once seen her half carry a man twice her size — but Oney was no help.

The doc stuck a cotton swab in the honey jar and smeared the sweet stuff on Oney's gums. Oney was barely responsive. Why was she giving him honey? Seemed like the last thing a body with the sugar needed was more sugar.

"We'll give it a minute," Doc Lilly said, sitting back on her heels, one palm on

39

Oney's forehead. "How was Mrs. Evers today?"

"Friendly as a snapping turtle," Chanis said.

"Hmm," Doc said with a slight smile.

"I'm thirsty," Oney said, coming to himself.

"You'll need to take him to the clinic," Doc Lilly said. "I'll telephone someone to meet you there. I'll be along shortly."

Once Oney was settled into a hospital bed, and a treatment begun, Doc turned her attention to Chanis. "I want to have a look at you," she said.

He told her the story of the exploding sauerkraut as she went over each little cut on his head.

"Stick out your tongue," she said.

"Doc, I didn't swallow any glass," he protested.

"I'm sure," she said before she gagged him with a wooden blade. "But since you're here, I might as well check you over. Take off your shirt and your shoes."

Three kernels of corn popped out onto the floor when he pulled off his boots. Embarrassed, he picked them up and stuck them in his pocket.

By the time she was finished, he knew the

pumpknot on his head needed icing, that his heart was beating proper, that his lungs were clear, that he had no buildup of ear-wax, and that he was six-foot-three and weighed 180 pounds. He pulled his under-shirt on for the third time that day.

"Doc, what causes the sugar?"

"*Diabetes mellitus* is the medical diagnosis, Chanis. It's a disorder of metabolism — people call it 'the sugar' because traces of glucose, or sugar, will be found in the urine of a diabetic. We don't know what causes it or how to prevent it. Sadly, it's chronic and incurable."

"That means Oney is going to —"

"Eventually, yes. Meanwhile he's going to need good nursing care."

Chanis rubbed the back of his head, trac-ing the sore spot with his fingers. "I don't see Miz Evers being much help."

"People can surprise you, Chanis. Oney and Ina Evers have been together for a long time. I suspect they've figured each other out by now."

"I wonder how he survived the night under that hay seeing he has the sugar . . . I mean, the diabetes."

Doc Lilly gave him a thoughtful look. If you looked in her eyes close enough, you could almost see the gears turning in her brain — breaking things down so a regular person could understand. The doc was good like that.

"You told me Ina said he ate a big supper. I suspect his blood sugar didn't drop right away. You found him just in time."

Chanis could see it: Oney poking at the hay . . . it downloading right in his face, knocking him out . . . then him lying there all night getting weaker and weaker. It gave him goose bumps.

He picked up his boots. "I wonder if you'd have a minute sometime tomorrow, Doc. I could use your advice over at the general store."

Doc hung her stethoscope around her neck. "You have raised my curiosity. I would be glad to be of service."

"You know I'm fixing up that old house, but wallpaper's got me flummoxed. I'm kind of set on lilacs, but I don't know — maybe a girl would pick something else."

Doc smiled. "What young lady might that be, Chanis?"

Chanis could feel heat rising up from his chest. Doc knew he was sweet on her sister Mazy, but she might not suspect his full intent.

"I was thinking my mom's front room could use some paper and, you know, Mazy

— I was hoping Mazy might like the same."

Doc's face did not reveal what she was thinking. "You'd best go home and clean up a bit, else folks will think you've been mauled by a bear," she said.

"Or that panther that prowls Becker's Ridge," he said, reaching for the doorknob. "That would make a real good story."

Doc laughed. "I suppose anything's better than being attacked by sauerkraut."

"You got any remedies for these iodine stains on my shirt? My work shirt's beyond saving. I hate to lose them both."

"That undershirt will make a good dust rag."

Chanis missed his hat. Slapping a hat on his head was the perfect exclamation point to any conversation. "Later, Doc," he said.

"Later, Chanis."

CHAPTER 4

Mazy's stomach roiled. Mrs. Carpenter had sprung a surprise on the class. Not only would they take a letter she dictated, but they must also type it, and there could be no errors.

She had managed to convert Mrs. Carpenter's words into the symbols of shorthand without too much difficulty, probably thanks to Eva, but now the real pressure was on — typing under the tyrant's watchful eye.

As if discerning Mazy's thoughts, Mrs. Carpenter rapped her desk three times. Caught off guard, Mazy jerked with each strike of the wooden pointer. It seemed to Mazy that Mrs. Carpenter was way too fond of striking things. As often as she used the pointer to direct their eyes to a particular spot on the blackboard, she used it to smack the back of a hand or to emphasize a point or to get their full attention, as if there were one student who wasn't practically standing at salute.

Poor Polly, whose desk was directly in front of Mazy's, was nearly rigid. Polly seemed to bear the brunt of Mrs. Carpenter's ire. Mazy didn't know why because Polly was studious, but her hand often sported a long, thin bruise. Maybe it was because she sat in the front row, making her an easy target. Polly was a tall girl with wide shoulders, and Mazy was ever so glad to sit in her shadow.

Mrs. Carpenter tapped the desk. "Position," she said with one more decisive rap.

Keeping her back perfectly straight, Mazy crossed her ankles and tucked them under her chair. Flexing her fingers, she held them lightly over the keyboard; pressing the keys too hard would blur the print.

"Begin."

Don't pound; stroke, Mazy reminded herself as she glanced from steno pad to keys. She hoped Mrs. Carpenter didn't catch her looking at the keys. She knew it was forming a bad habit, but she couldn't help herself. Back and forth, back and forth, back and forth until she was practically dizzy — glad to hear her machine's bell announce the end of each row, glad to set the carriage if only to begin again.

Concentrating with all her might, Mazy

closed out the clacking and shifting noises of the other machines, focusing only on her own. She ignored the odor of nervous perspiration emanating from Polly's chair and the piquant scent of Eva's favorite Midnight in Paris, instead relishing the nose-tingling fragrance of ink released with each tap of her fingers.

Quickly she flipped a page of her stenographer's pad, letting the turned sheet rest over the back of the small wooden stand, not taking time to secure it, hoping the warm breeze coming in through the half-open windows didn't flip it back. Finding the perfect rhythm, her fingers flew, making each word a testament to her finesse.

Relief flooded through her; she was nearing the end of the letter. *Therefore, it is with great pleasure that the* Four Track News *announces the acquisition of "New York from an Airship," by Miss Bertha Smith.*

A few more strokes and she finished with the standard business closing. Reversing the rollers, she released the smudge-free, perfectly typed communiqué.

Reading back over the missive, Mazy could scarcely believe she'd wrought such a thing of beauty. The page was crisp and clean, the left margin justified, the right ragged. There were no breaks of hyphenated words at the ends of lines, and every paragraph was indented half an inch.

With a flush of pleasure, she inserted the letter inside a manila folder and placed the folder squarely on the desk beside her machine, careful to retain her posture until Mrs. Carpenter released them with another sharp rap. Maybe secretarial school wasn't so hard after all.

"Class," Mrs. Carpenter said, "you will find your graded papers on your desks in the morning. Polly, if you would be so kind."

Polly knew the drill. She leaped to her feet, nearly upending her chair, and hastened to collect each student's manila folder before stacking them atop the instructor's large oak desk.

Finally free, the students filed out of the room one by one, keeping order until the wide double doors of the academy swung closed behind them. Eva's group reassembled at the shaded low rock wall that separated the schoolyard from the sidewalk. The day was warm with just enough of a breeze to make a sit-down pleasant.

Eva took her usual seat on the wall right beside the stone steps. In an unspoken but recognized agreement, the other girls found their seats. Mazy sat beside Eva, then Polly, Clara, and Ernestine. The driver of an automobile tooted the horn as he drove past, sending Mazy and Clara into a fit of giggles. Ernestine waved at the car and the man blew the horn again.

Polly stood, wielding a short stick, and addressed the group in Mrs. Carpenter's nasally whine. "Ladies, compose yourselves. The academy will not tolerate such ill-mannered behavior. Never acknowledge a toot. Proper comportment is ever important."

Mazy could hear Mrs. Carpenter's heels clicking down the walk. The sole on one of her shoes was thicker than that of the other, causing a slight slap on the pavement. Oh, dear. Polly would be in trouble if she was caught mimicking their instructor. Mazy kicked up her legs and sent one of her own shoes flying. The shoe sailed a little farther than Mazy intended, but Polly dropped the stick in surprise.

Mrs. Carpenter paused where the walk opened onto the sidewalk. "Ladies?" she said, looking down on Mazy's shoe.

"Goodness," Mazy said, hopping on one foot to retrieve the offending footwear. "I'm ever so sorry, Mrs. Carpenter."

Mrs. Carpenter's hand twitched like it was itching to swing a switch. "Comportment, Mazy."

From where she stood, Mazy could see the other girls shaking their index fingers at her.

"Yes, ma'am," Mazy said. "Thank you, ma'am."

With a slight but regal nod, Mrs. Carpenter continued on her way, her skirts swaying awkwardly in response to her limp. Polly began to mimic her halting walk.

Mazy clamped her lips together to keep from chastising Polly. That wouldn't do. She knew Polly was a kind soul and only hoped to entertain Eva, who smirked condescendingly. Mazy took her seat and smoothed the toe of her stocking. She wondered if Mrs. Carpenter's leg hurt and where she got her specially made shoes.

"So," Eva said, "who did well on the test?"

Mazy wanted to shout, *Me! Me!* but a tiny seed of doubt held her back. Pride goeth before a fall, she'd learned in Sunday school.

"I think I did well," Polly said.

"I know I did," Ernestine said. "This was a snap — especially since Mazy cued us in on what was needed to answer the very first question." She leaned out from her seat to face Mazy. "I never would have known the answer without your telling us about the memoirs of Socrates."

"Why does Mrs. Carpenter always try to trip us up with her surprise questions?" Polly grumbled. "It's not a history class."

Mazy flushed from Ernestine's compliment. Ernestine didn't seem to care what Eva thought. Mazy supposed she'd never met anyone else so sure of herself, except for her sister Lilly, who was a doctor, for goodness' sake. How anyone could stand up under all the years of schooling it took to be a doctor, Mazy couldn't fathom. She fingered a pleat in her skirt, remembering how proud her parents had been when Lilly graduated from medical school. And her mother was prouder still when Lilly presented her with twin grandbabies. Mazy shuddered. She could hardly stand to think about having babies. A body could die in childbirth — her sister nearly had.

"Can you not bear to answer?" Eva said, dragging Mazy's attention back to the low rock wall. She draped her long arm around Mazy's shoulders and gave her a squeeze. "Don't worry your silly little head about it. We'll just have to study harder before the next one."

Oh, Mazy thought. *Eva is going to be green with envy tomorrow when we see our graded papers. She won't be able to bear it if both Ernestine and I get big A's.*

"Hold your noses; there she is again," Polly said.

All eyes followed Polly's as she looked across the street. Mazy saw the same girl they'd seen yesterday, the one who'd been looking through the tea shop window. She was wearing the same tatty shift-like dress that didn't quite cover her thin ankles. It was obvious she wore no stockings. A lumpy burlap sack was slung over one shoulder.

"What could she be carrying in that bag?" Polly said.

The sack shifted, pulling the girl's shoulder down. Reaching back, she rearranged the contents without breaking stride, clomping along in oversize shoes.

"This is so offensive," Eva said. "People like her shouldn't be on the streets this time of day."

"She has pretty hair," Mazy said. "Such an unusual color."

"Dirt colored," Polly snorted. "Red clay after a rain."

They watched as the girl scooted down the alley between the drugstore and the millinery. The alley-side door to the drugstore swung open and the girl stepped inside.

"At least she had enough sense not to use the front entrance," Eva said.

Mazy felt a pang of homesickness. At the

general store in Skip Rock, everyone was welcome to use the front door. Closing her eyes, she could see Mr. Rogers standing behind the meat counter, slicing rounds of red-skinned bologna and thick slabs of yellow cheese with a razor-sharp butcher knife. Mr. Rogers always had a big smile and a teasing word. For reasons she could never discern, he called her Lolly. Maybe he called all the young women Lolly.

The store bustled at lunchtime, when dust-covered men with sweat-stained faces would get a fat bologna sandwich or a tin of Vienna sausages along with a sleeve of saltines to eat where they stood. Usually the men who congregated at the store would be taking a break from working at the huge tipple that loaded coal into railroad cars. The belowground miners carried pails of food inside and would not see the light of day for many hours.

Sometimes Lilly would send Mazy from the clinic to the store to get a mason jar of sweet tea poured over shaved ice for them to share with their own lunch. Mrs. Rogers made gallons of tea every morning. Mazy bet Mrs. Rogers had made a river of tea in her time — enough tea to quench a working-man's thirst.

Mazy's stomach grumbled. "Where are

52

we going for lunch?"

Eva stood and smoothed the back of her skirt. "How about a chocolate shake and a pimento cheese sandwich from the soda fountain? We can satisfy our appetites and my curiosity at the same time. I'm dying to know what that urchin had in her bag."

The girls trooped across the street, dodging a streetcar and a newspaper boy on his bicycle.

"Traffic is terrible," Eva said.

"You could get killed just crossing the street," Polly said.

The bell over the door tinkled as they made their way into the interior of the drugstore. The air inside was cool and dry and scented with a curious mix of aspirin powder, sticking plasters, and baby talc. At the back of the store, Mazy spied the pharmacist preparing a prescription. She'd often seen her sister doing the same thing, and a few times she'd been allowed to wield the pestle herself. The rub and pound of the pestle against the mortar as the potions were mixed was a satisfying task. She also liked measuring the drug in tiny increments, scooping it onto a scale, and then pouring the mix into a tiny paper envelope. Lilly said she was a natural with weights and measurements.

Eva meandered up one long aisle, stopping to peruse a rack of hairnets and a jar of Sanitol liquid tooth cleanser. She popped the top and waved it under Mazy's nose. The antiseptic smell was not pleasant and made Mazy sneeze.

"Can you imagine cleaning your teeth with this?" Eva said.

Mazy looked at the price marker on the shelf. "It's expensive, too. Fifty cents, my goodness."

"May I help you, ladies?" the pharmacist said when they stopped in front of the counter.

"Thank you, just looking," Eva said, craning her neck to see behind the pharmacist.

"Anything in particular?" he asked.

Eva rested her hand on her delicate collarbone. She looked as charming as a kitten. "I thought I saw someone I know coming in there," she said, nodding toward the door that opened directly behind the counter. "I wanted to say hello."

Mazy blushed at Eva's blatant lie. Her curiosity was getting the better of her.

"Nobody's come in that way but Cinnamon," the pharmacist said, "and I doubt you know her."

Eva fluttered her hand in a coquettish gesture. "I must have been mistaken."

54

The other girls waited at the lunch counter. Mazy pulled herself up onto one of the high stools. Thank goodness there was a metal ring around the stool on which to rest her feet, else she would have slid right off.

A waitress pulled the stub of a pencil from behind her ear and flipped open a small pad. "What can I get for you?" she said as she stopped in front of Eva, pencil poised.

"We," Eva said, indicating Mazy, "will split a pimento cheese sandwich and a chocolate shake, two straws. Thank you."

The sandwich turned to dust in Mazy's mouth. The milk shake was too thick to sip from the narrow straw. She hadn't wanted it anyway. The strawberry cream soda Polly was sharing with Ernestine looked much better. And Eva's lie sat like a lump in Mazy's throat. She had to say something or be guilty by association.

"Eva," she said, patting the corners of her mouth with her napkin, "why did you tell the pharmacist that you saw someone you know?"

Eva turned her steely gaze on Mazy. "What are you implying, Mazy?"

"I don't know — nothing, really. It just didn't seem right, somehow," Mazy stammered, backtracking like a crawdad.

"I have seen the girl before; therefore I

'know' her. There's not a thing wrong with me wondering what she was up to with that sack. She might have been a robber for all we know."

"That's true," Mazy said, more confused than comforted. Maybe the girl had been up to no good. She shouldn't be so quick to judge Eva.

CHAPTER 5

Beyond a doubt, selecting wallpaper was the most frustrating thing Chanis Clay had ever done. He'd already been in the store for half an hour looking at stripes and prints and even solids when Mrs. Rogers pulled a roll of stiff white paper from a shelf. "Whichever else you choose," she said, "you'll need several rolls of this for the ceilings."

Chanis had not even considered the ceiling. Who looked at ceilings?

At his side, Doc Lilly looked through a book of samples. There seemed to be dozens of different styles of wallpaper. "This is pretty, Chanis. What do you think?"

Chanis rubbed his jaw between thumb and forefinger. The paper Doc had chosen was a dainty flowered print. He squinted, trying to imagine what four walls of rosebuds would look like. "Where's that lilac?" he said. "I want to see that again."

"Here," Mrs. Rogers said. "I pulled it. It's in stock."

Chanis would rather have been chased by a wild hog — which he had once been — than try to figure this out. He'd grown up in a house papered with newsprint and colored pages torn from magazines. The paper was cheap, clean, and kept out the wind on cold winter days. Once a year they glued another layer on. He and all of his siblings had learned to read from those walls turned classroom. Unlike Mazy, his mother didn't lean toward fancy. Somebody might think she was taking on airs. With her gray hair in a no-nonsense bun, her print housedress and black lace-up shoes, Esther Clay was as solid and stalwart as the mountain behind her simple cabin. And he thanked the Lord for that.

Still, his mother and Mazy both might like the lilac paper. That would be nice — his two favorite women enjoying the same thing.

"You want my opinion?" Mrs. Rogers said.

"Yeah, please."

The clerk laid a roll of the lilac paper on a long table, beside the sample square the doc had picked. She tapped the lilac. "This here for the front room, this pretty pink for the bedroom, and this —" she unrolled a fraction of paper printed with teacups and saucers that looked to be dancing across a green background — "for the kitchen. It's washable and I can get you some oilcloth to match. You know, for the table."

"Excellent," Doc Lilly said.

"All right then," Mrs. Rogers said. "I'll have to send over to Jackson for the pink. How many rolls will you need altogether?"

Chanis pulled a piece of paper from his pocket. He'd measured the rooms minus the windows and doors and set the measurements down. "Can you figure the ceilings from this? I never thought about the ceilings."

"Sure. Do you have the other supplies you'll need?"

Chanis shrugged. He was at a loss.

"Have you never hung wallpaper before?"

He thought of his mother's newspaper-lined walls. "Not this kind," he said.

"There's an art to it. You want me to come by and help you get started?" Mrs. Rogers said.

"I've got it covered. No pun intended." Chanis was determined to take care of the house himself — all for Mazy.

"One clue, then," Mrs. Rogers said. "Always start in the middle."

When Chanis left the store, he had dozens

of rolls of wallpaper, borders — evidently you cut them out and stuck them atop the paper — scissors, two brushes, a long washtub sort of thing, and a few boxes of paste.

He dropped Doc Lilly off at her front door. "Would you like to come in?" she asked. "The children would love to see you."

Chanis waved at the two little figures pressed up against the screen door. "Nah," he said, "not today. I've got to stop by the jail before I go home, and I'm kind of anxious to get started on the paper."

"Don't be too proud to ask for help, Chanis."

"I won't. Thanks, Doc."

It was 3 a.m. before the front room's ceiling was done, but it was done and plumb, although that had taken several attempts because the ceiling and the walls did not square. With aching arms, Chanis folded the stepladder and leaned it against the wall. This evening he'd cut out the border and start on the walls. Once he finished with the wallpaper, he needed to drain the well, clean and seal it; then he'd tackle the root cellar.

He'd first noticed the boarded-up house a year or so ago when he and the doc were walking up Becker's Ridge on the way to check on one of her patients. Even from a distance, he could tell the house had good bones. With an eye to the future, he'd been there to place a bid when the stove-up house had been auctioned off in January. Now he owned the place — which sucked down money quick as a sinkhole sucks mud.

As soon as the weather was fit, he'd shingled the roof, figuring that was the place to start. Once that man-size job was done, he ripped out all the warped floorboards. The hickory hardwood planks he'd cut and planed himself gave the house a natural feel, not to mention he liked the homey scent of wood. In the kitchen he'd laid linoleum, figuring it would be easier to keep clean.

He couldn't quite picture Mazy with a mop in her hand. That was okay; he knew how to man a mop. And the house sported double-hung windows he'd ordered from Sears, Roebuck and Co. They put a dent in his pocket but made the house more open and airy.

Taking a glass of water outside, he sat on the porch to sip it. The moon hung over the mountains like a beacon. This same moon and the same shining stars were looking down on his sweetheart. He longed to see her again. The last time she'd been home from that fancy school she was attending, they'd gone sledding. Now it was summer. He couldn't figure why she needed to be away, why she needed to study typing and shorthand. Didn't she know he'd always take care of her?

He dashed the last of the water on the moonflower plant that glowed whitely in the moonlight. It would be romantic to sit out here with Mazy and watch the flowers unfurl of an evening. She'd be finished with school come fall; then they could start their real lives.

Back inside, he pulled off his boots, folded his pants neatly across the foot of the bed, and pulled on a nightshirt. He was happy to be sleeping under the same moon as Mazy.

A rooster woke Chanis at six. He staggered toward the kitchen, glad he'd measured the coffee the night before. Once it was brewed, he went to the front room to admire his handiwork.

"What the — ?"

On the floor, strips of ceiling paper curled around like the vines of the moonflower. One lone piece, held up by the light fixture he'd replaced, drooped like a wet sheet from the ceiling. With a choice word, Chanis ripped it down and flung it out the door with the rest of the soggy paper. He'd have to start all over, but it would have to wait. He had to transport a prisoner to the next county so the man could stand trial in the courthouse next door to the bank he'd robbed.

He set up the ironing board and heated the iron. While drinking his coffee, he pressed a shirt — one job he was an expert at. It could be worse, he figured as he started on the collar. He could be the prisoner instead of the sheriff.

Once dressed, with his badge properly pinned, he retrieved a hat from the hall closet, mourning the one he had lost. Whenever the doc called for him to pack Oney Evers home, he'd take time to search for it. More than likely it was in that wretched cellar. With any luck, it wasn't covered in sauerkraut.

When he got to the jail, Tully, his deputy, had the prisoner ready. The man was freshly shaved and had on a relatively clean striped shirt and drawstring pants. He had a faded jacket folded over his arm.

"Eat yet?" Chanis asked.

"Sweet rolls and milk. He doesn't take coffee," Tully said, as if the white ring around the prisoner's mouth needed explaining.

Choosing a key from a heavy ring, Tully

unlocked the cell door.

"You ready for an outing?" Chanis asked.

"Ready to get out of this low-rate dive," Frank Cheney said.

"I'm sure the digs over to Jackson will suit much better," Chanis said. "I hear they feed you at least once a day."

The man was big as a skinned ox and just as bald. His shoulders barely fit through the door. "Can I have the rest of them?" he asked, pointing toward the nearly empty sack of sweet rolls on the desk.

Chanis cuffed him with his hands in front so he could finish his breakfast. "Watch your head," he said as Frank got into the truck, making it list to one side.

"Heavy load," Tully muttered.

"Yeah, well," Chanis said, "it's not too far to Jackson."

Tully jangled the keys. "See you later, then."

"Later," Chanis said. "Keep the peace."

The truck jounced down the road, dust flying, the springs groaning at each bump. Frank finished the sweet rolls and leaned against the door. Seesawing snores soon filled the air.

With one hand on the wheel, Chanis shifted his shoulders and began to enjoy the drive. It was three hours to town, but the roads were tolerable, and maybe Frank would sleep the whole way.

He let his mind wander, and it went where it always did — straight to Mazy. He'd first noticed her at church, year before last. She was pretty as a speckled pup. Her hair was the color of sunshine on a summer's day, more golden than yellow. She'd worn it pulled back but not so severely that you couldn't tell how lush it was and what it might look like flowing freely over her shoulders. Not that he had a right to think about her in that way — at least not yet. She'd been wearing a sort of brown-checked dress with white trim. A small brown hat perched atop her head like a little nest. He was smitten from the start. He'd held back, though, that summer, afraid he'd scare her off. She was only seventeen to his twenty-one. Not to mention, her sister watched her like a hawk. He was glad for that — Mazy was special. Sweet as honey from the comb, but not silly like some sweet girls. She definitely had a mind of her own.

Lulled by the heat of the sun streaming in through the driver's side window, the rhythmic snores of the sleeping man, and the syrupy scent of roadside honeysuckle, Chanis relaxed. He rested his elbow on the window ledge. Man, he appreciated his truck. Yes sirree, the power of twenty horses in one sweet engine. This trip would have taken all day back when the only transport they had was a horse. He'd seen only two other vehicles on the road today, and he recognized both of them. In his job it was important to know the patterns of people's lives — their comings and their goings. Just like with Oney Evers — it was a broken pattern, missing his appointment with the doctor, that led Chanis to find him in time. And if he'd known more about Miz Evers, he would have known to stay out of her cellar.

Thinking about the cellar set all his cuts and scrapes to itching. He rubbed the back of his head as he steered around a sharp curve.

Just feet ahead, a cow stood chewing her cud in the middle of the road. With a stomp on the brakes, the tires screeched and sprayed gravel up onto the hood. Chanis flung out one arm in a futile attempt to keep Frank Cheney from smashing into the windshield.

Frank thudded forward, then jerked back against the seat when the truck stopped short. "Cow," he said.

"Yep," Chanis replied, blasting the horn.

The cow swung her big, square head back

and forth, causing the bell on her neck to ring, but did not move.

"Give her a minute," Frank said. "Cows are slow."

They waited while she thought over her next move. Delicately, she pulled a few pieces of tender new grass from the side of the road and kept on chewing.

"Stupid thing," Chanis said with another toot of the horn.

"I always favored that sound," Frank said.

"Car horns?"

"No, cowbells. My folks had a dairy when I was a boy. I'd get up before dawn and go up to the pasture to bring them back to the stable. Did the same of an evening — alls I had to do was listen for the toll of the bell." He made a milking motion with his fingers curled against his palms. "You ever drink milk fresh from the cow? That's good stuff."

"I don't know your folks," Chanis said. "They still live hereabouts?"

"Ma and Pa died of the pox back in 1895. Me and my brothers and sisters got broke up. I wound up in an orphanage in Dayton, Ohio. Every day I snuck out. Every day I took a whipping." He picked crumbs from the bottom of the sweet-roll sack. "I pretty near starved to death before I turned fourteen — then they set me out on the street

67

with nothing but the clothes on my back. Said I was the most ungrateful young'un they'd ever tried to help."

Chanis wondered if Frank ever found his brothers and sisters, but stopped himself from asking. It wasn't good to get invested in the lives of folks you were helping to incarcerate. He kept his mind on the good folks Frank had stolen from. They all had stories too.

He cracked the door. Bossy had had enough time to make up her mind. It was time to help her along.

"You say they only eat oncet a day there at Jackson jail?" Frank said around a belch.

"I'm sure they'll feed you plenty." Chanis regretted what he'd said earlier. He snapped one of Frank's cuffs onto the passenger side window frame. "You sit tight. I'm going to get the cow out of the road."

When Chanis approached, the cow turned and ambled back the way she had come. "Get," he yelled, swinging his hat, hoping to steer her off to the side, but the road had narrow shoulders. He'd have to get her to a wider spot.

Around a bend he was relieved to see a woman turning a piece of fencing back upon itself.

"Sorry, Sheriff," she said, holding out a

small bucket of mash. "Sally gets to wandering."

Chanis watched the cow through the makeshift gate. "I was calling her Bossy."

"She is that," the woman said, allowing Chanis to fix the fence back in place with wire ties. "Thanks again."

Just about the time the cow and the woman disappeared over a hillock, Chanis heard the truck start up. By the time he got back around the bend, all that was left was a puff of exhaust and a trail of dust. With a flare of anger, he swept his hat off his head, meaning to fling it to the ground. But he'd only get it dirty, and he'd need it to protect him from the glare of the sun. It was a long walk back to Skip Rock.

He'd walked half a mile, berating himself all the way, when he saw the truck straddling a ditch. Frank stood in the roadway; his head hung down like a piebald mule's. The twisted window frame dangled like jewelry from the free end of the handcuff.

Chanis kicked a stone so hard it hopped up the road like a gigged frog. "You broke my truck!"

"And popped a tire," Frank offered. "You gave me a chance. I took it."

Chanis swallowed anger that burned his throat. "So why're you still here?"

"It's hot, and I'm hungry. What time of the day you reckon they serve dinner there in Jackson?"

Chanis didn't say a word, just went to the cargo box and fetched a canteen, a jack, two tire irons, a file, a tin of talcum powder, and a tire patching kit. Taking his sweet time, he drank a long draught of water, then wiped his mouth on his sleeve. "Ah, that was good."

Frank licked his lips. "Can I have a drink of that?"

"Sure," Chanis said, pitching the tire patch Frank's way, "just as soon as you fix this problem you got yourself in."

Frank turned the kit over and over. "You ain't going to help?"

"I'll be taking a little siesta — sleeping like a snake with both eyes open." He freed Frank from the handcuff, then unsnapped his holster and rested his hand on the butt of the gun. "You're on your own."

Frank eyed the six-shooter. "I heard you was a quick draw."

Chanis leaned back against an ash tree that grew straight as an arrow alongside the narrow road. "You heard right."

Frank proved adept at detaching the wheel and rotating the irons to remove the white-wall tire. Easy as peeling a grape, he slipped the inner tube out. The hole in the tube was obvious. Frank roughed the rubber surface with a file before applying the adhesive from the kit.

"About five minutes and she'll be good to go," he said, mopping sweat from the top of his head. "I'll take some of that water now."

Chanis took him the canteen. It was nearly empty before Frank passed it back. If they had any more delays, Chanis would have to find a well.

Back in the shade, he watched Frank study the tin of talcum before he sprinkled some over the patched area to keep the tube from sticking to the tire. Then he did a curious thing — without even a glance at Chanis, he pulled off his black- and white-striped shirt and doused himself with the sweet-smelling powder.

"Might be a long time before I smell so good again," he said as he screwed the end of the pump onto the valve of the tube.

When Frank was finally finished, Chanis snapped the cuffs back on and waited for him to seat himself before he fastened the door with a piece of twine he scrounged from the box.

He went to the front of the truck, inserted the crank, and gave it a whirl. For the first time ever, the truck wouldn't start. He took off his hat and set it atop the hood. Man, it was hot. He gave it another mighty crank — the motor turned over but didn't catch. He popped the hood. Maybe the truck just needed a minute to cool down; he sure did.

"All right," he said, waving the tool around like he was coming up to bat. "Let's try that again."

"And then what?" Frank asked, leaning out the broken window.

"And then we walk," Chanis said.

"I ain't walking."

Chanis didn't reply. He was too close to the edge. Instead he focused his attention on the crank and the truck. "Come on, Ray. Come on, buddy," he said as he turned the crank. The motor sputtered, then caught — sweet music to his ears.

"Who's Ray?" Frank asked once they were on the road again.

"The truck."

"Truck needs a name?"

"Yeah, you know, like you'd name a horse."

"Hmm, well, Ray's a good, solid name, I reckon — sounds dependable."

"Yep."

"Think I'll name my feet Bob. Bob's taken me many a mile and hasn't once let me down."

They were on the outskirts of Jackson before Frank spoke again. "Sorry about the truck."

"It's all fixable," Chanis said. He wanted to say a lot more, like *"Sorry life's given you a bum deal"* or *"Hope inside's not too hard on you"* or *"Watch your back in there."* But he didn't; it seemed like too little much too late. It was hard to figure why some folks got so much and others so little. His mother would quote her favorite Scripture, about how the last will be first. She would think that made all the inequality going on down here okay. She'd also say that was a mighty good reason to treat everybody with respect.

Chanis parked in front of the jail. "Here we are," he said as the door to the squat building swung open. "Looks like the jailer's been waiting for you."

"Reckon me and Bob's at the end of the line."

"Reckon so."

Frank hauled his good-smelling self out of the truck. "Thanks for the ride," he said with a light smack to the truck's hood.

"Good luck."

"Smells like fried chicken," Frank said, sniffing the air. "Hope there's taters to go along."

■ ■ ■ ■

On the way home, Chanis stopped by an auto repair shop. Frank had not only pulled the window frame loose, he'd destroyed half the door panel. That one act had cost Frank two more years on his sentence.

"I'll have to send off for a new panel," the repairman said, quoting a price. "Stop back in a couple of weeks."

"Two weeks? I can fix it myself quicker — and cheaper."

With one grease-blacked finger, the repairman tapped the work sheet Chanis was holding. "We gave you a discount, seeing as how you're the law. Have at it if you think you can do better."

"Sorry," Chanis said. "Call me when you get the parts."

Chanis drove home in a sour mood. The last couple of days had been as aggravating as a cloud of gnats. Maybe he'd stop at the diner for supper. Maybe that would cheer him up. When Mazy was home, he'd often drop by the doc's house and take supper with them. Doc always made him feel welcome. And Mazy . . . well, Mazy was the sunshine of his life.

He turned his head as far to the right and then to the left as he could and still keep his eyes on the road. The muscles in his neck screamed in protest. That session with the wallpaper had left him stiff and sore. But still, he couldn't wait to tackle the ceiling again. He drove right past the diner and on up the road toward home. He had to finish so that he could start on the other projects. Thinking how happy Mazy would be to see the house all prettied up lifted his spirits.

But a sense of unease crept up his backbone when he reached the house. The back door was propped open, and he could hear voices through a window he was sure he hadn't left up.

Chanis eased out of the truck and slipped his gun from the holster. It was already loaded. Crouching down, he duckwalked to the window. He laid his hat down in the grass before raising his head in order to look in.

He could hardly believe what he saw. His house was full of women. Mrs. Rogers smoothed lilac paper with the long, flat brush she'd sold him yesterday. A lady he recognized from church sat in his favorite chair coiling narrow strips of border into a roll. Another woman — he thought she was

75

Tully's wife, Rhoda — swept debris into a dustpan, and two others (one being the doc's housekeeper, Miz Armina Tippen) busied themselves in the adjoining kitchen, which he could see through the pass-way. The air was heavy with the scent of starch and damp paper.

Stooping back down, he made his way to the front door he rarely used. He knocked his boots against the scraper, making all the noise he could before he jiggled the door-knob.

The ladies greeted him with "Surprise! Surprise!" as soon as he stepped inside.

Surprise was a weak sister to what he actually felt, for the front room was awash in lilacs. The ceiling was pristine white.

Mrs. Rogers stepped forward. "I hope I haven't overstepped my bounds, Sheriff, but I came by to drop off the rose print for the bedroom. I found enough rolls in the store-room to fill your order. Anyway, I saw you weren't home. I told my husband about it, and he said you were gone to Jackson for the day. So I got the ladies together." She swept the air with her arm. "Well, we hope you're pleased."

What could he say? *"You're trespassing on private property"*? Nobody locked their doors hereabouts; it wasn't like they were breaking and entering. And he had left the ruined ceiling paper on the porch for the whole world to see. Besides, the ladies were beaming with pride.

"You sure caught me off guard," he said. "I don't know how you got that ceiling so straight."

"I'll have to order more rolls to replace what you . . ."

"Made a mess of?" Chanis said with a grin. "I reckon it wasn't as easy as I thought."

The women tittered and tee-heed.

"Some things take a woman's touch," Mrs. Rogers said. "Now, if you'll give us about an hour, we'll be out of your hair. All that's left to do is the border."

Chanis turned the truck around and drove back into Skip Rock. He pulled up at the diner and went inside. When he came back out, he was balancing two pies in his hands — one butterscotch and one chocolate. The ladies deserved a treat.

CHAPTER 6

Mazy laced her fingers in her lap as the instructor finished the day's lesson on carbon copies. It was one she dearly needed, for the pads of her fingers were often smudged with ink. How clever to carry an old soft glove in one's pocket for handling the carbon sheets, but it was hard to keep her mind on the lesson. The desire to open the manila folder on her desk was as strong as twice-brewed coffee. She could hardly wait to see the big navy-blue *A* on yesterday's test.

Mrs. Carpenter stood straight as a rod behind her desk. "Ladies," she said, "you may open your folders."

Mazy's eyes saw red — red, not blue, and *D* not *A*. She closed the folder and looked for someone else's name. But *Mazy Pelfrey* was neatly printed in the right-hand corner. She closed her eyes tightly before opening the file again. Very slowly she unclenched her eyes and stared at the grade through the fringe of her lashes. How could she have done so poorly?

The explanation was printed just below the *D. Mistakes in spelling will not be tolerated.* Spelling? Spelling was Mazy's long suit. She hadn't missed a spelling word since third grade. She had nine blue ribbons from nine spelling bees to prove it.

Quickly she scanned the page. Her heart sank. There it was near the end of the letter. *Anounce* — she'd left off an *n,* of all things. Heat stained her cheeks. She wished to be a tiny brown wren so she could fly right out the open window and wing her way anywhere but here.

"If you received a passing mark on your test, you may leave," Mrs. Carpenter said. "If you did not, reapply yourself to the task."

Every chair pushed back except hers and mousy Mirada Pottage's. Poor Mirada — she had earnestly earned her nickname. Mazy wondered what her own should be. Family lore was that her mother had named Mazy and Molly after favorite cows. At the moment, Mazy felt sure that was correct. There was nothing dumber than a cow — unless it was a chicken. Thank goodness Mama hadn't named her Biddy.

Mrs. Carpenter's rod struck Mazy's desk.

"Begin," she said.

Mirada's typewriter was already clacking before Mazy loaded a fresh sheet of paper into her own. It was easier this time. She remembered the letter's content from yesterday, but she was still nervous because there was no Polly to block her from Mrs. Carpenter's all-knowing gaze. She cocked her head sideways so it would appear that she was looking at the steno pad and not the keyboard. Her fingers felt thick as cold molasses, and halfway down the page she hit the keys so clumsily it caused them to jam like piglets at a foul-smelling trough. The page was smudged. She would have to start all over.

Mirada curtsied and scurried from the room after presenting her typed sheet to Mrs. Carpenter. Now there was no one left to be the dunce but Mazy. And a dunce she felt when, nearing the closing remarks, the carriage suddenly stopped.

"The machine has reached the end of the ribbon, and I have reached the end of my patience," Mrs. Carpenter said. "We are on a tight schedule, and you must try harder to keep up."

Mazy blinked back a shimmer of tears.

"You wouldn't want to hold the rest of the girls back, would you, Miss Pelfrey?"

"No, ma'am."

"You may go."

Shoulders slumped, Mazy shuffled toward the door. Humiliation was a heavy load.

"Miss Pelfrey." Mrs. Carpenter called her back.

Mazy stood sobbing in front of her instructor. Mrs. Carpenter put the pointer on her desk and lifted Mazy's chin with one hand. Mazy couldn't meet her eyes.

"A bit of advice, Miss Pelfrey. You must learn to master your mind if you want to be good at this. The machine doesn't respond well to woolgathering. It requires a steady hand."

"I'll do better."

"You must if you wish to complete this course with your companions."

Mrs. Carpenter turned her attention to the folders on her desk.

"I'm truly sorry," Mazy said, her sobs turning to soft hiccups. She felt just like Socrates. She only knew that she knew nothing.

"We all have something to overcome," Mrs. Carpenter said. "Now, head up and shoulders back. Good posture is an essential element to the wardrobe of a typewriter girl."

■ ■ ■ ■

In her room, Mazy blew her nose and splashed cold water on her mottled face. The other girls were probably having lunch. No one had waited for her. More than likely she was off Eva's list for good. She knelt beside her narrow bed, asking the Lord for strength to make the right decision. Finished with her hasty prayer, she pulled the suitcase out from underneath the bed and unclasped the locks. In the silk pouch pocket was the envelope of money Lilly had given her to keep for emergencies. There was more than enough for a train ticket to Lilly's house.

The thought washed over her with a longing so fierce she was glad she was already kneeling. By late evening she could be sitting in her sister's kitchen. Lilly would be disappointed, but she would understand that Mazy was not cut out for higher education. And Chanis — dear Chanis, he would take her homecoming as a sign she was ready for marriage. Maybe she was. In her humiliated state, the thought of someone else caring for her, releasing her from worry over tests and studies, was as enticing as a soft breeze on a hot summer night. Marriage — the tie that binds. And binds . . .

and binds.

With a decisive snap, the suitcase closed. She would give secretarial school one more try. Shoving the case back under the bed, she got to her feet, shaking a rim of dust from her navy skirt. Even on her knees she had been woolgathering.

At the dresser she shared with three other girls, Mazy dabbed a bit of face powder under her swollen eyes. She'd see if she could find the others. Hopefully it wasn't too late for dessert.

Mazy peered through the plate-glass drugstore window. She didn't see any of the girls. Phooey. She'd already checked the tea shop. They must have gone to the library.

"Your hair's the same as mine, only different."

Mazy jumped, startled to hear a strange voice addressing her. It was the girl with the sack on her back. She was slight of build and decidedly unkempt, but very pretty. The spray of freckles across her pert nose matched the color of her hair — more sassafras tea than red-clay dirt. And her hair was indeed as curly as Mazy's.

"My goodness," Mazy said. "Where'd you come from?"

"The dump," she said.

"The dump?"

"Yeah, where they leave the garbage."

"I see," Mazy said, though she didn't. The girl's sack was enticingly close. Eva would be very pleased if she found out what was in it.

The girl turned away and cupped her hands against the window, peering in. "I like to watch people eat," she said. "Look, you can see the soda fountain. See, that lady's having a sandwich and potato chips. I might have some of those chips."

Mazy opened the door and indicated for the girl to go ahead of her. She could watch what she did with that bag on her shoulder.

"I'm not allowed in this way," she said.

Mazy could hear the girl's stomach rumbling. She doubted she had money for chips. "Would you share some lunch with me? We could walk over to the park and sit at one of the picnic tables."

The girl looked at Mazy with the biggest brown eyes she had ever seen. They were perfectly round with thick, dark lashes. "I've got work to do — but there's a bench around back. You want to go around back?"

"All right. I'll meet you there. What would you like to eat?"

"It's been a long time since breakfast. I'd eat a bear if I could catch one."

Mazy carried two chicken salad sandwiches, a side of kettle chips, and two orange cream sodas around to the back of the drugstore. The girl was washing something under an outdoor faucet. White bones gleamed in the glare of the sun. Bones! The girl was washing bones. Even though Mazy was a farm girl, the sight made her squeamish.

When the girl saw Mazy, she laid one more bone atop those already set aside to dry. Upending the burlap bag, she shook it until a sliver of soap plopped out. After washing her hands vigorously under the flowing faucet, she dried them on her skirt tail.

The bench was under the shade of a spindly catalpa tree. Huge green seed pods hung like Christmas decorations from its branches. Mazy had once caught her brother Aaron trying to smoke one of those dried beans. He'd coughed and gagged and threatened her direly if she ever tried to do the same.

Mazy spread a napkin on the bench and arranged the sandwiches. The brown-paper poke was already stained with grease from the potato chips. The grease and a generous shaking of salt were what made them so good. When the girl sat down, Mazy handed her a soda. "Oh, dear, I should have had them opened."

The girl popped up from the bench like a sprung jack-in-the-box. Her sassafras curls bounced wildly around her small face. Taking her bottle and Mazy's, she pried the lids off with a bottle opener fastened to the side of the tree. "Lots of folks use this church key," she said, "especially on Saturday nights."

Mazy nearly choked on her chicken salad. Church key? She'd never heard such. She'd have to ask Chanis if he knew the term next time she saw him. But she suspected that the folks using the "key" on Saturday nights weren't in church come Sunday mornings.

While the girl crunched chips, Mazy searched her mind, trying to find a delicate way to ask an obvious question. "I'm curious," she finally said, "as to why you were washing bones."

"The drug man won't take them if they have stuff on them," the girl said with a shrug.

Mazy fished. "Drug man?"

"You know — the pharmacist. I trade him stuff for medicine. Sometimes I have enough extra that I make money, too, but not very often, now that Pa's taken a turn."

The girl neatly folded the potato chip sack and asked, "You want this?" When Mazy shook her head, she stuck the bag in her pocket. "I've got to be going. The bones look better when they're still wet."

"Wait," Mazy said, touching the girl's arm. "What's your name? Mine is Mazy Pelfrey."

"Cinnamon Spicer. Glad to make your acquaintance."

"Pretty name."

"Yeah, I like it," she said, rinsing the bottles before offering them to Mazy. "You can get a penny apiece."

"You keep them."

"Okay," Cinnamon said, putting the bottles in her sack. "Well, see you sometime."

Stacks of musty books muffled Mazy's footsteps as she made her way to the reading room of the library, where she hoped to find her friends. Her heart sank when she saw Clara at Eva's right hand — Mazy's spot until now. Embarrassed, she turned to leave, but it was too late. Ernestine, book in hand, was waving her over.

As Mazy slid in next to Ernestine, Eva glanced up from a note she was taking. The smile on her face was as self-satisfied as the

Cheshire cat's in Mazy's childhood copy of *Alice's Adventures in Wonderland.*

"Gracious, Mazy," Eva stage-whispered, "I thought Mrs. Carpenter had eaten you for lunch."

"You for the main course," Clara simpered, adjusting her spectacles, "and Mousy Mirada for dessert."

The girls all chuckled under their breath except for Ernestine, who held her book to cover her mouth and whispered, "Consider the source" for Mazy's ear alone.

Mazy was thankful for her comment, but it wasn't Ernestine's attention she hankered for. "I found out what was in that girl's sack," she said.

Eva licked her lips and leaned toward her. "Pray tell."

"Pop bottles," Mazy said, put off by the gleam in Eva's eyes.

"Oh," Eva said, "how common. How did you find out?"

"I saw her outside the drugstore. She was putting some in her bag."

Eva fanned her face with an open hand. "Boring," she said. "Fishing for pennies."

"She needs more than pennies," Clara said. "She needs a case of Ivory soap."

"It will take more than a case to make her 99 percent pure," Eva said. "Now on to something important. Let's go to High Bridge tomorrow afternoon. We can take a picnic supper and stay for the music and dancing."

"Who will we dance with?" Mazy asked, her mood lightening considerably.

Eva raised her eyebrows. "That remains to be seen."

CHAPTER 7

The room Mazy shared with Clara, Polly, and Ernestine looked like an explosion in a dress shop. Polly, unfortunately dressed in yellow sateen, hogged the standing mirror while Clara begged for someone to loan her some dress shoes.

Mazy held a pair of black patent pumps up for perusal. "What size? These are fives."

"I'll make them work," Clara said.

Mazy had her doubts as she watched Clara squeeze her feet into the shiny black shoes.

"Perfect," Clara said.

Mazy shrugged. They were Clara's feet, and Mazy was glad to lend the shoes. She would wear the pretty kid slippers that were dyed to match her lavender empire-line frock.

"Is it true what they say about patent leather?" Polly asked.

Clara looked askance. "What do they say?"

"That the shiny surface reflects the wearer's underthings," Polly said.

The girls gathered around Clara's feet.

"It's snowing down south, but that has nothing to do with your shoes," Polly said.

"Sit, Clara," Mazy said, "and I'll fix your straps to keep your slip from peeking out under your dress."

"All my slips are too long now that dresses are shorter," Clara said, taking a seat at the dresser and sliding her dress down from her shoulders.

Mazy threaded a needle and whipped two stitches in each strap.

Clara caught her eye in the dresser's mirror. "I'm sorry for teasing you yesterday, Mazy."

"That's okay, Clara. I thought Mrs. Carpenter was going to eat me too."

Looking sophisticated and older than her years, Eva swept into the room. Her moss-green gown was a perfect complement to her creamy complexion and auburn tresses. "Mazy," she said, "what did you do to your hair?"

Mazy fretted with the lavender ribbon capturing her Goldilocks curls.

"You look like you're twelve years old," Eva said, motioning for Mazy to turn her back. Mazy was so much shorter than Eva she didn't even have to stoop as Eva untied the ribbon and, with quick upward twists and turns, shaped Mazy's boisterous curls into a sleek roll much like her own. "There, that's better," she said as she tied the ends of the ribbon into an off-center rosette. "Now you look like a Gibson girl."

Mazy looked in the mirror. The transformation was amazing. With her hair pulled back into an updo bouffant, she looked like a Charles Gibson print come to life. The newly fashionable long-line corset she'd purchased at the dress shop didn't hurt the look either. Her figure suddenly sported a tiny waist and just a hint of a top. With her boyish build, all she could hope for was a hint. "How do I keep my hair in place?" she asked.

Eva demonstrated tucking errant strands back into the roll. "That's the best I can do. Your hair is so fine it might not stay put, but pomade is too heavy for this style."

"We could shellac it," Mazy said, drawing a laugh from the girls.

"The car is here," Ernestine said from her perch in the window. "Let's go. The driver we hired is paid by the hour."

On the outskirts of town, the driver pulled the topless touring car over. "When we leave Fayette County, the roads are going to be

dusty," he shouted over the throbbing motor. "Do you want me to put the side
curtains on?"

A chorus of noes came from the girls, who
were all heady with the thrill of speed and
the anticipation of the night to come.

"We don't want to be closed in," Eva said.

"Then you'll want these," the driver said,
passing around a set of goggles for each girl.
He demonstrated putting them on and
tightening the stretchy strap.

"I don't think we'll want them," Eva said.
"They'd simply ruin our hair."

"Suit yourselves." The driver stuck his arm
out the side of the vehicle to signal any
oncoming traffic and drove on.

He pulled over again after a smut of oil
struck Polly right between the eyes. He
revved the motor while they each put their
goggles on and readjusted their head
scarves.

"We look like bugs," Polly said.

"Ladybugs," Mazy said.

"Crazy ladybugs."

Mazy loved the way the road flew by, the
wind stinging her face. It was as if they were
one unit hurtling through space: the car,
the driver, and the girls all squeezed together, each making room for the other. She
had never had so much fun.

The driver changed gears more than once as the car climbed Renfro Hill and then entered the town limits by going under the railroad and through an underpass. They sped by a grocery store and the post office. A cloud of dust enveloped the vehicle as they motored between the High Bridge Depot and a mammoth rock quarry.

Clara tightened the scarf beneath her goggles. "Why is it so dirty here?"

"They're digging rock at the quarry," Eva said.

"Why?"

"It's for building roads and such. The bridge has twin towers constructed with rock from the quarry," Mazy said.

"But it makes such a mess. I thought we were going someplace pretty."

"Don't be a ninny, Clara. We're not picnicking in the quarry," Eva said.

Their car lined up behind others until a man cued them toward an open field and a parking spot. Their driver stepped out and held the door to the backseat open for them. "You young ladies should be back here by nine o'clock. Nothing good happens here after that." He fetched the picnic hamper from the front floorboard. "I'll find a table and get you set up."

"Thank you," Eva said.

Nearly giddy with excitement, Mazy followed the others along a whitewashed fence and through the park gates. Outside a food stand, a man hawked the "world's finest hot dogs" and "cold, refreshing ice cream." Mazy wondered what a hot dog would taste like.

A little way farther along were two gazebos made of cedar poles, two rope swings, and two lavatories. The outhouses sat side by side, one marked Ladies and one marked Gents. How embarrassing. Mazy determined to drink very little while in the park.

Oh, but there was the dance hall. It was like the gazebos but much more ornamental and much larger. Eva had said that it was the finest outdoor pavilion in the country. Mazy could see members of the band milling about on a raised platform at the far end of the spectator area. The plinking and plunking of various instruments being tuned was already music to her ears. As they passed by the platform on the way to the picnic shelter, a loud *root-a-toot-toot* filled the air. Mazy nearly jumped out of her skin. She and Clara stopped and stared.

"He winked at us." Clara pointed to the sharply dressed man swinging the horn. "I swear he did."

"Don't point," Mazy said. "He probably

winks at all the girls."

"Well, spoil the moment, Mazy," Clara said in a little huff. "I've never had a wink before."

"Neither have I," Mazy said as they hurried to catch up with the others. "What do you do with one when you get it?"

"I think you're supposed to flirt back — if you're interested. Are you interested?"

"No, I don't think so. Are you?"

"Maybe just a little," Clara said, pushing her spectacles up her nose with her index finger before looking back over her shoulder. "I think that's a saxophone he's playing — do you know?"

"No, I don't. If we only had an encyclopedia, we could look it up."

"Mazy, this is hardly the time to be thinking of looking things up. We're here for fun."

Stung, Mazy took a seat at the picnic bench. See if she'd go out of her way to be so nice to Clara again. She took a bite of her ham sandwich and bit the end from a tart pickle. Her mouth puckered. Did she come across as a girl who didn't know how to have fun — a timid librarian spending dry days with her nose in a book, only coming up for air when she was stamping cards or saying, "Shush"?

A tendril of hair tickled her cheek, escaping the confines of her pompadour. She tucked it into the roll as Eva had shown her. If she looked like a Gibson girl, then she could act like a Gibson girl: remote yet accessible, serenely self-confident — a perfect blend of Eva (without the haughtiness) and Ernestine. She could be a modern woman who knew how to have a good time, within reason.

Mazy was not expecting the beat of the music that drifted their way as supper was finished and the table tidied. She was most used to hymns or lilting melodies. Sometimes in the evenings when she lived with Lilly, they'd crank up the gramophone and listen to something like "My Wild Irish Rose" or "In the Shade of the Old Apple Tree." Lilly liked opera, and on rare occasions she'd put the needle to an operatic record. Lilly's little terrier would howl when he heard opera. Mazy understood. But this music made her feet twitch and her heart beat fast.

As daylight faded into dusk, a crowd formed in front of the bandstand. Mazy stood between Eva and Clara. She didn't know where the other girls were. Eva swayed to the beat of the music, the short slits in her sheath skirt revealing her high-heeled bronze pumps and her slender ankles.

Standing beside the coolly elegant Eva was a good place to be if you didn't want attention. There was Chanis waiting back home, after all. Wouldn't he be upset if Mazy were in another man's arms? Or did dancing count? She might want to find out.

"Who is that?" Clara asked, pointing to a group of young men standing several feet away.

Mazy grabbed Clara's index finger and pushed her hand down. "You're calling attention."

"I'd like to call his attention."

There was no doubt whom she meant. One man had an air about him. He was taller than the others but slim. His hair was dark and swept back from his brow. His nose was perfectly straight and his lips were the fullest Mazy had ever seen on a man. He was wearing a white linen jacket with a pink rose in its lapel.

"What sort of fellow wears flowers?" Mazy whispered.

"That's Loyal Chambers," Eva said. "His family owns half of Lexington."

Mazy held her breath. Loyal Chambers was coming her way — as if her words had beckoned him. She was about to learn what sort of man wore a rose in his lapel.

"I would love to," Eva said as she placed

her white-gloved hand on Loyal's extended palm.

Mazy could feel a dreaded blush climb her cheeks. What had made her think he was going to ask her to dance? At least she knew the answer to whether she would take to the floor or not.

"He's the most beautiful creature I have ever seen," Clara said, nearly in a swoon.

"I don't think men can be beautiful," Mazy said, glad to be grounded by Clara's chatter.

Clara polished her glasses with a cotton hankie before reseating them. "That one boy's looking at you, Mazy. He's just your type."

"What does that mean?"

"Short," Clara said.

Mazy didn't mind short — everyone was taller than her — but she kept her eyes averted just the same. Thinking of a guy looking her over turned her shy.

"I can't stand still one more minute," Clara said as the band struck up "The Downtown Rag." Grabbing Mazy's hands, she pulled her out onto the floor. Mazy wasn't the best dancer, but she could keep up with Clara. It was as if the music took control of her feet. Over Clara's head, she could see the short guy approaching. He tapped on Clara's shoulder. She turned into his arms, leaving Mazy dodging other dancers.

Mazy backed up a step, bumping into someone behind her.

"Sorry," a deep voice said. "I was just going to ask if I could have the next dance."

A perfectly respectable-looking young man was holding out his hand to her. Mazy was suddenly tongue-tied. Should she say yes? If she said no, would his feelings be hurt? Thankfully, the dance song ended. People broke out in applause as four men illuminated by a spotlight took center stage.

"That's the Hayden Quartet," the man standing beside her said. "Have you heard them?"

"Only from my sister's Victrola," Mazy replied, rubbing her arms as a shiver overtook her. How exciting. Maybe they'd sing "Sweet Adeline," her very favorite. She might die if they did.

"I'm Billy, by the way. Mind if I stand with you?"

She took one sideways step away. "I'm Mazy."

The first strains of a song wafted their way.

"In the evening by the moonlight, dear Louise,

I'll do what you want me to do; life is too short for crying. . . ."

"They sound great, don't they? Close harmony — I sing in a quartet also. We call ourselves the Lone Bandits. Catchy, huh?"

Mazy shot him a stop-talking look. Surely he could read it.

"I'm in university. You?"

She put one finger to her lips — the staid librarian again, but she wanted so much to hear the song.

Suddenly he was twirling a straw hat on the end of his finger before flinging it upward. "Catch it," he said.

Reflexively she did and handed it back. Her eyes darted around the pavilion. Where was Clara? Was there no one to rescue her from this bore?

The crowd clapped vigorously as the song ended and the lead singer stepped forward. " 'Sweet Adeline,' " he crooned. " 'You're the flower of my heart.' "

Mazy's pulse sped up. Billy stepped closer. His arm snaked around her waist.

"Let's get out of here," he whispered in her ear.

Someone clamped Billy's shoulder and jerked him slightly backward. "Do you mind?" Loyal Chambers said. "We're trying to hear the music."

"Tease," Billy said under his breath before he faded into the crowd.

Mazy shook with indignation. What a vile thing for him to say. She knew she hadn't invited that sort of advance. Loyal and Eva stepped up beside her. Hopefully they hadn't heard the crude remark. The stupid guy had caused her to miss most of "Sweet Adeline," and now it was intermission.

Polly and Ernestine and a couple of fellows joined them. They laughed and chatted among themselves, sharing introductions, giving Mazy the perfect opportunity to pull herself together.

Loyal Chambers inclined his head toward her. "You okay?" he said quietly.

"Yes, thank you," Mazy said, his gentlemanly ways nearly bringing tears to her eyes. Chanis would have hauled off and socked Billy in the jaw. She could just imagine the commotion. Of course, if Chanis were here, none of it would have happened. She wondered if Chanis could dance.

"We're hiking up to the bridge before it gets too dark to see," Polly said. "Want to come?"

It was not an easy walk for the girls in their fancy shoes, but seeing the imposing structure made it worth the effort. The marker said that the 275-foot-tall High Bridge was built in 1877 and spanned the deep gorge of the Kentucky River between Jessamine and Mercer Counties. Featuring twin towers, it was the highest railroad bridge in the world. They walked a few steps out onto the tracks. It took Mazy's breath away to look down at the dark waters below.

Loyal threw a small rock over the side. "Nobody has ever survived a fall from this bridge."

"Why would anyone be falling off?" Mazy asked, hearing the faraway splash as the rock broke the water.

"People walk across it," he said, looking intently at Mazy. "It's sort of a rite of passage for guys hereabout."

"But what if a train comes?" Mazy asked.

"Exactly," Polly's swain chimed in. "Come on, Loyal. Let's show the girls how it's done."

"Go! Go! Go!" Eva, Polly, and Ernestine chanted.

Mazy grabbed Loyal's arm. "Please don't. It's too dangerous."

Loyal laughed and stripped off his white linen jacket. "Here," he said, "you can hold this for me."

Eva jerked the coat from Mazy. "I'll take

care of it."

The guys swaggered around for a bit, guffawing and slapping each other's backs. The one with Polly dropped to his knees and put his ear against one of the tracks as if reading the rails. "Nothing's coming," he said.

"Come on, chumps," Loyal said, strolling onto the high span as casually as if he were taking a walk down a country lane.

"My word, Eva," Ernestine said as the guys walked away. "How did you snag Loyal Chambers?"

"Class calls to class," Eva said, lifting her perfect chin. "Who's the guy you're with? I've never seen him around town."

"He crews for the band — sets up equipment and such. He'll be gone after tonight, but, boy, can he dance."

"So you're learning some new moves?" Eva said.

"Mind your own business, Eva," Ernestine snapped.

"Has anyone seen Clara?" Mazy said. "She shimmied away and never came back."

"This is not the first time she's disappeared with a guy," Ernestine said. "She's just asking for trouble."

"Clara's a big girl," Eva said. "She knows to meet us at the car."

Night had fallen as they talked. The light of a full moon showed the boys were halfway across.

Arms straight out, Polly stepped onto a rail. "See if you can balance."

Eva stood with Loyal's jacket draped over her arm. "Don't be silly," she said.

Mazy took the challenge. If she put one foot right in front of the other, it was easy, but she was too scared to go very far. She didn't like being so close to the long drop to the water.

Polly walked several feet before, with an elegant pirouette, she came back. "I used to take ballet."

Mazy tried the move but lost her balance and teetered on the rail. Her slick-soled slippers were not made for pirouettes. Laughing, she righted herself. "Good thing I didn't go out on the bridge." Her feet tingled. The tingle turned into a quiver that traveled to her knees.

"A train is coming," she said, jumping from the rail. "Are the boys across?"

The ground began to shake, and way up the track, a bright, round light appeared. Polly jumped up and down, waving her arms frantically. "Run," she screamed to the fading backs of the boys. "Run!"

The light came closer and closer as the

train bore down on them. Now everyone, even steady Ernestine, was screaming, "Run! Run! Run!"

Ernestine was standing near the track, mesmerized by the thundering train. Mazy grabbed her arm and dragged her down the incline, away from the track. There was danger in standing too close to a passing train. Lilly had once had a patient who lost an eye when the wheel of an engine flung a pebble into his face.

The train's whistle blew a shattering warning.

"They'll all be killed," Polly said, falling to her knees.

"We should pray," Mazy said.

The girls knelt. "Words won't come," Polly said.

"The Lord's Prayer always works," Mazy said. By the time the prayer ended, the train was beyond the bridge. One long, mournful whistle blasted the night.

"Should we go check on them?" Polly said.

"I'm not stepping on that bridge," Mazy said. "We should go tell someone. I saw a police officer standing by the gazebo. He'll know what to do."

"This was supposed to be a fun night," Polly said.

"For pity's sake, Polly," Ernestine said.

"I know," Polly said. "I'm sorry . . . but those guys shouldn't have been playing that way."

Eva adjusted the shawl she'd draped around her shoulders. "Don't you think the train would have stopped if it had hit anyone?"

Another sort of whistle greeted their ears. Here came the fellows walking back up the track.

"I'm sorry if we scared you," Loyal said in his gentlemanly way.

"We weren't afraid," Eva said, "just sorry to be missing the dance."

"I was," Mazy said. "I was terribly frightened. You fellows should never do anything of this sort again."

Taking his jacket from Eva, Loyal shrugged it on before pressing Mazy's hand with his. "Well then, Miss Mazy Pelfrey, I'm sorry I frightened you."

Mazy's heart gave a little flutter. He stood so close she could smell his shaving lotion. Limeade — Loyal smelled like limeade. When he released her hand, a pink boutonniere rested in her palm. She was glad it was too dark for Eva to take notice.

The driver was busy installing the side curtains when the girls got back to the car.

No one complained — it was too dark to watch the scenery anyway. He opened the door and they piled in, except for Eva, who took the passenger's side of the front seat as she had done before.

Once the motor started, the driver eased the car forward, dodging folks in the parking lot. People were hooting and hollering and dancing in the lot — the music was nearly as loud as up by the pavilion. The whole place was one big party.

Mazy felt revved up — like she'd drunk a whole bottle of Coca-Cola all by herself. The band, "Sweet Adeline," the walk to the bridge, the thundering train, the boys challenging the train — whew, it was a lot to take in. It was the most exciting night of her life. Stroking the silky petals of the rose she sheltered in her palm — she dared not bring it to her nose — she leaned back against the roomy leather seat.

Roomy — why was there more room than on the trip here? "Wait! We've left Clara behind."

As the car slowed to a crawl, Mazy got on her knees and looked out the back. She could see poor Clara running their way. "Here she comes. Oh, thank goodness."

Ernestine opened the door and Clara tumbled in. She looked a fright, her face all blotchy from running to catch up. "I can't believe you were leaving me," she said as she fumbled with her hair.

"You girls should have stuck together," the driver said, taking none of the blame.

"You knew we were leaving at nine," Eva said.

"I was with Mazy." Clara's voice cracked, then broke as she began to sob. "Mazy left me there all alone."

Mazy kept silent. She didn't want to make Clara feel worse by reminding her that she was the one who left Mazy standing alone in the middle of the dance floor. With a twist of the clasp on her small clutch, she slipped the rosebud inside. Her fingers searched for a couple of the hairpins she kept in the bag along with a tube of red lipstick (which she'd bought at the drugstore but had never been brazen enough to wear) and the dollar bill Lilly had cautioned her to always keep on her person.

"I'm sorry you got left, Clara," she said. "Want me to help you with your hair?"

Clara twisted in the seat, turning her back on Mazy. "You've done enough already," she said.

Quick as pulling the string on a ceiling bulb, Clara had switched off the fun.

"Hush, Clara," Ernestine said. "There's

109

no harm done. We would have missed you soon enough."

CHAPTER 8

It didn't matter that Clara's feet were so swollen from dancing in Mazy's too-tight shoes that now she couldn't get her own on, or how tired they all were from Saturday night's fun — the girls had to go to church. Sunday morning service was mandated by Mrs. Carpenter. Missing church, save for severe cramps or a migraine headache, would lead to expulsion from school.

Clara clomped around bumping into things and trying on various pairs of shoes — sadly no one else's feet were bigger than her own. Ernestine handed her a couple of shoe boxes. "Try these."

Clara burst into tears. "What am I going to do?"

"You'll have to make do with house slippers," Polly said.

Clara rubbed her eyes. "I think I'm getting a headache."

"Where are your glasses?" Mazy asked.

Clara fell forward onto her unmade bed and buried her face. "I lost them."

Mazy sat down beside her, patting her back. "Don't worry. I'll help you look. Are they on your bedside table?"

"I lost them last night."

"Why didn't you say something then?" Ernestine said.

Clara mumbled something into her pillow. To Mazy it sounded like she said, "I'm so ashamed."

"For goodness' sake, Clara, sit up so that we can understand you," Ernestine said.

Clara sat up, shrugging off Mazy's hand. Her face tightened. "I said I lost them running to the car. I didn't want to hold the rest of you up."

Church bells chimed from down the street.

"We'd better get going or we'll all be expelled," Polly said, fetching Clara's leather mules from beneath the bed.

Mazy smoothed the chenille spread on the bed and fluffed the pillow. An untidy bed was one demerit poor Clara wouldn't get.

St. Luke's was old and beautiful. Sunlight streamed in through stained-glass windows, sending prisms of color dancing across the backs of the long wooden pews. Just walking through the heavy double doors put Mazy in a positive state of mind.

The girls took their usual places in their usual pew. Mazy sat farthest from the aisle next to the window that depicted Jesus in the garden. She could just sit there all day in the light of His glory. Wouldn't it have been something to live in Bible times? What if she were going to the well with a jug upon her shoulder and happened by while Jesus was kneeling there? She wouldn't have interrupted Him, but He might have sensed her presence. He might have spoken to her — maybe called her *sister.* It wasn't far-fetched to think so — after all, Jesus was her brother.

Mazy tried to focus on the sermon, but her eyes kept closing. She pinched her index finger with her thumbnail — a trick she'd learned to keep her mind on the boring lectures in school. Her eyes drifted to the stained glass. Would she have helped Jesus carry the cross? She liked to think she would have.

Clara sniffled — poor dear. Mazy unclasped her purse and retrieved an embroidered hankie to pass along. The rose sprig, now limp and browning, fluttered to the floor. Afraid to reach for it for fear of calling attention, Mazy stood with the rest of the congregation and turned the pages of a hymnal to the doxology — always her favorite. But she could barely concentrate on the blessings of the song for fear the bud would catch Eva's eye. Mazy moved her foot to hover just above the rose. She couldn't bear to trample it.

" 'Praise Father, Son, and Holy Ghost,' " she sang, taking a deep breath for the ending solid agreement. With the combination of the breath and the hovering, she lost her balance. The songbook slipped from her grasp. It slapped against the floor, a loud rebuke against the lingering resonance of the *amen.*

Eva leaned to fetch the hymnal; so did Mazy. Their heads met with a tooth-rattling jar. Mazy saw stars. Eva spied the rose. The look she cast at Mazy from her stooped position stopped the stars midspin.

Mazy hustled down the aisle. It was obvious from the possessive way Eva had acted that she was partial to Loyal. But was he partial to Eva? Why had he given the blossom to Mazy anyway? And why had she kept it? Now she was in trouble again.

It was Sunday, so all the shops were closed. The girls took their lunch at the boardinghouse — fried fish and fried potatoes with a blob of boiled cabbage.

"My word," Ernestine said after lunch was

finished. "We need an airing out. Let's walk to the park."

"I can't walk that far," Clara said. "My blisters have blisters. I barely made it home from church."

"We have to do the dishes," Mazy said. "Remember?"

"I don't understand why we girls have to wash dishes today," Polly said. "If no one else can work on Sunday, why must we?"

Wiping her hands on a red-and-white dish towel, Mrs. Pearl, their housemother, stepped across the threshold from the kitchen. "It's your ox in the ditch," she said.

Eva lifted her chin. "I am not a simple servant. My father pays well for my room and board."

"Even a princess should know how to scrub a pot," Mrs. Pearl said, "just in case her prince turns into a frog."

Mazy would have laughed if she were brave enough. Eva never helped with their turn at washing up. She always had an excuse. Last Sunday after lunch she'd left to powder her nose and hadn't come back until the last dish was dry.

"Clara and I will do them," Mazy said. "She doesn't feel like walking as far as the park, and I don't mind."

Mrs. Pearl draped the dish towel over her

shoulder. "The water's hot," she said. "Don't forget to save the scraps for the cats."

"Those stupid cats," Polly said after Mrs. Pearl left. "You'd think they were her children."

"Maybe they are," Mazy said, thinking about the five kittens in the kitchen pantry.

"You're very agreeable today," Polly said. "You must have had a really good time last night."

"I just like to do what I'm supposed to," Mazy said, fudging the truth when what she really wanted was to get away from Eva's glaring eyes.

"Suit yourself," Eva said, fetching her hat from the stand near the outside door. "The park should be lovely today."

Mazy took two bibbed aprons from the linen press. She tied the strings around Clara's neck, and Clara returned the favor but said, "I can't see well enough to wash. I'd leave spots."

Mazy added Gold Dust powdered soap to the hot water in the granite dishpan. Bubbles rose to her elbows. She blew one off and it landed on Clara's nose.

"Why are you always in such a good mood, Mazy? Doesn't anything ever get you down?"

"You should have seen me Friday after the test," Mazy said. "I was so upset I cried."

"In front of Mrs. Carpenter?"

"I couldn't hold back, but you know what, Clara? She was nice as she could be to me."

Weaving a dry cloth through the handle of a white stoneware mug, Clara snorted. "She's lying in wait."

"Maybe, but I did fail the test. I'm glad she's giving me another chance."

"The school's not going to throw you out over one bad test, Mazy."

Soapy water slopped over the rim of the pan and splashed on the floor. "Gracious, I've made a mess." Squatting, Mazy parted the printed flour-sack curtains that hid the sink's plumbing and retrieved a stained rag from the stack Mrs. Pearl kept there. After running the rag over the spill, she put it in the laundry hamper. "This floor could stand a mopping. Maybe I'll do that in the morning before class."

Clara's cloth went round and round over a dinner plate. She looked sideways through red-rimmed eyes at Mazy. "Are you on work-study?"

Mazy scrubbed grease from a skillet. "I don't know what that is."

"It's a program to help girls whose families don't have the money to pay for their education. I thought since you are always helping Mrs. Pearl . . ."

"My sister takes care of my expenses. But I like to keep busy. It keeps me from getting so distracted. And I like being of help to Mrs. Pearl."

"Can you keep a secret?"

"Surely."

Clara took the heavy skillet. "I don't work here in the boardinghouse; that's why you and the rest don't know. I work after hours in the office helping the teachers."

Mazy emptied dirty wash water down the drain, releasing a fine mist of steam. She patted her cheeks with the hem of her apron. "But that's a good thing, Clara. You must be learning a lot."

"You're from the mountains, so you don't know how these things work, Mazy. If the other girls find out — especially Eva — they won't like me."

"I understand that part," Mazy said, untying Clara's apron strings.

"Let's go outside," Clara said.

Mazy opened the pantry door and fetched a bushel basket squirming with tiny bits of fluff. "We can take the kittens and give them some air."

The mother cat followed them out to the shade of a maple tree. Clara spread a woven blanket. Mazy sat down and emptied the basket one kitten at a time.

"I could get some tea and see if there are any of those sugar cookies left in the cookie jar," Clara said.

Released from their bed, the kittens swam across the blanket. Mazy laughed to see five sets of miniature legs paddling through the woolen waves. Leaning back on her hands, she wondered how long it would be until they found their feet. The yellow tabby looked on in alarm until her offspring nestled against her side.

Clara came scurrying out the door, laughing. "Mrs. Pearl caught me," she said, handing the tea to Mazy before taking two cookies from her pocket. "She said, 'Don't let the kittens get lost.' "

"Mmm," Mazy said, biting into the luscious confection and offering a crumb to the cat.

"I don't know what I'm laughing about — really I just feel like crying."

"Because you lost your spectacles?"

Clara leaned her head on her bent knees. "Yes, that and . . ."

Mazy scooped one tiny golden kitten from the blanket and tucked it into Clara's lap. "You can tell me, Clara."

"My boyfriend broke up with me last

night. I saw him with someone else a few days ago, but when I confronted him last night, he turned it all around and blamed everything on me."

"Boyfriend? You have a boyfriend?"

"Had," Clara said. "*Had* is the key word. He moved here from back home, but now he says he's moving on. We were supposed to marry when I finish school. You know you can't attend if you're a married woman? I knew he was going to be at High Bridge, so I danced with that other fellow. I thought it would make him jealous and he'd come back to me. But it just made him mad."

Mazy couldn't think of a thing to say. She knew about the marriage rule. She'd signed the pledge.

"Did you know I'm on probation already?"

Mazy took in Clara's fair complexion, now mottled with splashes of red, her wispy brown hair, her sharply pointed chin, her smallish, watery eyes. "I don't even know what that means, Clara."

"It doesn't matter — it just means I have to work harder than everyone else."

Mazy riffled through the grass at the edge of the blanket. Maybe she could find a four-leaf clover to cheer Clara up.

"It took me a long time to get here," Clara

said. "I was raised on a farm. Our barn straddles the Kentucky-Tennessee line. It was work, work, work from sunup to sundown every single day. My poor mother . . ." Her voice trailed away and she petted the kitten before looking up. "There were sixteen of us kids — can you even imagine?"

Mazy could imagine. She'd often visited the small cabin where Chanis's mother raised his twelve brothers and sisters. It was always a happy house with gingerbread in the oven and kids playing Mother, may I? in the freshly swept yard. It wasn't a stretch to imagine there would have been more children if Chanis's father had not died. Mazy did not want that many kids — two would be plenty.

"I hated every inch of that place — flies and noise and mess. When I saw an advertisement for secretarial school, I determined to come here. I cleaned houses for three years to save the money for tuition. Then Dad got sick — he's a good man, but to him one penny earned is two pennies spent. Anyway, the money went for his hernia operation. Then Mom got TB. The sanitarium in Bourbon County is where I met Mrs. Carpenter — her husband was there for two years. Did you know that?"

Mazy shook her head. This was a lot to take in.

"She encouraged me to apply for a scholarship here. It's one of those bad things turning out for the good — for me at least." Clara rubbed her eyes with the heels of her hands. "I don't know what I'll do, Mazy. I can't see to read or type without my glasses."

Mazy clapped her hands as if to dispel the gloom. "We could take the train to High Bridge and go look for them. It would be fun — we can have another picnic."

The mother cat's ears perked. She nosed her kittens, then hurried to claim the errant one from Clara's lap. The yellow ball of fluff dangled like a dead mouse from the feline's mouth as she carried it to the side of the house and dropped it in a patch of weeds. Back at the blanket, the mother mouthed another of her kittens.

Seeing that the tabby was about to secrete all her babies, Mazy gathered them into the basket. She would never have found the little one in the tall weeds if she hadn't seen where the mother dropped it. Cats were so clever. "I'll take them back in," she said, pulling sticker weeds from her skirt tail. "I think they've had enough of the great outdoors."

Clara grabbed Mazy's hand. "Don't tell the others what I've told you, okay?"

Mazy turned an imaginary key at the corner of her lips.

Without warning, Eva, Polly, and Ernestine appeared. "Tell the others what?" Eva asked.

"That we swiped sugar cookies," Clara said without missing a beat.

Eva plopped down. "Go swipe some more."

Mazy stood with the load of kittens. "I'll ask Mrs. Pearl."

"You're so pedestrian, Mazy," Eva said.

"I know what *pedestrian* means," Mazy snapped. "You've called me that before. Just you remember the turtle wins the race."

Eva twirled the withered rose between her thumb and forefinger. "Turtles are sooo attractive."

The other girls laughed — even Clara.

Mazy bit back a sharp retort. Were any of these girls really her friends? Homesickness overcame her once again as she fiddled at the door, trying to open it without setting the basket down. The tabby cat rubbed against her ankles and rushed through the door when she finally got it open. Inside the pantry, she placed the babies on the rag rug Mrs. Pearl had provided for them. Ready for a nap, the kittens snuggled so closely it was hard to tell where one began and another ended. Taking a pint of cream from the icebox against the wall, Mazy poured a tat into a saucer. The tabby lapped delicately at the treat.

Mazy didn't ask for cookies and she didn't ask for tea. Instead she found her hat and her gloves before going out the front door. She had to get away for a while.

The streets were nearly deserted. Sunday afternoons were for families and for rest. The church bells wouldn't ring vespers for hours yet. She strolled aimlessly, each step reminding her of how far she was from home. At Lilly's house they'd be sitting in the side yard reading or talking — just passing time. The little ones — Lilly's twins, Julia and Simon — would be napping on a quilted pallet under the apple tree. If Lilly's husband was home, instead of traveling for work, he might crank a churn of ice cream, hopefully strawberry. If so, the yard would soon be full of passersby. Lilly would send Mazy inside for dessert bowls and spoons.

While she was indulging in a pity party, Mazy had walked as far as North Broadway. A pebble had made its ornery way inside her shoe, pressing irritably against the arch of her foot. She paused on the sidewalk where a riotous rosebush spilled over an iron fence. From beyond the open gate, a circle of red begonias framed a stone urn filled with white petunias and tall spiked greenery. A cast-iron bench in the same design as the fence beckoned her to come and sit awhile. It would be the perfect place to shake the pebble from her shoe. Did she dare?

Gargoyles stared down from the turreted roof of an imposing gray stone house. The ugly statues belied the cheery garden scene. On the one hand, the house· said, "Keep away"; on the other, it said, "Come on in." Taking a breath, she stepped through the gate and made her way along a curving flagstone path to the bench.

Thankfully, the garden was screened from the house by charming latticework that supported even more of the sweet-smelling climbing roses. Unless looking in from the street, no one would even notice her here. Sitting, she slipped off her shoe and shook it. No pebble popped out. Leaning forward, she examined the bottom of her foot as best she could without exposing her legs. A cocklebur stabbed her searching fingers. The bothersome thing was enmeshed in her stocking.

"Fiddlesticks," she said, picking at the

burr, causing a run up her ankle. "What a bother."

A shadow fell across the flagstones. "May I be of assistance?" a male voice said.

Not daring to look up, Mazy slid her foot under the bench. "No thank you. I'm fine."

"You seem to have lost your shoe," the man said.

"It's hardly lost," Mazy said. "I don't need help — now please run along."

"You're in my garden," he replied.

Mazy wished the ground would swallow her up. She shoved the shoe back on her foot and stood. "I'm so sorry," she said. "I didn't mean to trespass."

"Mazy?"

Startled, she took a backward step. "Loyal?" The burr dug into her foot and she gave a gasp of pain.

Loyal Chambers proffered his arm. She clung to it as he settled her back onto the bench. "Let me," he said, sliding off the shoe.

His fingers probed her foot. She jerked it away. "Please stop," she said.

"It's okay," he said.

"Turn your back."

With a chuckle, he did.

"Would you mind to step in front and block me from the street?"

"Of course," he said as he complied, "but there's no one watching."

Mazy could feel a thousand eyes bearing down on her — judging her foolishness. The burr stuck her fingers with spines as sharp as needles. Try as she might, she could not dislodge it.

Loyal peeked over his shoulder. "Any luck?"

She cried out as a needle drew blood.

Loyal turned to her. "You leave me no choice," he said, bending to lift her from the bench. "I'm taking you to my mother."

There was no way to protest Loyal's forwardness without calling even more attention to her plight; besides, he'd said his mother was inside. For just a moment, Mazy allowed herself to enjoy the strength of his arms and his clean citrus scent. Goodness, what a turn this day had taken.

At the front door, Loyal gently set her on her feet. "Lean on me," he said as he reached for the knob. The door swung open. "Mother, you have a patient. Mazy, meet Dr. Chambers. Mother, this is Mazy."

Mazy was at a loss to describe the tall, thin woman who met them at the end of a long hallway, but if Loyal Chambers had been a girl, he would look exactly like his mother. Since Loyal was so handsome,

Mazy would have expected Dr. Chambers to be a beautiful woman, but she wasn't. Her jawline was too pronounced, her eyebrows too thick, her eyes a too-piercing light blue. Her white hair was tidily twisted into a knot atop her head. She peered at Mazy through a pair of half glasses.

"Mother," Loyal said, "my friend Mazy has hurt her foot."

"In here," Dr. Chambers said.

Mazy recognized the room: the swing-arm lamp with the oversize bulb, the white-sheeted exam table, the autoclave, and the bookcases full of leather-bound tomes. It was not much different from her sister Lilly's office.

Leaning heavily on Loyal's arm, she hopped on one foot to the end of the cot-like table. She couldn't possibly hop up onto the step.

With his hands around her waist, Loyal lifted her to the end of the table.

Dr. Chambers switched on the lamp. "Let's have a look," she said, pushing Mazy's skirt up over her knees.

Mazy tucked the skirt under her legs. "I'd like some privacy."

"Sorry," Loyal said, heading toward the door. "I'll see you after."

Dr. Chambers selected a pair of needle-nose tweezers from a metal tray beside the table. Mazy thought she might faint when the doctor probed the sole of her foot with the instrument. This was sure to hurt.

The doctor pulled Mazy's cotton hose away from her foot with the tip of the tweezers. In her other hand she wielded scissors, which she used to free the offending burr. "Your foot will be fine, but you'll have to patch your hose," she said, upending a bottle of iodine. "This will sting a bit."

"I'm sorry to interrupt your Sunday afternoon," Mazy said.

The doctor capped the iodine, then wrapped the tweezers in brown paper and placed them in the autoclave before turning her sharp eyes on Mazy. "Is this all you need, young lady?"

"Yes, ma'am." Mazy took some folding money from her pocket. "What is your charge?"

"Seventy-five cents will cover it."

"Thank you," Mazy said. Receiving the quarter in change, she stepped down from the table. "I must have left my shoe under your garden bench."

Dr. Chambers opened the door that led to the hall. "Loyal will help you find it," she said. "Stay out of the weeds."

Mazy colored. "Yes, ma'am."

CHAPTER 9

On Monday morning Mazy entered the classroom with trepidation, still smarting from her failure. She kept her eyes on the floor as she sidled past Mrs. Carpenter's desk. Last evening, after vespers, she'd spent an hour with a mock keyboard trying to memorize the placement of the alphabet letters. It brought back unpleasant memories of torturous piano practice when she was eight years old. She still got a stomachache when she thought of that. Her fingers just wouldn't work in tandem with her brain. After a few months of limited success, her mother had taken pity on her and canceled her lessons. The only song she could still play was "Here we go, up the road, to a birthday party." Pathetic.

She was an adult now, however, and her mother was not here to rescue her. Mrs. Carpenter would surely toss her out of school if she caught her peeking at the keys.

Besides, Mazy knew that careless habit slowed her word count; she was stuck at sixty words a minute. Maybe she was a turtle after all.

Taking the dustcover from her machine, she carefully folded it before placing it on the shelf beneath her desk.

Mrs. Carpenter rapped the corner of Polly's desk. "Today we will practice increasing your word counts." Putting the pointer aside, she retrieved a pocket watch. "You will be using the practice exercise on page 34 of your handbooks. Keep typing until I say stop."

A dry rustling sound filled the air as pages turned. Mazy moved her chair closer to her machine, sat up straight, and took a deep breath.

"Ready," Mrs. Carpenter said, pressing a stem on the watch, "begin."

This should be easy. We've practiced this a million times, Mazy thought as her fingers recalled the keys. *"The quick brown fox . . ."* She faltered — where was the *J?*

Mrs. Carpenter moved from the front of the room. Mazy was in her direct line of sight. *Don't look,* she reminded herself. *Don't look.* Forcing her mind to go blank, she took another breath and started again. *"The quick brown fox . . ."* In the middle — the J *is in the middle of the board . . . next to the* I? *No, that's the alphabet; the keyboard is not ordered the same way.* Her index finger hovered unsure over a key at the same time Mrs. Carpenter sneezed. Mazy sneaked a peek. Her blood turned to ice. The letters had all been blacked out. She couldn't read a thing. She stared at page 34 and kept typing. It was either that or leave the room — grab her valise from under the bed and head for the train station. If she did that, she'd never see Loyal again.

He had insisted on driving her home yesterday afternoon . . . insisted on helping her from the car . . . insisted on walking her to the door, and she allowed him, even though her foot was only slightly tender. She could still recall the feel of his hand on her elbow.

"Where in the world have you been?" Polly had asked when Mazy found all the girls studying at the dining room table. "We were thinking we'd have to go to vespers without you."

"I went for a walk," Mazy said. "I needed some air."

She felt like she needed some air again as a dozen sets of typewriter keys *clack-clack-clack*ed all around her.

"Stop," Mrs. Carpenter said.

Mazy's fingers trembled as she removed her page from the machine, exchanging her work with Polly's. As per usual, they'd grade each other's efforts. There were no mistakes in Polly's work. If an error was found in a word, that word wasn't counted. Mazy made a slash mark at the end of each five letters, which would count as one whole word. When she reached the end, she added the words up. Polly had typed sixty-eight words in one minute. Not a great effort, but certainly better than Mazy had ever done.

"Call out," Mrs. Carpenter said, aiming her pointer toward the first row of students.

"Sixty-two. Sixty. Fifty-four," and so the tally went until Eva's turn. "Thirty-two," she said.

A collective gasp filled the air. Mazy glanced at Clara, who sat directly in front of Eva. She was white as a sheet.

"Continue," Mrs. Carpenter said, pointing to the next row.

"Seventy-two," Polly said.

Mazy's head spun like it had the time she'd been on a ride at the county fair. Had she really done that well? "Sixty-eight," she squeaked, finishing the count.

Polly gave her a smile as she handed the test paper back. Mazy's hand trembled as she received it. *The quick brown fox jumped*

. . . ," typed over and over with no mistakes — indeed, that counted as seventy-two words in sixty seconds. Mazy entertained the swell of pride until a commotion in the middle of the room caught her attention.

Clara was bawling — not crying with tearstained cheeks, but bawling and heaving like a two-year-old told no. At the direction of Mrs. Carpenter, Ernestine escorted her from the room.

Polly turned toward Mazy. "For pity's sake," she said, "you'd think someone had died."

"She lost her glasses," Mazy whispered back. "That's why she did so poorly."

"Care to share your conversation with the class?" Mrs. Carpenter said.

Mazy colored. She and Polly had broken a cardinal rule by whispering among themselves. She stood. "I was saying Clara is upset because she lost her glasses."

"Being properly prepared is a matter of no little importance." Mrs. Carpenter raised her voice over the clanging bell in the hall. "Class dismissed."

Hurriedly, Mazy brushed her machine's keys with a type brush before settling the cover over it. There'd be fifteen free minutes before the next class, and she couldn't wait to catch up with the others, sure she would be congratulated for her seventy-two.

Mrs. Carpenter's hand on her shoulder stopped her haste. "I am pleased with your progress today, Miss Pelfrey. The blacking of the keys can only improve your timing."

"Yes, ma'am, thank you," Mazy said, all the while thinking it wasn't the blacking of the keys that made the difference. It was Loyal. Just thinking of him gave her confidence — not to mention butterflies.

The girls were in their meeting place on the wall. Clara's face was a splotchy red, but she'd pulled herself together. Nobody mentioned Mazy's score, but at least Polly scooted over to give her a seat and Ernestine threw her a smile.

Mazy leaned across Polly to pat Clara's knee. "I'm sorry about the test," she said.

"I might as well drop out," Clara said. "I can't type if I can't see."

"Can't you buy some more?" Polly asked. "They have reading glasses at the drugstore."

"Mine are a special prescription. I can't see up close or far away. It will take weeks to have another pair made."

"Maybe the readers will do in a pinch," Mazy said. She wouldn't mention looking for the lost pair again. That was up to Clara.

The bell called them back inside for their

135

last class before lunch. Even though it was dictation, Mazy felt confident. All she needed to do was keep half a mind on the lesson and the other half on Loyal. A sweet breeze wafted in through the open windows at the back of the room, ruffling the pages of Mazy's steno pad. She fancied it carried the fresh scent of lime.

Class was over, but the bell had not yet rung when Mrs. Carpenter dismissed them. Mazy followed the others to their spot.

"Where's Eva?" Polly asked.

"Mrs. Carpenter asked her to stay," Ernestine said.

"Why?" Polly said.

Ernestine shrugged her shoulders. "We might as well go on to the drugstore."

"Shouldn't we wait for her?" Mazy said.

"She'll catch up. In the meantime, we can help Clara find readers."

Fox Lasso Eyeglasses, the sign above the display case stated. "Look, Clara, they have many different magnifications," Mazy said.

Clara squinted. "I can't see a thing."

"I'll read the sign for you. It says, 'Fox Lasso Eyeglasses. Laugh, eat, walk, and work in perfect comfort. Ordinary eyeglasses slip, joggle, tumble, and break. Our glasses hold securely to the center of the eye. They were conceived by Mr. Ivan Fox, who from long experience understands just how to make adjustments using tubular springs with screw lock ends, which make eyeglasses steady, secure, and good-looking.' "

Polly removed a pair from the case and stuck them on the bridge of Clara's nose. "I'm not so sure about 'good-looking,' " Clara said.

"But can you see?" Polly asked. "That's the important part."

Clara leaned closer to the advertising sign. "It says I should write today for 'eyes worth having.' I can definitely read this. But I still can't see very far ahead."

"Will you be able to type?" Mazy asked.

"I think so."

They were having lunch when Eva swept in. "Well, thanks for waiting," she said, taking an empty stool.

Mazy felt a moment's satisfaction. Hadn't Eva done the same thing to her just the other day?

"Why did Mrs. Carpenter hold you back?" Ernestine asked.

Eva raised one index finger self-importantly as she gave her order to the waitress. "It's really none of your concern, Ernestine," she said, "but someone has ratted on me for not doing dishes on Sunday.

As I remember it, I'm not the only one who went to the park instead of catering to Mrs. Pearl. And wasn't it you, Mazy, who insisted on playing Pollyanna? Maybe you were hoping to get me in trouble."

Mazy's stomach turned over and she set down her chicken salad sandwich "I didn't say a word."

"Always the innocent, aren't you?" Eva said. "Well, I had a tale of my own to share with Mrs. Carpenter. I saw who brought you home from your 'walk' yesterday. You may fool everyone else with your sweet-as-pie act, but you don't fool me. You know it's against the rules to see a guy on Sundays."

The other girls twirled on the stools until all were facing Mazy. "Do tell," Polly said.

"I only meant to take a walk; really, that's all. But I got a cocklebur in my shoe. It hurt awfully, and Loyal's mother —"

"You met his mother?" Eva said, sounding more indignant than ever.

"Well, when Loyal carried me into the house —"

Polly gasped. "He carried you?"

"Inside his house?" Ernestine said.

Clara pushed her new spectacles up the bridge of her nose. "Well now," she said.

138

Eva's eyes flashed fire. "You know I like him."

"I didn't mean to like him, Eva; it's just that he is so nice."

Polly looked all swoony. "What did it feel like?"

"It stung when she put iodine on it," Mazy said, "but it's much better today."

"Not your foot, Mazy," Polly said. "His arms. What did it feel like when Loyal Chambers lifted you up into his arms?"

"Embarrassing," Mazy said. "I was embarrassed to death."

"I wouldn't be embarrassed if he put his arms around me," Polly said.

"You're a silly twit, Polly," Eva said. "And you, Miss Sugar Wouldn't Melt, he'll tire of you soon enough."

"There's nothing to tire of. It was just happenstance. He was only being a gentleman." The last thing Mazy wanted was to upset Eva. She had been good enough to help her with her studies and to invite her into this study group. Besides, a girl like Mazy had no chance with a guy like Loyal Chambers when he could choose someone like Eva.

"I'm sure you're right," Eva said, sounding mollified. "You can't help your naiveté, considering where you were raised."

Ernestine laid a quarter beside her plate, prompting the others to do the same. "It's time to get back to class."

Sliding from her seat at the counter, Mazy fished a quarter for the bill and a nickel for a tip from her purse. As she stepped out onto the sidewalk, Mazy could see the bone girl — Cinnamon Spicer — coming down the street. She ducked her head and hurried away, praying the girl didn't call out to her. That was all she needed.

A light rain set in that evening. Supper was quiet — no one seemed eager to talk over Eva's subdued mood. Clara's glasses falling into the tomato soup lightened the atmosphere for a moment, but the laughter didn't last.

Clara wiped the spectacles on her napkin. "I really need my prescription glasses," she said, catching Mazy's eye. "What do you all think about helping me look for them?"

Mazy played along. "That might be fun. We could take the train to High Bridge on Saturday."

Before they could discuss the trip, Mrs. Pearl walked into the room and slapped a dish towel onto the table beside Eva's plate. "You're on dishes tonight, princess."

As if it were contagious, Eva pinched the

rag between two fingers and held it at arm's length. "But why? We aren't responsible for supper dishes."

"Not we," Mrs. Pearl said. "You."

"This isn't fair. I'm not the only one who didn't do dishes yesterday."

"Play your violin somewhere else, princess. I'll be setting in the parlor with my feet up. Come and get me when you're finished, and don't forget the pots and pans."

"Hateful old hag," Eva whispered at Mrs. Pearl's back. "She's the one who told on me."

"That's just mean," Polly said. "She should have let it go."

When the other girls nodded in agreement, Mazy began to scrape the plates, saving bits of cheese from the toasted sandwiches they'd had with the tomato soup. The mother cat would enjoy the treat. Surely she was tiring of having nothing but milk.

The tabby wound around her ankles when she opened the pantry door. Mazy sat on the floor and let the cat sniff at the cheese before she delicately ate each bite. The cardboard box of dirt needed changing, she noticed. That box was so clever of Mrs. Pearl. At her mother's house the cats were allowed to come and go freely, so there were no accidents indoors, but Mrs. Pearl wanted to keep her eyes on the kittens. She had told Mazy that the rangy old tom who hung around the back porch might kill the babies — such a dreadful thought.

Mazy scooped one of the silken fur balls up and let it nestle in the curve of her neck. "I won't let that mean cat hurt you," she said. "No, I won't let that old tom hurt you." Funny, she sounded like her mother did when she talked to one of the newborn babies in her care. Mama always repeated words she said to babies — teaching them to talk, Mazy guessed. Mama was a midwife, so she would know.

The tabby circled the inside of the wicker basket before she plopped down on her side. Mazy put the kitten back in the basket. Soon it was climbing over the backs of its siblings searching for a place to nurse.

"I'll be right back," Mazy said, picking up the cat's jury-rigged toilet. "Be right back."

A misty rain spun a halo around the porch light as Mazy stepped outside. Holding her breath against the stink, she dumped the box in a patch of weeds. Now what would she replace the filler with? Sometimes she was so dumb. Hadn't Lilly always reminded her to think before she acted? Well, she'd just have to find a shovel.

There was a shed in the back corner of the yard. Mazy unlatched the door and let it swing wide. Chances were that's where Mrs. Pearl kept her garden tools. A shovel or a hoe would do nicely to dig some fresh dirt. She stepped inside the scant circle provided by the porch light. In the corner by the door, she saw a tangle of long wooden handles. One was attached to a shovel.

"Aha," she said, "success."

Balancing the box awkwardly against one hip and dragging the shovel, she went to the edge of Mrs. Pearl's vegetable garden. With one foot on the blade, she shoved the pointed end into the soft earth. She'd spent many an hour in a garden when she was a girl. Oh, the heat and the bugs and the calluses. It was a job she was glad to leave behind. Releasing a good-size clod of earth from the ground, she shoveled it into the box before breaking it into fine pieces with her hands. One more clump should be plenty.

Raindrops soft as moths' wings landed on her shoulders as she rushed to set the box by the kitchen door, where it would be protected from the rain. Dragging the shovel behind her, she ran to the shed, anxious to put the tool away and get back in the house before the rain got serious. She flung it in the corner. With a clatter the shovel, the rakes, and the hoe fell over. "Good grief," she said, stepping inside the shed to set them right.

A figure filled the doorway. "I waited out front for more than an hour," a man said. "Are you playing games with me?"

Mazy's heart jerked in her chest as a scent of tobacco and stale sweat tainted the air. She clutched the shovel like a shield. "Who are you?"

A man lifted his hands in a surrender gesture. "Sorry; thought you was somebody else."

"I'm going to scream," Mazy said.

"Now don't do that," he said, backing out the door. "I mistook you. That's all."

Mazy swung the shovel. "You've got no business here."

"I'm gone," he said, turning on his heels and running off into the darkness.

The blade of the shovel was now stuck in a crack between floorboards. Mazy leaned on it until her heart stopped its runaway gallop. The soft night air with its pattering rain suddenly felt as creepy as a cemetery at midnight. Was the stranger waiting for her? Maybe she should scream after all.

From the shed she could see the porch door open. "Mazy?" Ernestine called.

Relief flooding through her, Mazy pulled the door to the shed closed and sprinted toward the light.

"What were you doing out there?" Ernestine asked. "Meeting your boyfriend?"

Mazy carried the box of soil through the door that Ernestine held open. "There was a man out there, Ernestine. He scared me."

"Probably a tramp looking for a handout. You know Mrs. Pearl's always feeding them."

"Maybe," Mazy said with a shiver. "Get the pantry door for me, would you?"

"Hurry and finish with those cats. We're all in Eva's room discussing going to High Bridge on Saturday. We can't take a vote until everyone's present."

Mazy set the box in the corner, then counted the kittens. All five were curled up asleep against their mother's belly. Good. "What's the discussion?"

"Whether to hire a motorcar like Eva wants or to go on the train."

"What do you want?"

"I vote the train. It's considerably cheaper," Ernestine said.

"Then I do too. I vote for the train."

"You'd go against Eva?"

"Eva's already cross with me. Besides, I really like trains."

"I'm going back up," Ernestine said. "Are you coming?"

"In a minute. I'm just going to get a drink of water and switch off the light."

After her drink, Mazy rinsed the glass and nearly dropped it when she heard the kitchen door open. "Gracious," she said when Clara came in. "You startled me."

"I slipped outside while you were in the pantry. I heard you tell Ernestine about seeing someone. I knew it was my boyfriend. He often comes around so we can have a moment alone. I thought he'd come back to apologize." Her voice broke. "At least he told me where he's going. But he doesn't want a tagalong. Can you believe he called me a tagalong?"

Mazy searched for some way to console her friend. "At least he came to tell you, Clara. Maybe when you finish school, you'll get back together."

"You're a dreamer, Mazy. If I can just get through the rest of this semester . . ."

Mazy checked the door to see if it had closed properly and then followed Clara up the stairs. She was glad Clara had begun to confide in her — everybody needed a friend — but she wondered why Clara was worried about one semester. They had two more

146

before they graduated. But it was best not to pry.

CHAPTER 10

Chanis wiped sweat from his brow. It was hot as hades. Not the best day to dig out the well. The *Farmers' Almanac* predicted a change in the weather, and he wanted to get the project finished before the rains set in. Of course the almanac was not always right, but his mother was, and her rheumatism had been acting up something fierce.

Thinking of his mother often put an ache in his heart. He wished he could do more for her than hand over half his pay. Money could never make up for the loss of his father in such a terrible way. She remained fiercely loyal to his memory — still wearing the thin gold band he'd put on her finger twenty-six years ago come September. "Some men are replaceable," he'd once heard her say, "and some aren't. I was both blessed and cursed to marry one that wasn't."

He couldn't wait to see her face when she

saw the paper he'd picked out for her. He'd bet she could put it up so that it would stay put. The newsprint she had on the walls now should make a good base. He was learning more about wall covering than he'd ever hoped to know.

Pulling a makeshift ladder from the depths of the well, he used the claw end of a hammer to pry a broken rung loose before nailing on another. Blamed thing had broken under his foot, and him halfway down the fifteen-foot hole. He'd borrowed every ladder he could beg to go from narrow ledge to narrow ledge in the deep hole. Falling wasn't what he feared, however. What killed men in a well hole was a silent killer — carbon monoxide gas. Once it crept into your lungs, you were a goner. Cautious words from his father entered his mind as they so often did. *"Take your time, Son. Think things through — don't plunge ahead with a project till you know what you're going to do backwards and forwards."*

At least he wasn't spring-poling the well with green saplings and a two-hundred-pound bit. Some other poor sucker had done that hard work many years ago. All he'd had to do was drain the water before he began to haul up bucket loads of gunk, old jars, a pair of waders, two or three rotten bushel baskets, and a soggy parlor rug hand over hand with a rope and pulley — so far so good. He figured it would take a week to finish at the rate he was going. He should have put a notice in the paper for all the local ruffians and roustabouts. *For the Time Being: No shootings, no knifings, no loitering, no skillet-swinging fights. The sheriff's got other things to do.*

He was loading another bucket when his deputy's voice echoed down the shaft. "Hellooo down theeere!"

Shucks. He'd have to climb out. Tully wouldn't have come out unless it was important. At the top of the ladder, Chanis leaned his forearms on the lip of the well.

"You look like a gopher," Tully said.

"I feel like one too. What's up?"

Tully crouched down. "Got a call from the sheriff over in Jackson. That Cheney fellow you hauled over there is giving him fits."

"How so?"

"Cheney's supposed to be transported to Lexington."

"Yeah, I know. He has to stand trial there also. Seems Jackson Bank and Trust wasn't the only place he hit."

"Therein lays the problem. Cheney says he won't go unless you take him."

Chanis spit dirt from his mouth. "He has

150

a choice?"

Tully laughed. "Funniest thing I ever heard — seems they can't get him out of the cell. Sheriff there says he don't have a shoehorn large enough to pry his lard butt out. His only other choice is to shoot Cheney, but he don't want to waste the bullet."

Chanis laughed so hard the ladder shook. He hauled himself on out. "You're right, Tully; that is funny."

"So you want me to call back and say you'll come?"

"Yeah, I reckon."

Tully cuffed him on the shoulder. "Thought you wouldn't mind a little trip to the city — see your girl while you're there."

"That too. When's he want me to pick Cheney up?"

"He sounded like the sooner the better — Cheney's eating him out of house and home."

"I'd like to get this finished before I go. Might take a few days."

Tully peered down the shaft. "I'll bring my boys around. They're good hands. You oughtn't be doing this alone anyhow. There's safety in numbers."

"Thanks, Tully."

Tully's word was good as gold. His boys

made short work of the well. Big and burly, the three weren't afraid to bend their backs or muddy their boots. They came early and stayed late. When Chanis tried to pay them for the two long days of hard work, they just grinned. "No need. You're a friend of Pap's," one said, slapping Chanis on the back so hard he nearly toppled into the shaft.

Chanis put his wallet back in his pocket. "I thank you kindly."

"We was that glad to do it," another said. "Reckon you could give us a ride in that truck? That'd be pay enough."

"What say I ride you over to the diner and buy your supper?"

"You'll be in the hole for sure if you try to fill these three up," Tully said with a touch of pride.

Chanis felt a swell of pride himself as he drove the truck into Skip Rock. It was rare as hen's teeth to have a motor vehicle in these parts, and here he was squiring folks around in one. When he pulled up in front of the diner, Junior hopped out of the bed, followed by his younger brothers, Jonah and Samuel.

"That's a way smoother ride than a wagon," Junior said.

"Could you pop the hood?" the youngest

brother asked.

With a little effort, Chanis lifted the hood. The motor gleamed in its power.

"You need to get us one of these, Pap," Tully Jr. said.

"Money don't grow on trees, boy. Besides, what'd we do with Samson and Delilah?"

Junior dropped the hood back in place. "Put them out to pasture. This here's bound to be cheaper."

"I don't know about that," Tully said. "Gasoline's seven cents a gallon. Besides, the horses are already paid for."

Once the fellows were full of country-fried steak, white gravy ladled over Mrs. Rogers's light-as-air buttermilk biscuits, and tangy-sweet coleslaw, Chanis ordered a whole chocolate meringue pie for the table.

Junior pounded his fist on the tabletop. "Man, oh, man, this is good eating."

Tully selected a toothpick from a small glass container set between the salt and pepper shakers. He began to work it through his teeth. "Cheney'd hang himself for us if we was to offer this meal as his last supper," he paused his plundering long enough to say.

Chanis shot him a look. Idle talk started gossip. "Nobody's talking about a hanging, Tully. Most he'll serve is ten to fifteen, I'd expect."

"That's a mighty long time to be hungry," Tully said. "Ain't no jail I know gonna be able to keep Frank Cheney full."

"Yeah, well, there's a price to be paid for stealing." Chanis pushed back his chair. "You fellows enjoy the rest of the pie."

Esther Clay's cabin sat so near the river, one good shove and it would be a houseboat. Chanis parked the truck at the end of a narrow dirt road and walked the rest of the way in. His mother swore the sound of the truck's motor scared her hens so bad they wouldn't lay eggs for a week. Not to mention the way the cats climbed to the top of the tallest pine tree they could find if he dared to pull in closer. He thought it would be a good idea to leave the cats up there — they could live on birds — but his mother fretted over them. He couldn't count the times he'd climbed that tree to rescue an animal too stubborn to back down what it had just climbed up. Chanis always accommodated his mother's strange fears and premonitions. It was something he could do.

She'd sworn it broke her heart when he moved out. Of course it hadn't. She was stronger than she thought she was — just not eager to lose her eldest. He'd been the first to go, but three sisters followed, all married to decent guys. And the two boys next to him in age were boarding at the Bible Mission School in Breathitt County, getting a good education. That left seven — three boys, four girls. You'd think that was more than enough to keep her company, but if she had her way, her kids would be like her cats, always within arm's reach.

True to form, a passel of fat cats stirred from a patch of sunlight on the porch. A black-and-white shorthair sauntered across the yard to meet him, probably curious as to what was in the pie boxes. "Ma," he called at the screen door, "call off the cats."

His ma inched open the door, keeping her foot in the space. As much as she loved her cats, she didn't like them in the house. "Chanis, I would have waited supper if I'd known you were coming by."

"Where's all the kids? I brought pie."

"They're over to church. You know the revival's going on this week."

He put the boxes on the table, lifting the lids. The meringues stood up in brown swirls, pretty as you please.

"Where'd you come by these? I'd make you pie anytime you asked me."

"Now, Ma, let me treat you once in a

while. They're chocolate. Your favorite."

"Maybe just a taste," she said, reaching for saucers and a knife. "There's coffee on the stove."

Hiding a smile, he set two steaming mugs on the table. Ma had already eaten half a slice. "So how come you didn't go to meeting?"

"Church is just too far to walk when my knee is acting up."

"I'd have been glad to drive you."

"I don't like that fool truck. Anything could happen in that thing. You could run into a tree or get stranded — no telling what."

"I wouldn't let you get stranded. Church is only two miles up the road."

"Johnny's doing the service tonight. You know he's as good a preacher as Brother Taulbee. He'll tell me the sermon when he gets back, and the girls will line me the hymns. It'll be near as good as being there. Besides, if I'd gone, then I'd have missed you."

"Johnny's good for a twelve-year-old. That's for certain. You think he'll be a minister?"

"Who can figure what will become of young'uns," she said, pinching a bit of crust. "I wanted the same for you, Chanis. You was always such a good hand at preaching."

"That's just a mother's pride talking. I was too green whenever I did that service to be any good."

"That's not true. Folks talked about it for months afterwards. And your daddy was so proud." She stirred her coffee round and round, her eyes distant and sad.

"Now, Ma, don't you think Daddy would like for me to follow in his footsteps?"

"You aren't turned the same as your daddy, Chanis. I never wanted you to take to the law."

Chanis choked down a bit of too-sweet pie. He'd heard this speech way too many times. It didn't make him feel good to know his mother thought him too soft for the job. She never said that exactly, but he could read between the lines.

One of the cats clawed at the screen door, hanging on and meowing a pitiful wail.

"Pouncer's stuck on the door again," Ma said while scooping chocolate filling out from under the meringue on her sliver of pie.

Chanis put his fork across the top of the saucer before he stood, practicing the manners his mother had so diligently tried to instill. He eased the door open and plucked the cat from the other side of the screen.

"Pouncer, you dummy, why do you keep doing this?"

Pouncer arched his back like a Halloween cat and hissed as though Chanis had done him a great disservice.

"Come get him a bite of this meringue, Chanis," Ma said. "That's all he wants."

"I brought it for you, Ma, not these critters," Chanis said, receiving a saucer's worth of the sticky sweet.

"They have bellies too, Son."

"I guess I'll head out if you don't need anything else." Chanis hated this part of his visits — the leave-taking. He never felt like he spent enough time with his family.

"I'm fine as frog's hair. You go on . . . get on the road before dark."

You'd think he had a thousand-mile journey ahead of him instead of just five. "The truck's got lamps, Ma."

"They might go out on you, or you could run out of gasoline." She pointed her fork in emphasis. "Now a horse could find its way home in the dark even with an empty stomach."

He was sure his mother was thinking of the time their horse carried his dad home through a blinding blizzard. That horse had become a hero in all their eyes.

She made a show of scraping the saucers

while Chanis went to the sideboard across from the table, where she kept the china teapot that had belonged to her mother. The pretty pot painted with pink flowers had been brought over from Ireland when Lydia Taylor emigrated. It was kept on the top-most shelf, away from little hands and eyes. Gingerly, Chanis removed the lid — still afraid of breaking it — and put some rolled bills inside. Ma didn't say a word and he didn't either. It was a little dance they played at each week — him giving what he wished was more and her receiving what she wished she didn't need.

"Tell the kids hey," he said at the door. "Tell Johnny I can't wait to hear his sermon."

"I will, Son. Now give your old ma a buss."

Leaning down, Chanis put a light kiss on her cheek. "See you next week, Ma."

"Be extra careful, Chanis. I had a bad dream last night."

"I will. I might be gone to Lexington later on. You call on Tully if you need anything."

"Go by the henhouse on your way out if you don't mind, Son. It's nigh on dark and the kids aren't here to open the door to let the chickens in for the night."

Ma always gave him a small job to do as he left. Somehow it made his leave-taking easier. "Will do, Ma."

Stepping into the chicken yard, Chanis propped the door to the coop open. The hens fussed their way inside. The over-proud rooster strutted in last. Turning the wooden latch, Chanis fastened them inside, safe from gimlet-eyed possums and sly red foxes. One of the girls would let them out come morning.

The chicken house was next to the bunk-house his dad had built for the boys. Chanis poked his head inside to make sure his brothers were keeping everything tidy. The beds were made — if a little sloppy — and there were no clothes on the floor. Good enough. The bunkhouse had a potbellied stove at the safe end. The one farthest from the door. It kept the room cozy warm in the winter. This time of year the boys would be sleeping in hammocks in the side yard. Even with all the windows open, the bunkhouse could get unbearably hot.

Two of the cats followed him all the way to the end of the lane. Once he got the truck fired up, he had to determine where the cats were before he could back out onto the road. He hoped Mazy would never want a cat. Maybe she'd like a dog, though. He was partial to collies and had always wanted one. Last year Mrs. Rogers's dog had a litter of six, but he hadn't been in the position to take one. He could picture a fine collie sitting shotgun in the truck. Maybe he'd name it Laddie — if Mazy agreed. She might rather have a girl to keep around the house.

A rumble of thunder made him step on the gas. He needed to get back and set the well before the rain began.

CHAPTER 11

Mazy woke to the sound of rain pattering on the roof. She wondered what she'd done with her umbrella and if her galoshes were still under the bed. Sometimes Mrs. Pearl threw the girls' stuff in the trash if she deemed it out of place when she ran the dust mop over the floors.

"Do I smell bacon?" Clara asked from the bed next to Mazy's.

Mazy stretched and yawned. "If it's Friday, it's pancakes and bacon." She was glad it was Friday. It had been a long week. Every muscle in her body was tired from the hours and hours at the typewriter.

"Almost makes it worth getting up," Clara said, swinging her feet to the floor. "Dibs on the lavatory."

Mazy drew her cotton wrapper around herself and cinched the tie at her waist. "I'm going on down. I'll dress later."

She would have liked the chance to wash

her face and dress her hair before going downstairs and usually got up fifteen minutes before the others in order to do so, but she'd overslept. Someone had to make concessions — might as well be her. Thankfully, Mrs. Pearl didn't mind if they came to breakfast in nightclothes as long as they were decent. One morning, Eva had come down in a pink silk ensemble, and Mrs. Pearl had sent her straight back upstairs. The silk was a tad too clingy for Mrs. Pearl's taste. Mazy wished she had the curves a silk robe would cling to. She might ask Eva where she had gotten the lingerie, but since the incident with the rose on Sunday, Eva was barely speaking to her. Every night after dishes, she would stare at her pruny hands and then give Mazy the evil eye.

"Morning, Mrs. Pearl," Mazy said. "Do you need any help?"

Mrs. Pearl sifted flour into a yellow bowl. "You could pour the milk if you don't mind, Mazy."

Taking glasses from the middle shelf of a kitchen cupboard, Mazy made two trips to the table with them. The cupboards were painted white with black trim. The upper shelves had glass fronts so that you could see everything inside, but the bottom cabinets were closed. Mrs. Pearl kept pots and pans and such in them. On top of the tall cabinet was a collection of chalk figurines: an elephant, a clown, a garishly painted parrot, and a bulldog. Eva called them tacky, but she didn't know that Mrs. Pearl's husband had won them for her at various county fairs when they were young and in love. Mazy could see why she would find them valuable.

Mazy's favorite kitchen was her sister Lilly's. It was kind of spare with only useful things in it, like the sink under the window, a modern stove, and a Hoosier cabinet (where Lilly, going against the grain as always, kept medical supplies). The walls were plastered and painted a sunny yellow and the woodwork was just stained, keeping the natural look of the wood. Lilly didn't like things too homey — and she couldn't abide knickknacks.

The pantry door was stuck. "Give it a good yank," Mrs. Pearl said. "It always sticks when it rains."

Mazy jerked it open and went to the wooden icebox to get the milk. She poured a bit in the cat's saucer, surprised that the mama hadn't come to greet her. Mrs. Pearl must have let her outside. Holding the bottle of milk by the neck, she went to the basket in the corner.

"Mrs. Pearl, the kittens aren't in here."

The jars and cans on the shelves shimmied as Mrs. Pearl pounded across the floor. Her footsteps were always heavy — she said her knees locked up. A fine swirl of flour beat her through the pantry door. Her wooden spoon still worked the pancake batter in the yellow bowl. "The mother must have hidden them. They do that sometimes. Look behind the laundry hamper."

On her knees, Mazy checked behind the hamper, then crawled across the floor to look behind the icebox. Feeling panicky, she pulled a sack of potatoes and one of pinto beans out from under a shelf. "They've disappeared."

"Did you close the door good and tight when you left them last night? Maybe they got out in the house."

"I did, and I counted them after I put fresh dirt in their necessary like I've done all week." Mazy stirred the rags in the bottom of the cat's basket. "They were all right here."

"Don't fret about it. They'll turn up. Someone must have come behind you last night and left the door ajar. Believe you me, you can't get rid of cats this easily."

At breakfast, the pancakes were tempting with melted butter and maple syrup, but

Mazy could barely swallow. An uneasy feeling caused a lump in her throat. Maybe the tabby would hide her kittens, but she would still come out to eat. She couldn't make milk if she was hungry.

Friday was a half day of classes. Mazy vowed to look all over for the cats when she got home. She'd turn the house upside down if she had to.

A crazy wind whipped around the girls as they made their way to class. Clara's umbrella turned inside out, so she had to huddle with Mazy under hers.

"Are you ill, Clara? You didn't eat a bite of your breakfast."

"You didn't eat much either, Mazy. Maybe we're both coming down with something. Does your stomach feel queasy?"

"No, I'm fine. I'm just worried about the kittens." Mazy stepped over a puddle, but Clara missed a step and splashed them both with muddy water.

"Sorry."

"It's just water, Clara. We'll dry."

"If this rain doesn't let up, we won't be able to go to High Bridge tomorrow. I was counting on finding my spectacles."

Mazy tilted the umbrella against the wind. "I predict buttermilk skies tomorrow."

"That makes no sense, Mazy. You can't

drink the sky."

"My mother used to say that — it means the clouds are fluffy and break up easily, like creamy buttermilk."

"Don't talk about food. It's making me ill," Clara said.

"Maybe you should go home and lie down."

Clara grabbed Mazy's elbow, hurrying them along. "Not a chance," she said. "I've already got two strikes against me."

Once settled at her desk, Mazy uncovered her machine and started the day's practice. She surprised herself when she began to enjoy typing. Once she'd figured out that the keys were somewhat like a puzzle, she hadn't missed a stroke. She had Mrs. Carpenter to thank for that.

From the corner of her eye, she kept watch on Clara, who had turned a peculiar shade of green. Ernestine had read snippets of the *Lexington Herald* to them over breakfast. The paper warned of an outbreak of the Russian influenza in the nearby town of Midway. Maybe that's what Clara had, although a green face wasn't noted in the list of symptoms reported in the newspaper: chills, fever, lassitude, hoarse cough, and an anxiety to be near the fire.

Mazy hurried home after classes were

dismissed. It meant missing lunch at the tearoom, her favorite place, but she was too worried about the kittens to eat. She thought perhaps Clara would skip also, but she seemed to have perked up. Thank goodness.

The rain had stopped, but Mazy kept her umbrella unfurled against the fat drops that plopped down from the trees. The sun popped out from behind a cloud, causing the puddles along the street to sparkle and wink. Nearing her street, Mazy paused to look behind her, hoping to see a rainbow. Already-fading bands of pink and lavender blue arched across the sky. She would count it as God's blessing and claim it for the kittens.

In her room, she shook the damp from her skirt and hung it from a hanger before putting on one of the dresses Lilly's neighbor had made for her school toilette. A modified suit dress with a fitted bodice, it was Mazy's favorite. In the foyer, she pulled her galoshes back on and went to find Mrs. Pearl.

"Drink this," Mrs. Pearl said by way of greeting.

Mazy sniffed at the glass Mrs. Pearl thrust at her. "What is it? It smells like grass."

"It's an infusion against the grippe," Mrs.

Pearl said. "The recipe was handed down from my grandmother's mother. You take a measure of mullein, a pinch of flaxseed, a bit of slippery elm, stir them all up in warm lemonade, and . . . down the hatch."

Mazy held her nose and took a gulp. The taste made her shiver. "Ugh, this is worse than castor oil."

"Not a soul in my family has ever got the influenza — not even during the epidemic of 1889."

"My goodness, Mrs. Pearl, they probably all died on the spot from drinking this concoction."

Mrs. Pearl didn't give an inch. Mazy downed the rest. Vile though it was, she would get the recipe and send it to her mother. Lilly mostly practiced modern medicine, but she might like a copy also.

"Please tell me you found the kittens."

Mrs. Pearl frowned, turning her double chin into three. "I've found nary a one, and I've turned this house upside down. Alls I can figure is they somehow got outside."

The yard was dripping wet. Rivulets of water formed tiny creeks that raced across the yard as if they might make it to the ocean if they were only fast enough. Mazy plucked a leaf from the maple tree and set it to sail down one of the streams; it didn't get very far before it ran aground.

She spied something furry and gray in a puddle under the downspout at the corner of the house. Two of the kittens were gray; three were yellowish like their mother. Mrs. Pearl said if she found a gray male cat in the neighborhood, she was sending his owner a bill and at least two kittens.

The gray lump was not moving. Swallowing hard, Mazy found a stick and gently probed the dirty water. The lump broke apart. She could make out three hairless tails. She lifted the minute mouse bodies from the water with the end of her stick. Poor little baby things. Now they'd never have the pleasure of running wildly from the cats or eating the corn in the garden. Gathering sodden leaves and twigs, Mazy covered them where they lay.

"Kitty, kitty, kitty," she said, letting her voice lilt like Mrs. Pearl's did when she called the tabby cat to supper. She vowed to give the mama cat a proper name once she was found. When she had asked Mrs. Pearl why she'd never named her, Mrs. Pearl said once you name a cat, you're stuck with it forever. Mazy figured that had happened when Mrs. Pearl let the cat come into the house.

After an hour of looking under every bush

and tromping through the garden, Mazy had found not one cat.

"You look a fright," Ernestine said when, following lunch, she came out to help.

Mazy tucked a hank of hair behind her ear. "Let's search the shed."

They looked through everything, carefully moving heaps of junk and some treasures. "Look, Mazy," Ernestine said as she tugged a set of handlebars from a musty corner. "It's a bicycle. Let's try it out."

"I don't have the heart to have fun right now. Besides, the tires are flat."

"Where you find a bicycle, you'll likely find a pump," Ernestine said. "Listen — did you hear a meow?"

Mazy strained her ears. All she could hear was her own muffled heartbeat.

Turning her ear toward the floor, Ernestine paced the cluttered shed.

"Here," she said, pointing to a large knothole.

Mazy scrambled over a stack of moldy newspapers. Dropping to her hands and knees, she looked down into the darkness. There she spied the tabby with some kittens curled close beside. "What should I do? Should I get them out or leave well enough alone? I can bring food out here, and water."

"I don't know," Ernestine said. "I'd say leave them alone."

Mazy shuddered thinking about the dead mice. "But they're so little. Anything could happen to them."

"Ask the expert," Ernestine said. "Mrs. Pearl will know what's best."

"You're right, but I want to see them first — make sure they're all there."

Back outside they studied their options. Set three feet off the ground on a stacked stone foundation, the shed listed to one side; it had definitely seen better days. Patches of white paint clung here and there from the weathered wooden siding. Most had flaked off, giving in to the ravages of time and weather.

"We'll have to move some rocks," Mazy said. "Then I can crawl under."

"That's not a good idea. The whole thing could collapse on you."

"I guess we could saw a hole in the floor instead."

"We could just drop food down through the knothole. Obviously the mother can get out whenever she wants."

"How do we know that?" Mazy asked.

"She got in, didn't she?"

"Well, yes, she did, but I still want to count the kittens. Let's look around."

At the back of the shed, they found a gap in the underpinning. "It's like a chink in armor," Mazy said as, kneeling, she pried one lichen-covered rock loose and then another.

Ernestine stood with her arms crossed. "I am not going to help you get yourself killed, Mazy Pelfrey."

"Would you fetch me one of those old dusters we saw hanging in the corner of the shed? I'd hate to ruin this dress."

In two shakes, Ernestine was brushing the dust from a faded cotton coverall. She helped Mazy slip it on over her dress.

Mazy lay facedown on the ground and began to inch through the gap in the wall. Pulling herself along by her elbows, she slid several feet under the shed toward the cats. The tabby hissed and spat. "There, there," Mazy murmured. "I won't hurt you. I wouldn't hurt you for the world."

The tabby untangled herself from her babies and beat a retreat back out the way Mazy had come in.

Ernestine gave a shocked yelp. "She nearly ran me over. Are you okay in there, Mazy?"

"There are only four kittens," Mazy said. "One of the grays is missing."

"Well, four is better than none. What are you going to do with them?"

"Please go get Mrs. Pearl. I'm not sure what is best."

The babies' tiny mews mingled with the squeaky sound of Ernestine's feet running through the wet grass. Mazy's heart turned over as she gathered them close to her chest. Like a tipsy clown, a tiny body staggered toward her from the farthest corner — the missing gray. Mazy laughed aloud. "Thank You, Lord," she praised. "Now please help me put this little family back together."

"Bring them out, Mazy," Mrs. Pearl shouted through the gap in the wall. "They'll likely die of shock if they stay under there, as wet as it is."

"I'll go get the basket," Ernestine said.

"Do you need me to come under there and help?" Polly said.

At the girl's willingness to help, Mazy felt a warmth that had nothing to do with the kittens. "No, but thanks, Polly. I'll hand them off to you, though."

In three backward trips clutching kittens, they were all safe. "It's going to be harder to get out than it was to get in," Mazy said, squirming on her belly until her feet were outside the gap.

"It seems you have company," Eva said, her voice dripping icicles. "Your beau is standing on the front porch."

Mazy let her head fall on her folded arms. It must be Loyal. Who else could it be? Eva was just being her condescending self — saying he was her beau. Why, she hardly knew him. He'd been really nice on Sunday, though, and he had given her that rose. And, my, wasn't he handsome — and didn't he smell good?

"For heaven's sake," Mrs. Pearl said. "Where's your manners, Eva? Go let him in. Have him wait in the parlor."

Mazy inched backward until strong hands gripped her ankles and pulled her out. "Thanks, Polly," she said.

"You simply can't see company looking like that," Ernestine said.

"She's right," Polly added. "You're an allover mess."

"Wash up in the kitchen," Mrs. Pearl said, taking the basket of kittens from Ernestine. "I'll make some cocoa. The girls can keep you company."

Mazy didn't mind sharing her visit with Loyal. She understood Mrs. Pearl's rules about not being alone in the house with a fellow. Besides, she couldn't think of a thing she could talk about with Loyal Chambers.

In the kitchen, Ernestine sponged a bit of mud from the hem of Mazy's skirt while Polly fluffed her hair. Mazy felt like she was in court, preparing to see the king.

"Where's Clara?" Mazy asked.

"She took to her bed as soon as we got back," Polly said. "She thinks she's coming down with something."

Ernestine tweaked the collar of Mazy's dress. "There, that's better. Now come on; we don't want to keep your 'beau' waiting."

"Don't say that. You'll upset Eva."

"A pox on Eva," Ernestine said. "Someone needs to put her in her place."

CHAPTER 12

Mazy pinched her cheeks for color just before opening the parlor door. She'd never had a gentleman caller before. Except for Chanis Clay maybe, but he'd never been unexpected — he was just sort of always there, especially at suppertime.

Polly and Ernestine were right on her heels, and Mrs. Pearl wasn't far behind. Mazy took a breath and turned the knob.

Goodness gracious, Chanis Clay perched on the edge of Mrs. Pearl's fancy horsehair sofa, looking as out of place as a pickle in a fruit salad. And there was Eva, sitting a little too close in Mazy's estimation, looking like an exotic maraschino cherry.

"Chanis? What are you doing here?"

Chanis stood so quickly, his hat dropped from his lap to the floor. Polly swooped in and picked it up. "I'll just put this on the hall tree for you," she said.

"I just came from the jail," he said. "I had

177

to transport a prisoner — thought I'd stop by, see how you're doing."

Mrs. Pearl extended her hand. "Dorothy Pearl. My father was a sheriff."

"Local?" Chanis asked.

"Twenty years right here in Fayette County."

"I'm sorry; I should introduce you," Mazy said. "Chanis, these are my classmates Polly, Ernestine, and Eva; and this is Mrs. Pearl, my housemother. Ladies, this is Chanis Clay, a friend from back home."

She didn't miss Chanis's raised eyebrows at the "friend from back home." It made her feel uncomfortable — like he was claiming her. When she'd left home to come to school, she thought she'd made it clear that she was not pledging herself to him. She'd thought he understood.

"I hope you'll stay for supper," Mrs. Pearl said.

"Thanks for the invite, ma'am, but I have to get on the road soon."

"Well, it was good to meet you. Stop in anytime." Mrs. Pearl walked to the doorway. "Girls," she said, "let's give Mazy a few moments with her friend."

"Special rules for special people," Eva said just loud enough for Mazy to hear. Now she'd never get on Eva's good side.

"It's good to see you, Chanis," Mazy said as soon as the others had left.

"Mazy, I wish you would come home." He rested his hands lightly on her waist. "I can't tell you how much I miss you."

She crooked her head to look up at him. She'd forgotten how tall he was and how muscular. She traced a red mark on his chin. "I don't remember this."

"I had a little dustup," he said. "It's healing. Nothing to worry about."

His voice resonated with the sound of home, drawing her closer. For a moment she allowed herself to feel comforted in the circle of his arms.

"I really want to kiss you, Mazy."

"You know better, Chanis Clay."

"But I shaved twice this morning," he said.

Laughing, she stepped away. His sense of humor always caught her off guard. She patted a spot on the sofa. "Sit with me awhile. Tell me of Skip Rock."

They spent a pleasant twenty minutes catching up, reconnecting. Mazy was surprised at how right it felt to be with him. He told her the goings-on in Skip Rock, and she shared about how Mrs. Carpenter had blacked the keys and about how homesick she grew at times.

"Come back with me and you'll never be

lonesome again," he said.

"You can't guarantee another person's state of mind, Chanis."

Capturing her hand, he turned it palm up and stroked it with his thumb. "I'd sure try."

Slowly she removed her hand. His touch made her feel guilty. Maybe she needed to tell him about Loyal, but what was there to tell? Surely it was better to let it lie and not make a big to-do about what might be nothing. She'd wait and see how things went. She wasn't in charge of Chanis's feelings any more than he was in charge of hers. Even though it seemed he'd always tried to be.

She remembered the first time she'd taken real notice of Chanis Clay. It was the summer before last, when Lilly had sent her on an errand to the sheriff's office. His uniform, the holstered gun on his hip, and the star on his chest had bedazzled her. With Lilly's permission, they started stepping out, just walking close to home, Sunday school picnics, and visits with his family and hers. Once she had let him kiss her. It had seemed right, natural, at the time. But in retrospect, she should not have let it go that far. A kiss was a promise, and now he seemed ready to cash that promise in.

"A penny for your thoughts," he said.

180

She stood and walked to the window. "Is that your vehicle?"

Coming up behind her, he pulled the heavy drapes farther apart. "Sort of. It belongs to the city council, but I drive it. I reckon I can keep it until the next election. Who knows what will happen then."

"Oh, Chanis, everyone in Skip Rock likes you. I'm sure they'll keep voting for you."

"You never know," he said.

Working a wrinkle from the curtain's tieback, she dared a question. "Do you ever want to do something else?"

"Like be something besides a sheriff?" he asked. He stood so close she could feel the deep masculine timbre of his voice.

"Yes, that and . . . I don't know, maybe live somewhere different — meet different people."

"I don't want to meet anyone but you, Mazy."

She took a breath. "Let's not get too serious. I don't know for sure what I'll want to do once I finish secretarial school."

"I'm willing to wait. I hadn't thought about living somewhere else, but I'm not married to that place or that job."

Mazy began to think Chanis Clay was stuck to her like that prickly burr that had torn her stockings.

A weight tugged at the hem of her skirt, dragging the fabric down like a fishing sinker. Mazy swatted at her ankles and caught a handful of fur.

She lifted the tiny thing to her chest. "Oh, it's one of the gray kittens. How in the world did he get in here?" She stroked the kitten's head as she filled Chanis in on the day's excitement. "This kitty must be looking for his mother. Let's take him back to his basket."

In the kitchen Mrs. Pearl tucked the kitten in the basket with the others. "Still no sign of the mother."

Polly took hold of Chanis's elbow. "Sheriff, surely you can help us track her down."

"Do, Chanis, please," Mazy said.

"Show me exactly where you found the others," Chanis said, rolling up his sleeves.

Thankfully the skies had cleared. The girls held their skirts up against the wetness lingering in the grass. Mrs. Pearl stayed on the porch. Eva stood behind her in the open door, her hand held to her throat.

Chanis walked around the shed before heading toward the shade tree. "Two to one she's up the tree."

Mazy looked up through the branches. "There she is."

"I'll get a saucer of cream to entice her

down," Mrs. Pearl said.

Chanis reached for his holster. "Don't bother."

"Don't shoot her," Polly gasped.

Chanis removed his gun belt and handed it to Mazy. "Here, hold this."

Even Eva oohed and aahed when Chanis grabbed a high branch and pulled himself up. Mazy took notice of the way his muscles stood out on his arms and bunched up across his shoulders. Chanis was a good-looking man and hers for the asking.

A rustle high up in the leaves signaled that Chanis either had the cat or was about to fall from the tree. "Got her," he said, dropping down.

"Praise the Lord for small favors," Mrs. Pearl said, receiving the tabby. "And thank you, Sheriff Clay."

"You're more than welcome," Chanis said. "I'm always rescuing my mother's cats." He took his gun belt from Mazy. "Walk me to the truck?"

They lingered awhile as the sky darkened, threatening a rainy evening. Gas lamps winked on up and down the street, catching them in a yellow glow.

"I've never seen a rainier summer," Chanis said.

"Everyone says the same. Wonder why."

"Don't know. The winter was wet too."

"Why are we talking about the weather, Chanis?"

"I'm stretching out the time. I don't want to leave you. If there weren't so many eyes upon us, I'd take you in my arms."

"Eyes?"

"Don't look now, but the windows are full of women."

"Did you like Eva?" Mazy teased. "She's quite beautiful, don't you think?"

"There's something about that one," he said. "She's got eyes like a snake."

"She dresses beautifully and is so sophisticated. I'd like to be half as fashionable as Eva is."

He captured her chin between his thumb and the knuckle of his index finger, lifting her face. "Sweet girl, there's not a woman in the world who holds a candle to you."

Here was her moment. She had to mention Loyal Chambers. It wouldn't be fair for Chanis to go back to Skip Rock not knowing that she'd begun to dream of time with someone else.

He gave her chin a caress with his thumb and looked at her with such longing it stilled her voice.

"I've got to go, Mazy. When will you be home for a visit?"

"We have a break in a couple of weeks — I thought I'd told you."

"No. No, you didn't. I would not have forgotten. Maybe you told your sister in a letter. I haven't had one in a while."

Mazy felt like a third grader — chastised for not memorizing her times tables. Suddenly she was right back at the blackboard, her nose full of chalk dust, missing recess while she ciphered her times tables.

"That's okay, Mazy. I know you're busy, and usually Doc Lilly saves all your letters for me." He struck his forehead with the heel of his hand. "I nearly forgot. She sent you a package."

"She did? What's in it?"

Chanis lifted a box wrapped in brown paper and tied with string from the truck. "I don't know — she said something about clothes."

Mazy took the box. A gift from her sister took away the sting from Chanis's chiding. Lilly always made her feel better, no matter what the circumstance.

"All right, then," Chanis said. "I'll see you in a couple of weeks. I have a big surprise waiting for you at home."

Mazy was itching to get back in the house, where she could tear the paper from the box, but she stood on the sidewalk and waved until his truck turned the corner, leaving nothing but a puff of dark exhaust hanging in the lamplight.

Busy fiddling with the string, Mazy didn't notice the girls had come outside until she stepped up on the porch.

Polly was still waving. "He's just divine, Mazy."

"And nice," Ernestine said.

"But who'd want to be squired around in that thing he drives?" Eva said.

"Me," Polly said.

"You're just jealous, Eva," Ernestine said. "I notice you came out to see him off."

"I simply followed you. I wanted some fresh air. Those stupid cats make me sneeze."

Mazy led the way to the kitchen. She put the box on the table before she fetched the scissors from the cabinet drawer. Lilly tied a mean knot.

"Did you notice how firmly he handled the cat?" Polly asked. "And did you see the gun in the holster? I'll bet he has to shoot people all the time. Do you know, Mazy?"

"Hmm?" Mazy asked as she unfolded the box flaps.

"Does Sheriff Clay shoot folks with that gun?"

"I shouldn't think so," Mazy said. "He

mostly just threatens to."

Polly busied herself by folding the white tissue paper Mazy flung from the box. "I wish he'd threaten me," she said.

Holding a middy blouse in front of her, Mazy danced around the kitchen. "I forgot that my sister was having some clothes altered for me." She draped the blouse over the back of a chair before taking another article out. "Oh, this is so nice. Now I won't have to tie a ribbon around my waist to keep my skirts up."

"You're so lucky," Polly said.

Ernestine rolled the string into a ball and put it in the drawer with the scissors. "A person makes their own luck," she said.

"Or steals someone else's," Eva said with a sniff.

"What's that supposed to mean?" Mazy asked while breaking down the cardboard box.

"Mazy, clear the table," Mrs. Pearl said. "Supper's running late, what with all the excitement. It's just cold cuts and cheese tonight."

"Good," Eva said. "The dishes will be easy."

Mazy stacked her new outfits. "I'll take these up and see how Clara's doing."

Clara was sleeping on her side with her

hands tucked under her chin. Mazy hated to wake her, but she must be hungry by now. "Clara?" she said gently, shaking her friend's shoulder. "Are you feeling better?"

Clara woke and reached for her readers. "Is it morning?"

"No, evening — you've slept the afternoon away. Come to the table. Supper's ready."

It was Mazy, not Clara, who woke feeling ill in the middle of the night. Throwing back the covers, she stumbled toward the bathroom in the hall. Nearly there, she doubled over in pain. It felt like her stomach was gripping her backbone. When she pulled the string to the bulb hanging from the ceiling, the bathroom flooded with harsh light. Clinging to the rim of the porcelain sink, she turned the handle, then splashed her face with cold water. The pain let up.

She studied her reflection in the mirror. Her skin was bright red despite the cold water dripping on her cotton gown. After using the facility, she patted her face dry with the soft flannel squares Mrs. Pearl kept there for their use.

Feeling shaky and cold, she started back to her room, wanting nothing more than to pull the cover over her head and sink into sleep. Another searing pain took her to the floor. Crying out, she curled on her side and pulled her knees to her chest.

"Mazy?" Polly said. "Whatever is the matter?"

"Oh, Polly, it hurts. It hurts. Please get Mrs. Pearl."

Soon she heard Mrs. Pearl's heavy tread on the stairs. Mrs. Pearl struck a match and lit the coal-oil lamp on the hall table. The sharp scent of sulfur melded with the warm smell of oil, turning Mazy's stomach.

"Get a basin from the lavatory," Mrs. Pearl instructed Polly.

Mrs. Pearl helped Mazy into a sitting position while Polly hurried to get the granite pan. The commotion had wakened the others. Their soft murmuring comforted Mazy. If she died, at least she wouldn't die alone.

Polly held the basin under Mazy's chin while Ernestine placed a cold, wet cloth to her forehead. The pain faded. "I'm okay now," she said.

"See if you can stand," Mrs. Pearl said.

Feeling shaky, Mazy stood balancing with one hand against the wall. "If I can only get back to bed," she said before the hallway began to swirl and the floor came up to meet her.

"Call Dr. Chambers," Mrs. Pearl said. "Her number's in the front of the phone book by the telephone in the foyer."

"I'll call," Ernestine said.

The next thing Mazy heard was Dr. Chambers calling her name. "Mazy! Mazy!"

Mazy tried to focus, but the discomfort in her belly was so intense she couldn't attend to anything else.

Dr. Chambers poked her fingers into Mazy's right side, causing her to cry out and push the doctor's hand away from her tender abdomen.

"Lie still," Dr. Chambers said sharply. "I'm trying to help you."

Mazy puckered her lips around a glass thermometer. It didn't feel like help to her.

"Appendicitis," the doctor said, shaking the thermometer down. "I'll make arrangements at St. Joseph's for surgery as soon as possible."

"Can't it wait until I notify her sister?" Mrs. Pearl said. "She's a doctor also."

"Really? Where does she practice?"

"Somewhere up in the mountains. I don't remember exactly. I'd have to look it up."

Mazy felt like someone had thrown her a lifeline. "Please, please call Lilly," she whimpered and clutched the doctor's hand. "Please call my sister."

Dr. Chambers hung her stethoscope

around her neck. "We have a small window of time since she hasn't developed a temperature, but not long. If her appendix ruptures, she could die."

"Do you have to cut her open?" Polly asked. "Will she have a scar?"

"For pity's sake, Polly," Mrs. Pearl said.

Mazy writhed in fear and pain. She didn't even know what an appendix was, but if God had given her one, she badly wanted to keep it.

"My son is waiting in the car. Someone go get him, please."

"I'll go," Eva said, pulling on a robe and tucking her hair behind her ears.

"The rest of you girls get decent," Mrs. Pearl said, "and bring Mazy's robe and slippers."

CHAPTER 13

Chanis Clay was dog tired well before he ever reached Skip Rock. He hadn't expected to like Frank Cheney as much as he did. Leaving him at the jail, knowing he was more than likely going to wind up in prison, was hard. He felt like he was turning his brother in. It was difficult to ascertain whether Frank was a con man or simply a man desperately down on his luck, but the outcome of his trial seemed like a sure thing. It was bad enough that he'd robbed a string of banks, but then he'd also held up a mail truck, another federal offense.

During the trip to Lexington, Frank had pulled a sheaf of envelopes from the inside breast pocket of his beat-up denim jacket. "I wonder, could you make a special delivery?" he'd asked.

Chanis pulled the truck to the side of the road and slammed on the brakes. "Where'd you get those?"

"They're left over from when I absent-mindedly ran upon that mail delivery."

Chanis let the *absentmindedly* slide. It was no use to engage Frank about everything he said.

"Why did you keep these? Were you hoping there'd be cash or money orders inside?"

Frank had swollen up with pride. With his double chins all aquiver, he put Chanis in mind of a bullfrog singing a sad song on a riverbank.

"I would never," he sputtered.

"Frank, you robbed the mailman. We know you took money from him."

Despite his handcuffs, Frank waved the envelopes in the general direction of Chanis's nose. "These here are all addressed in a feminine hand — probably mothers writing to their sons or maybe young women penning notes to their sweethearts. I figured to drop them in a mailbox somewhere."

Chanis thought of the old saw about honor among thieves. It was not a saying he believed in, but there was something about Frank.

"How in the world did you manage to keep these after you were arrested?" Chanis asked while springing the front of the glove box.

"Nobody checked my jacket. The deputies

just hung it on a coatrack when I came in and handed it back to me when I left out," Frank said, his leg irons rattling when he changed positions, getting his knees out of the way.

Chanis shook his head in disbelief. That was seriously stupid. There could have been a pistol in the pocket instead of mail. "You know I'll have to turn them in, Frank. They're evidence."

"How much evidence do you think the government needs? It's their fault anyway."

After a quick glance at the road, Chanis pulled back onto the highway. "How do you figure that?"

"All those slick government guys and toadying banker types are fat cats skimming the cream from the top — living off the workingman."

"When's the last time you held a job, Frank?"

Frank jangled his cuffs. "You think this ain't work? The pay stinks too." He looked over his shoulder. "You got anything to eat back there?"

While Chanis drove, his prisoner had eaten the two thick ham and cheese sandwiches and the packet of chips Chanis had purchased from the Rogerses' store. The handcuffs did not even slow him down.

"Want some?" he offered, thrusting the chips toward Chanis.

Chanis shook his head. The rank odor reminiscent of a pigsty emanating from the passenger's seat took his appetite. It wouldn't have been that hard for the deputy to have seen that his prisoner had soap and water for a bath and a shave that morning. At least his striped uniform was large enough and clean.

"Reason these letters mean so much," Frank said around bites, "is because my sister used to write to me. Her letters kept me sane last time I was in the pokey. I'll tell you that. Say, can you reach that jar of tea?"

Despite himself, Chanis had been sucked into Frank's world. "Where's your sister live?"

"Mason County. You ever been there?"

"Can't say as I have."

Frank fiddled with the jar lid. Thwarted by the short chain of the cuffs, he held the jar in place with his knees. "Has the prettiest town, Maysville, right on the Ohio River." He patted the dash. "You and me ought to run Old Ray here up there. What do you say?"

Chanis shifted gears, enjoying the power with which Old Ray maneuvered the treacherously steep road. "There's the little matter of a trial, Frank. I'm not looking to get arrested for harboring a fugitive."

Frank stared out the window. "If we was to stand on the top of this mountain, we could watch ourselves a-coming and a-going. They call this road a hairpin 'cause of the way it turns back on itself."

Chanis had traveled this mountain road many times, but he let Frank be the knowledgeable one. Sometimes a body needed to share something.

"So did you write your sister back?"

"Nah, I figured nobody wants to get a letter posted from Eddyville. My sister's a godly woman. Her mailman might talk — you know how folks like to gossip." Frank bumped the front of the glove box with his knee. "But that's why I kept these missives separate. Somebody somewhere might be desperate to hear from home."

"I can see that, Frank, but taking the letters was not your right."

"Don't you ever do anything just for the heck of it, Sheriff? Just because it feels right at the time? Maybe because it seems more right than what the law allows?" Frank looked toward the rear of the truck again. "I'm still empty as a rain barrel in August. You bring any dessert?"

The miles had dispersed like so much

smoke behind them. After half an apple pie, Frank slept with his head pressed up against the window. Lost in thought, Chanis kept Old Ray on the straight and narrow. He wondered what might happen if every prisoner had someone to talk to — someone who had a vested interest in listening and maybe even caring.

It seemed an odd coincidence now that both Frank and Mazy had challenged him with what was basically the same question. "Don't you ever want to do something else?" Mazy had asked, turning her sweet face up to his, nearly mimicking Frank's comment that had seemed more a challenge than a question: "Don't you ever do anything because it feels right at the time?"

He didn't concern himself with Frank Cheney's musings, but he greatly cared what Mazy thought. Did he come across as a stick-in-the-mud?

Famished, he stopped in Campton at a filling station. He'd had to rouse the attendant, who grudgingly opened up for his late-night customer. After filling the tank on the truck, the man had sold him a cold fried-egg sandwich and filled his thermos with stale coffee.

Chanis pondered his visit with Mazy as he chewed on the rubbery egg and sipped the scorched coffee. She'd seemed different in a way he couldn't put his finger on — maybe a little distant and definitely older. He supposed that was to be expected. It was hard to keep a relationship going when it was carried on with two-cent stamps, especially when he was the only one visiting the post office. With one hand on the steering wheel, he scratched the stubble on his chin. When was the last time he'd received a letter from her? Weeks — it was weeks, although he wrote her religiously every Sunday afternoon. Mostly he read the letters Doc Lilly shared with him. Mazy always mentioned his name. *Say hello to Chanis,* she would pen, or *Tell Chanis thanks for the letter.*

Suddenly he had a sick feeling in the pit of his stomach. He pitched the remainder of his stale biscuit out the window and capped the thermos. It took every ounce of discipline he had to not turn the truck around and head right back to Lexington, but what would it benefit if he did? What was he going to do? Kidnap her? Demand she reciprocate his feelings? He was flummoxed. It wasn't as if he had an example to go by. Whatever romance his parents might have experienced was now clouded by grief and lingering sorrow. His closest friend, Tully, had married when he was still a boy,

198

sixteen, and his wife even younger. They barely tolerated one another, mostly enjoying life through their three sons. The boys were all Tully talked about.

His preacher's marriage should have given insight. Brother Allen was a jolly, keys-to-the-Kingdom sort of man. It made you happy just to be around him, but his wife was sour as a green persimmon. She carried life like it was a heavy yoke upon her shoulders.

Chanis's mother said Mrs. Allen could do with a good meal, but then his mother believed in the power of food. She was always feeding somebody. Every summer she put up quarts and quarts of garden truck, much more than her large family needed, but not a quart or a pint would be left when the next summer rolled around. She would have given away every last jar that her family didn't eat. She'd quote that Scripture concerning not laying up stores while she packed a bushel basket with canned green beans, tomatoes (whole and stewed), sauerkraut, blackberries (jam and jelly), pears (whole in syrup), and apples (butter and sauced) for one of her kids to deliver to a neighbor or a church member. "The Rapture won't catch me with a full cellar while other folks go hungry," she'd say. His mother was a saint. She would have been right at home with the Israelites eating manna in the wilderness.

Doc Lilly and her husband, Tern Still, seemed happy to him, but the doc was awful independent. Her husband was frequently away on business, and she did fine without him. Chanis thought he'd like a woman more like his mother, strong in her own way but still deferring to her husband. No way would he want his wife to be out working. What if she made more money than he did? How would that look?

The best thing about driving was that it gave a body plenty of time to think. With Skip Rock within spitting distance, he stopped the truck on the side of the road and walked down to the river. It was early morning. Mist rose from the shallows like the ethereal remnants of a dream.

No matter what life had brought, he'd always soldiered on. The death of his father was the hardest, followed by his election as the county's youngest-ever (and certainly greenest-ever) sheriff. He'd figured out the best ways to deal with those things; why couldn't he figure out how to deal with Mazy?

With a practiced flip of the wrist, he flung a round, flat stone toward the opposite bank. The mist shrouded his effort, but he could hear the rock skipping across the surface of the river with a satisfying *thwip, thwip, thwip.* When he was a kid, they'd called it "walking on water," bringing a favorite Bible story about Peter to mind. He wished he had enough faith to walk on water if Jesus commanded him to.

The sun rising over the far mountain turned the sky golden red and cast a pink glow on the water. "Red sky in the morning, sailor take warning," the old saying went. Well, he was not a sailor, but he'd better heed the warning and get on home before the sky brewed up another storm.

He could swear Old Ray issued a heavy sigh of relief once Chanis turned onto the gravel road that led to his house and parked under a shade tree. This was when he most wanted a dog. He could picture a black-and-white shepherd running down the road to greet him. Considering Mazy's attitude, a dog might be the only thing that ever would. Thinking about a dog led him to thinking about cats — Mrs. Pearl's kittens, to be exact. Something nagged at him. Some bit of something did not fit. He cataloged his visit backward: telling Mazy good-bye, taking the cat down from the tree, the gray kitten in the parlor. Mazy coming into the room, Chanis sitting on the sofa waiting. That odd girl, Eva. The scratches on her wrists.

He was punchy from driving all night, but the scratches seemed important. For whatever reason, Eva had done something with the kittens. He was sure of it. What it had to do with Mazy, he didn't know. One thing was for sure: Eva didn't like Mazy. You could tell that by the way she looked at her — eyes narrowed like a cat's just before it pounces on a mouse.

His pillow was calling, but first he'd pump some water from his fine, new well. The water in Lexington was not as good as his. It might be more convenient turning the handle on a faucet, but the reward was tainted, faintly metallic.

Muddy water gushed into the bucket. He should have asked Tully how long it took for the mud to settle out. Hopefully there was still some water in the house. If not, he'd have to go to the spring. As tired as he was, that was a daunting chore.

In the kitchen, he scooped what little water there was in the bucket up with the granite dipper and poured it into a glass. His throat was parched from the bitter coffee he'd drunk on the way home. Turning from the sink, he went to set the glass on the table and noticed a piece of torn note-book paper anchored there by the sugar bowl. Setting the glass beside the bowl, he scanned the note. It was written in Tully's bold style.

Fri. 0700. Come to Evers place soon as you get in. Bad goings-on.

Chanis looked at his timepiece. Quarter to eight — he'd just missed Tully. Suddenly wide-awake, he scrubbed his face with the palms of his hands. Wishing he had time for a shave, he grabbed his hat and headed for the truck.

CHAPTER 14

Mazy kept her head just so on the pillow. Anytime she moved the slightest bit, the room spun like a carousel.

Last night had been the worst night of her life, even worse than the Christmas Eve when her brother told her that Santa Claus was not real. Worse than the night her cat Missy had died. Last night, Mazy thought *she* might die.

The pain had been so bad, she barely remembered Loyal lifting her into his arms and carrying her to the car. The hospital had been a blur: The smells of rubbing alcohol and iodine. A sound of moaning mingling with the whir of rubber wheels against a waxed floor. The cool, firm hands of a nurse called Sister who wore a hat with wings. The press of a metal rim against her mouth. The splash of vile liquid hollowing her insides. The prick of a needle. Her senses whirling into oblivion.

Where was she? The bed didn't feel like hers. The pillow was firm. The linens were heavily starched and drawn so tight she couldn't wiggle her toes. But the scent of Cashmere Bouquet comforted her. "Mrs. Pearl?"

She opened her eyes the tiniest bit, squinting against the light. The door was ajar and voices drifted in. One was her landlady's; one sounded like Dr. Chambers's. "I've talked to her sister again, and we agree that considering the circumstances it would be best to keep Mazy on bed rest for a week. Since the hospital is overrun with cases of influenza, she can stay here, where I can keep a close eye on her."

"I feel just dreadful about this," Mrs. Pearl said.

Mazy shut her eyes. She must have something terrible if it made Mrs. Pearl feel dreadful.

"I'm still not 100 percent sure the vomiting wasn't related to her appendix rather than the tonic you gave her."

"What can I do to help? I can send food."

"She'll have nothing but water for three days. Meanwhile, I'll keep her slightly sedated to control the vomiting, so you could send someone to stay with her during the night. Perhaps one of the other students?

My housekeeper will be here to help out during the day, and there's a girl I can hire."

"They can rotate night shifts. It'll be a good experience for them. I'll arrange it with Mrs. Carpenter."

"Do you need for me to send the car around this evening?"

"No, they can catch the trolley. There's a stop just one street over."

"We're all set, then."

"I'll just say good-bye," Mrs. Pearl said.

"She's sleeping. I'd rather you not wake her."

"You'll call me if she takes a turn?"

"Of course, and I'll send a report each morning with the girls."

"Do you think I should telephone Dr. Still? I can't imagine what she must think of me."

"I'm sure she would appreciate a call. Her own children are ill or she'd be on the next train out of Skip Rock."

"Oh, dear. I think they're tiny still. I hope it's not too bad."

Mazy could hear a rustle of skirts and footsteps retreating. "German measles," Dr. Chambers said, her voice trailing away. "She said they've already broken out and that the symptoms are mild, but of course she can't . . ."

The twins ill? Little Julia and Simon. Mazy hated to think of it. Couldn't the measles cause a body to go blind? When she'd had the red measles, her mother had made her stay in a dark room with a cold rag over her eyes. Mostly she remembered wearing mittens against the urge to dig at her skin because of the terrible itching. Her mother had daubed a paste of baking soda on the rash and warned her about scarring.

She ached to turn over but didn't have the energy. Her arms and legs felt as mushy as overcooked noodles. Sleep tempted her with yawns and heavy-lidded eyes. It felt so good to give in.

The room was flooded with light when next Mazy woke. She must have slept for hours.

A slight figure stood with her back to the room, tugging down the window blind. "I'm supposed to give you a bath," she said, turning around.

Mazy thought she must be dreaming. Why would the bag-of-bones girl be offering to bathe her? How embarrassing. She struggled to sit up, nearly upending the basin sitting on the end of the bed. "I can bathe myself."

With small but sure hands, the girl — why couldn't Mazy remember her name? — sponged Mazy's face, her hands and arms, her feet and legs.

"You're probably thinking I don't know what I'm doing, but I do. Dr. Chambers taught me so I could take care of my mother." Finishing the chore, Cinnamon — yes, Cinnamon — shook powder onto a puff. "This will feel good," she said. "Now scoot over and I'll make your bed."

Mazy shifted to the side of the bed while Cinnamon rolled the used linens toward the middle. She tucked clean bottom and top sheets under the edge of the mattress. When directed, Mazy moved over the lump of dirty linen to the freshly made side.

Cinnamon patted Mazy's hip. "Lift up a little," she said, smoothing the draw sheet underneath her. "There's a trick to this. I'd teach you, but I'm not supposed to talk too much."

"I like for you to talk," Mazy said.

"Do you like my hair?" Cinnamon said. "The housekeeping lady fixed it up for me. She made me take a bath too. I like that big tub. It's better than the swimming hole."

She picked up a glass from the bedside table, saying, "Doctor said you're to drink a little water. Here."

Mazy sipped a bit through a bent glass straw. The water soothed her parched throat. "Thank you. Could I have some more?"

"No, not yet — you might spit it up. I have to tell if you do."

The girl stepped into the adjoining bathroom with the basin. Mazy could hear the splash of water as the basin was emptied.

"Cinnamon, do you know where the appendix is?"

The girl stuck her head around the open door. "Umm, the library?"

Of course, Mazy knew you could find an appendix at the end of some books that needed to list additional information, but what did that have to do with the human body? It was a puzzle and so was Cinnamon. "Do you go to the library often?" Mazy asked.

"Every Wednesday I do the floors and dust the shelves. I'm good at floors. The librarian lets me look at the books if I'm careful. I have to wear white gloves to read this one book, *Birds of North America.* It's real pretty. You can look in the appendix for whatever bird you want to see a picture of. That's how I know about that. The snowy owl is on page 330."

"The next time I'm in the library, I will look for that book."

Cinnamon slipped a table saver under Mazy's drinking glass. "You know that church St. Luke's? I dust mop the floors

there on Saturdays, and on Sunday I wash
the tiny glass Communion cups and put
them back in the trays. That part's my
favorite job."

"You have a lot of jobs," Mazy said.

"I saw you there last Sunday. I liked your
dress."

It took Mazy a minute to remember what
she'd worn. It was the blue shirtwaist, a
hand-me-down of Lilly's, nipped and tucked
for Mazy. Seeing Cinnamon's faded, too-
short frock, she was embarrassed to remember how she'd fretted over wearing the dated
dress.

It was comforting to have Cinnamon
tending to her, but Mazy was growing
weary. A locust droned outside the window,
the sound lulling Mazy, calling her to sleep.

Everything seemed wrapped in gauze,
even her thoughts. She felt like a bug in a
cocoon. It must be because of the shots the
doctor was giving her. She didn't even
notice when Cinnamon left.

Sometime in late afternoon Dr. Chambers
came in, helped Mazy out of bed, plopped
her on the bedside commode, helped her
back into bed, and then popped her in the
hip. It seemed like the doctor woke her up
just to put her back to sleep. Mazy sort of
liked the shimmery feeling the morphine

gave her; she even liked the rich, medicinal smell, which she remembered from her sister's small apothecary. Relaxing, she let the drug's effect carry her away.

By the time her head cleared again, it was evening and Ernestine was coming through the door. Mazy had never been so happy to see anyone. Good, solid Ernestine. Mazy reached out her hand, and Ernestine took it.

"How are you? You look a mess."

Mazy's hand went to the rat's nest on her head. "I'll never get these tangles out."

Taking the chair by the bed, Ernestine fiddled in her carryall and pulled out a brush. "Mrs. Pearl sent your things. If you can sit up, I'll fix your hair."

"I guess it's all right. I've been up to . . ."

Ernestine looked to the necessary. The seat was covered with a towel. "It's good to have it handy like that," she said. "I'll prop you with pillows."

Mazy gave herself over to Ernestine's capable hands. If she closed her eyes, she could imagine it was her mother's hand working the brush. "A hundred times," she said. "My mother taught me to brush my hair a hundred times every night."

"That's why it's so shiny," Ernestine said as she twisted and braided. She gave Mazy a hand mirror. "How's that?"

Ernestine had wrapped her braid around her head. "It looks like a crown," Mazy said.

"Or a halo," Ernestine said.

Mazy giggled. "Hardly."

"Well, there is the matter of the stolen cookies. A real angel wouldn't always have her hand in Mrs. Pearl's cookie jar."

"Oh, Ernestine, I'm so glad you're here."

"Mrs. Pearl says she accidentally poisoned you."

The mirror seemed heavier than it should have been. Mazy laid it aside. The pillows felt good behind her back. "The doctor said I might have had an attack of appendicitis, brought on by something in the tonic Mrs. Pearl gave me. I hate that she feels bad about it."

Taking a skein of yarn from her bag, Ernestine settled in the bedside chair and began to knit. "Wouldn't you feel bad if you made someone ill?"

"I suppose, but it's not like she meant to."

"You really are an angel."

"Everybody makes mistakes."

The knitting needles clicked industriously. "It's time to spill the beans about that handsome boyfriend of yours, Mazy. You never dropped a word about him. Polly is green

212

with envy, and Eva's nose is seriously out of joint."

"Chanis is not really my boyfriend. He's just someone from back home."

Ernestine purled and raised her eyes. "Come on, Mazy. Polly was watching your every move."

Mazy sat up straighter. "She was not. We were alone in the room."

Ernestine laughed. "Polly was watching your reflections in the foyer mirror — the one over the telephone table. She reported everything to us girls."

Heat rose in Mazy's cheeks. She was ever so thankful she hadn't let Chanis kiss her. Her reputation would have really been ruined if she had.

Dr. Chambers hustled into the room. The doctor always seemed to be hurrying like she was constantly late. "You're looking flushed, my dear," she said, laying the back of her hand on Mazy's forehead.

Mazy opened her mouth for the thermometer and turned her hand palm up for a pulse check. She'd watched her sister assess patients a hundred times. She knew about temps and pulse rates and clear lungs versus gummed-up ones, so why didn't she know about appendixes, and why was she afraid to ask? Her cheeks flared again with unexpressed concern. If some of her parts had to be removed, would she still be able to have a baby? She didn't like to think about the physical part of having babies right now, but she might like one when she was older.

Just ask! her brain screamed. *Just ask!*

But she couldn't. Her tongue was frozen to the roof of her mouth.

"I've talked with Dr. Still twice today. She is pleased with your progress, and so am I. We'll try some broth tomorrow — see if that stays down." She turned to Ernestine. "My bedroom is downstairs, directly across from my office. Don't hesitate to come for me if you need me."

"Yes, Doctor," Ernestine said.

"Don't let her get out of bed without help. She's very weak still."

"I won't."

"All right, lights out at nine."

Ernestine pulled a footstool up to her chair. "This will be comfy enough tonight."

"I am so thankful for you, Ernestine. Will you loosen the covers over my feet?"

"I will if you'll spill the beans."

Mazy rolled her eyes, which wasn't smart because it made her head swim again. "About what?"

Ernestine tugged the sheet.

"Uncle. Uncle," Mazy cried. "My toes will

be permanently crimped. I'll have to be a ballerina."

"Sorry, you're not tall enough," Ernestine said as she loosened the sheets. "Now talk."

"I first saw Chanis Clay two years ago in the spring when I went to Skip Rock to help my sister."

Knitting needles clicked again. "The one who is a doctor?"

"Yes. My mother sent me to help Lilly in her clinic and also, I suspect, to get me away from a certain boy who shall remain nameless."

"My word, the guys all fall at your feet. No wonder Eva doesn't like you."

Mazy's words and the clicking needles fell into rhythm. "I liked Chanis right away. And he liked me."

"He very obviously still does."

"I don't know how to say this. . . . He weighs me down with his expectations, like he's already got everything planned out, and I'm supposed to follow his lead. It is strange because with one hand I want to draw him close and with the other I want to push him away."

"High-class worries."

Mazy snuggled closer into her pillows. "What does that mean?"

Ernestine stuck the two knitting needles

into the ball of yarn and reached for the chain on the lamp. "It means the rest of us girls would die to have one fellow look at us the way guys look at you. You should have seen how happy Loyal Chambers was to sweep you up off the floor. You are a femme fatale in disguise, Mazy."

With a yank of Ernestine's hand, the room went dark. "Good night; sleep tight," she said.

When Mazy was a girl, she had dreaded bedtime. The darkness seemed to rush at her, trying to pull her under its monstrous wings and carry her away. Her mother had taught her to recite a comforting Scripture when she was scared. The words of Jesus were more soothing than any medicine could ever be. " 'In my Father's house are many mansions: if it were not so, I would have told you. I go to prepare a place for you. And if I go and prepare a place for you, I will come again, and receive you unto myself; that where I am, there ye may be also. And whither I go ye know, and the way ye know.' "

She didn't realize she had said the words aloud until Ernestine spoke. "That's so pretty."

"They're my favorite verses," Mazy said.

Ernestine shifted in her seat. "I like the

216

way they sound. Can I borrow your Bible sometime so I can copy them?"

The doctor had cracked the window. The curtains billowed inward as if tugged by unseen hands. The night breeze was soft and humid and smelled of summer roses.

"The best way to remember Scripture is to write it on your heart. Do you know Jesus, Ernestine?"

"I go to church, Mazy," she said indignantly. "Always have."

"But do you know Him?"

"Well, not personally," Ernestine said with a snort. "He's been dead a long time, you know."

Mazy felt herself drifting. Fighting to focus her mind, she reached out for Ernestine's hand, which rested on the arm of the chair, and voiced words she'd heard her mother say a thousand times. "Jesus is as alive as this," she said with a gentle squeeze. "The best way to get closer to Him is to read His Word. Start with the Gospels."

"Maybe when school is over and I have more time," Ernestine said, her voice softening.

Mazy shivered with a sense of foreboding, as if a dark angel hovered at the end of her bed. "Don't put it off, Ernestine. None of us knows how long we have on this earth."

CHAPTER 15

Tully opened the truck door before Chanis had a chance to turn the motor off. "It's a bad one."

Chanis stepped out into the Everses' now-familiar farmyard and put his hat on. "So your note said. Give me the short version."

"Short's all I've got," Tully said. "Pete Munson's wife ran out of eggs this morning."

Chanis gritted his teeth. He just happened to be short on patience at the moment.

"So Pete walks over to the Everses' — Ina's chickens produce the best eggs in the county. Everybody knows that. Ina was nowhere to be found, but her apron's flung over the rail. One of the ties is torn off."

Chanis headed toward the house, where Oney Evers sat holding a hatchet. The porch and Oney had some splatters of what looked like dried blood.

"Pete saw the blood and all and hustled

to town to tell me." Tully pointed toward the well house. "He's laying low in there. Who knows what Oney might do next with that hatchet? He still ain't had his breakfast."

"Oney?"

"No, Pete."

The iron-scented odor of blood assailed Chanis's nose. He took off his hat and ran his fingers through his hair before he put it back on. "Do me a favor?"

"Sure," Tully said.

"Draw some water. And tell Pete to sit tight. I'll question him later."

The scene on the porch was a spine-chilling tableau. Oney sat on the floor with his feet planted on the second step from the bottom. His right arm was bent at the elbow and rested on his left knee. The hatchet hung from his right hand. The head of the hatchet was stained with something dark.

The pump handle in the well house creaked. Flies buzzed the porch. A mockingbird jabbered from the eave of the house. Chanis's brain whined like a tightly strung wire. He walked slowly across the yard.

"Hey, Oney, what's going on?"

At the sound of his voice, a rail-thin black dog slunk out from under the porch. With his tail tucked between his legs, the dog approached, sniffing Chanis's ankles. "This here your dog?" Chanis asked.

If Oney heard him, he didn't respond, didn't flinch, and didn't stop staring off into the distance.

The dog put his front paws on Chanis's leg. "Get," Chanis said. Startled, the dog loped off down the packed-dirt path that bisected the front yard.

Oney's hand began to quiver. The hatchet clattered to the ground.

Tully slipped up beside Chanis. Water sloshed from the full pail he carried. Chanis would have to slake his thirst later. He couldn't remember exactly how Doc Still had treated Oney, but he thought he had the basic idea. "Go in the kitchen and see if you can find some honey or molasses — anything sticky and sweet. Stir a couple of tablespoons into a cup of this water. Quick."

Tully high-stepped it through the door, the screen slapping closed behind him.

"Oney, where's Miz Evers? Where's Ina?"

"Pete said she wasn't here when he came by earlier," Tully offered through the door.

"Hurry up with that drink."

After a great clattering of dishes and clanging of pans, Tully came out with a delicate china cup. Chanis was certain Miz Evers was not at home, or Tully would have been full of holes by now.

"Drink this, Oney," Chanis said. He had to pry the man's chin down with his thumb. "Hold his nose, Tully."

Tully sniffed the drink. "It don't smell bad."

"Pinching his nose will make him swallow," Chanis said. Oney sputtered and spit but Chanis figured he got a quarter cup down his gullet. He came around a little, but his speech was so slurred, it was unintelligible.

"Pete," Chanis yelled. "Come give us a hand."

"What are you going to do?" Tully asked.

"You and Pete are going to take Oney to Doc's in the truck. I'll stay here and see if I can find Miz Evers. Once you get Oney settled, come back for me."

The place seemed deathly still when the sound of the truck faded away. Chanis dashed the last of the sweet water out in the yard and carried the cup into the kitchen, putting it in the dishpan on the washstand. The water had grown cold, but it was still sudsy. A butcher knife lay beside a slab of bacon. A skillet waited on the cast-iron stove. A yellowware bowl of corn bread mix sat drying on the counter; he broke the skim with a butter knife. The only thing out of place was the overturned chair beside the round oak table — and the few drops of dried blood across the floor. Everything indicated that Miz Evers had been here earlier this morning.

Chanis moved the skillet and used a prong to lift the burner. He could see pieces of burnt kindling in the fire well, but the wood box beside the stove was empty. He wondered if Miz Evers had started to cook breakfast before she realized she was out of fuel. Maybe she'd hollered for Oney to go get some from the wood stack. Maybe that's why he had the hatchet. Silently Chanis berated himself. He should have checked Oney to see if he had cut his leg or something. But if he had been actively bleeding since Pete came upon him earlier, wouldn't he have bled out before Chanis ever got here? Also, the blood on the porch, though obvious, was not abundant. It was more likely that the blood didn't come from Oney himself.

"Miz Evers," he called out, even though he didn't expect an answer. "It's me, Sheriff Clay."

His footsteps echoed hollowly when he walked through the house. In the small bedroom, a colorful quilt was pulled up neatly over the bed; the bolster pillow was plumped. A Singer sewing machine sat against the wall under the window. The treadle was even with the floor, as if Miz Evers had been interrupted in the middle of her task. Absently, Chanis released the needle. An unmoored piece of brownish fabric slithered to the floor. With a tiny insect's whir, thread slipped through the eye of the needle, tethering the yardage to the machine. Carefully, he replaced the fabric, abashed about the tangled thread. If his mother were here, she'd smack his hand for that one.

With his hands tucked under his armpits, Chanis moved around the room, scanning everything. The hair on the back of his neck rose when he looked at his own reflection in the dressing table mirror. A figure stood behind him. Unannounced, someone else had invaded the room.

Quick as a cat's sneeze, Chanis drew his gun and whirled to face . . . a lady's dress form wearing his own white hat, lost the day Ina had taken a shot at him. Blowing out a relieved breath, he holstered the weapon. Man, he was losing it.

He removed his hat from the form and took it into the kitchen, placing it in the center of the table beside an open toolbox. He paused a moment to drink a dipperful of water. It tasted of rock with a trace of coal smoke and went down smooth as silk. He should bottle the stuff and sell it out the back of a gypsy wagon like a snake-oil salesman. Maybe he'd better stick to law; nobody would be gullible enough to buy bottled water.

Well, he'd done everything but check the infamous cellar — might as well gird his loins and face the sauerkraut. With one hand on the butt of his gun, he turned the knob and pulled. Instead of swinging open, the door tilted sideways on a broken hinge, effectively blocking his entrance. He went back to the table and selected a flathead screwdriver and a hammer from the toolbox. With a few taps on the handle of the angled screwdriver, the remaining hinge pin was released. He lifted the door and set it against the wall, guaranteeing he wouldn't get trapped in the root cellar. Taking the steps one at a time, he started down, his senses on high alert.

The cellar was empty save for the jars and jars of canned goods. A pint of whole beets glittered like rubies in the scant light. He wondered if they were pickled. His mouth watered. His favorite meal was fried pork chops, pinto beans, mashed potatoes, and pickled beets. Or then again, there was chicken and dumplings, green beans, and sliced tomatoes. Maybe he'd stop by his mother's house for Sunday dinner.

Back upstairs and out the door, he started for the barnyard, keeping an eye out for the rooster. Miz Evers was out here somewhere, and he needed to find her.

In the side lot, a cow stood contently chewing her cud. Overhead, a chicken hawk circled relentlessly. A nervous broody hen gathered her chicks under her wings, settling down in the dust, assessing him with her frightened eyes. The black dog wrestled with something, dragging it toward the barn. Chanis's stomach turned. He was glad last night's biscuit and egg were long since gone.

"You mangy mutt," Miz Evers screamed, charging his direction from farther up the path. She pitched a stick at the dog, missing him by a country mile. With a yelp, the dog dropped its prey and skedaddled to the barn. Bending at the waist, Miz Evers picked up a pair of yellow feet. "Oh, would you look at this. Big Red was the best rooster I ever had. Now there's not enough left for a good stew." She shook her head in exasperation. "I've a mind to take the hatchet to Oney's neck — see how he feels."

She flung the bird into the scrub bushes.

"Might as well let the dog finish with it." She made a motion as if she were going to wipe her hands on her dress front and then stopped. "I don't even have my apron. Stupid man."

"Miz Evers . . ."

She studied him with eyes as beady and black as the chickens'. "What are you doing here anyway?"

"Oney's taken sick again, Miz Evers."

"Well, that just bakes the cake. I ask him to do one little thing and he decides to have a spell. Am I supposed to do my work and his too? 'Get some wood' was all I asked. Just a little wood so I could cook his breakfast." Her bony neck craned like Chanis had seen her favorite rooster do. She jutted her chin toward him. "Was that too much to ask?"

"Let's go the house. It's getting hot out here."

She slammed through the screen door and hefted the dishpan. Chanis hadn't yet closed the door behind him when she charged back through and slung the water out. The water sluiced across the porch floor. The china cup chimed like a musical note before it broke in two pieces, but she paid it no mind. "This will have to be scrubbed," she said, taking a straw broom from a hook on the wall.

When she began to whisk the broom around, Chanis grabbed the handle. They went hand over hand until he won. "We need to have a conversation," he said.

Her eyes sparking anger, she jerked the broom from his gasp and threw it like a spear out into the yard. Her chin jutted again. "Happy now?"

He thought about placing a hand on her shoulder or patting her arm in reassurance — sometimes a human touch calmed a body down — but he didn't know what Tully had done with the hatchet.

He squared his shoulders and held the door open for her. It was way past time that he assert his authority. "Ma'am, we'll talk inside."

She took a seat at the kitchen table. "I cleaned your hat for you. Cornstarch."

Chanis poured two glasses of water and set one before her, then took a chair himself. "I appreciate that. Thank you."

With a groan, she buried her hands in her hair and tugged. Strands of reddish hair tumbled down from a messy topknot, scattering pins and combs across the table. "I should heat the coffee."

"Just tell me what happened."

"You probably can't imagine that Oney and I was once young, can you? Twenty years ago we set up housekeeping." Her arm swept the kitchen. "We had just the one room then, this one and the root cellar." She smiled slyly. "Of course, you're well familiar with the cellar."

Chanis nodded. "I am."

"He was kind then, and a hard worker. That's what we did. We worked, but it was good." She sipped the water as her eyes turned distant. "We would sit of an evening out there on the porch. I baked him a pie ever' other day. Apple was his favorite. He ate two pieces ever' night before he went to bed. He said my pie made life worth living."

"Oney's still alive, Miz Evers."

"Maybe so, but he ain't my Oney anymore. First I thought he had that mad dog disease — the way he took those mean fits, flinging things around and cussing at me. See here's the thing: Oney never cussed, especially not at me." She stuck her index finger in the water and swirled it round and round. "And he was never, ever mean to any living soul nor any of our animals. Just ask that mangy dog. That thing is always underfoot. He let it sleep beside the stove all winter. Who ever heard of such, a dog sleeping in the house?"

Her eyes went flat like she was in some kind of a trance as she continued to talk. "I had already kindled the fire and I hollered at him, 'Oney, you lazy bum, you let the wood box go empty. What am I supposed to cook with — water?' "

Gathering her hair, she twisted it up and secured it with the errant pins and combs. Chanis thought he could see the young woman she used to be, before life got hard.

"I shouldn't have called him lazy. Oney was never lazy. I reckon that's what set him off."

Chanis was so far past tired he felt like his head was floating up near the ceiling. Without even asking, he went to the cookstove and poured cold, stale coffee into a mug. He drank it straight. "Tell me what happened here this morning."

"When I called him lazy, Oney got up from that selfsame chair you were setting in and walked out the door like it wasn't even there. If it had been latched, I reckon he'd have torn the screen out. So I busied myself mixing up the corn bread — Oney favors corn bread for breakfast — and getting ready to slice the bacon when I heard an awful squawking noise from the porch. Then Oney comes in with my rooster, missing his head. 'This here what you wanted?' he said whilst standing in the doorway. Oh, it was an awful sight. When he put that rooster down, the thing went running straight off the porch, never mind the steps, and took off down the path. You know how they do that — running before they're actually dead."

She shivered slightly though the room was stifling hot. "I never understood how chickens could do that — like if they go quick enough, they can catch up with their missing part. I reckon the dog must have caught the pitiful thing and drug it up there in the weeds beyond the barn. I was so mad, I tore my apron off and flung it out the door. I said, 'You see if I ever cook another meal for you, Oney Evers, let alone a pie.' I took out the door too. I was going to my sister's, but it was so far, and I was missing home before I was halfway there. So I came back."

She picked up Chanis's hat and dusted off a bit of cornstarch with her hand. "Now I ask you," she said, "who mistakes a rooster for a woodpile?"

"You know Oney's got the sugar. That might account for the change in his actions."

She smacked the tabletop with the flat of her hand. "I know that! I been fixing everything sweet I can think of — cream pies, angel food cake, devil's food cake, banana pudding — trying to make him better. But it don't do no good."

"You need to talk to Doc Still," Chanis said. "She can explain how the sugar works on a body."

Miz Evers shrugged. "I'll think on it. But right now, I'm going to gather the eggs — another chore Oney neglected."

Chanis let her go. He was scrubbing the porch with the broom and a pail of soapy water when he heard Old Ray coming. With one hat on his head and another in his hands, he walked up the lane to meet Tully.

CHAPTER 16

Mazy drifted awake. She vaguely remembered Ernestine's leaving. She wished her friend were still sitting in the chair beside her bed. Last night had been fun despite her illness.

Dr. Chambers's maid came into the bedroom carrying an invalid tray. She set the tray on the bedside table and helped Mazy into a sitting position.

Mazy couldn't believe how weak she felt. Her limbs had turned to jelly. She felt like a helpless baby. Once she was settled, the maid left her alone to eat her breakfast. There was a bowl of beef broth, a cup of tea, and a bud vase holding one long-stemmed pink rose. Her face flushed with pleasure. The sweet-smelling bud was a twin to the one Loyal had given her at High Bridge.

She tucked a fine linen napkin under her chin before sipping a bit of the broth. It tasted salty and made her wish for a cracker to go along. The heavy silver spoon she ate from was embellished with a *C* trailing into a curlicue.

A tiny pot of honey and a thinly sliced piece of lemon accompanied the tea. Mazy curled her pinkie finger as she drank the tea, pretending she was a princess held captive in a high tower. If she was allowed out of bed, she'd go to the window and let down her hair like Rapunzel. She could just see Loyal standing beneath her cascading blonde locks, holding a stupendous bouquet of pink roses.

Mazy nearly choked on her tea as Dr. Chambers came into the room in her take-charge way. "We're looking chipper today," she said, taking Mazy's wrist between her fingers. Mazy sat still while the doctor checked her pulse. "Broth staying down?"

"Yes, ma'am, my stomach barely hurts at all."

After checking Mazy's vital signs, the doctor stood back and studied her. "I believe some fresh air is in order today."

Cinnamon slipped through the door and stood quietly behind the doctor.

"Miss Spicer will help you get freshened up."

"Thank you, Doctor."

"You're certainly welcome. I spoke to your sister earlier. She's pleased with your progress."

"Did Lilly say how the twins are doing? I've been so worried about them."

"From what she said, it seems a mild case. They are quarantined, though she is not. Did you have measles as a child, Mazy?"

"Yes, ma'am, I did."

"That's good; best to get it over with before you have responsibilities."

When the doctor had left the room, Cinnamon laid a heavy book in Mazy's lap. "It's a dictionary."

"I see."

"And look what else I have." The girl beamed as she pulled a library card from her dress pocket. "Miss Scott at the library helped me get it. She said I could take any book I wanted home for two weeks. And when I bring it back, I can borrow another one. Except for the bird book; it's too fragile." Cinnamon ran her palm over the cover of the book in a sheet-smoothing motion. " 'A book's a beautiful thing,' Miss Scott said."

Mazy looked at the girl — truly looked. It was easy to see how she'd come by her name, for her hair was the copper color of the rich spice Mazy liked to sprinkle over apple-sauce. She could just as easily have been named Paprika. Her brown eyes sparkled despite the shadows beneath them. She was slight but sturdy in her too-short dress and run-down shoes.

Mazy opened the Webster's School Dictionary. "Are you planning on reading this, Cinnamon?"

"It's not for reading," Cinnamon said. "It's for looking up words. I got it for you — so you can look up that word *appendix.*"

"You are too smart, Cinnamon."

"My pa says I'm smart too."

"Your pa is right." With trepidation Mazy looked through the *a*'s and ran her finger down the line of words beginning with *ap: apart, ape, aperitif, aperture, apex, aphasia* until she found the word *appendix.* "Why didn't you just tell me what it means?" Mazy asked. "You wouldn't have had to lug this heavy book all the way here."

"Miss Scott says it's good to learn things on your own; then you won't have to ask so many questions."

Cinnamon looked over Mazy's shoulder as she read.

" '*Appendix* 1: supplementary material usually attached at the end of a piece of writing.' That's what we talked about yesterday. '*Appendix* 2: a small tubular outgrowth from the cecum of the intestine — called also vermiform appendix, from *appendere,* "to append." ' Next we'll find *cecum.*"

"See what I mean?" Cinnamon said. "You look up one thing and then you have to look up another."

Mazy ruffled pages. "It's a blind pouch."

"Does everybody have one?"

"Yes," Mazy said. "I'm sure they do."

"But what does it mean when it says it's blind?"

"I'm not sure."

"It should have pictures like the bird book."

Mazy laughed. "They wouldn't be very pretty pictures, would they?"

"It'd still be interesting."

"Thank you for bringing this for me to look at, Cinnamon. It helps me understand what Dr. Chambers is talking about."

"Speaking of her, I'd better get busy taking care of you."

When Cinnamon came out of the bathroom with a basin of water, Mazy felt embarrassed. Not because the girl would help her with a bath, but because Cinnamon, who had so little and worked so hard, asked for nothing, while Mazy lay abed fretting over everything.

Finished with her refreshing bath, Mazy

slipped her arms through her favorite night-gown. Ecru batiste over an attached pet-ticoat, the top of the gown had clusters of fine hand-run tucks and a decoration of white eyelet embroidery. Mazy had sewn the gown herself under the tutelage of her twin sister, Molly, who was born with a silver needle in her hand and a golden thimble on her finger. Everything depended upon the tucking. After many pulled stitches, Mazy learned that the correct way to do hand tucking was to pull two threads where each tuck is to be made, sewing the tucks with the thread that was pulled out. After that came the tedious part: each tuck had to be folded and the two lines where the thread had been pulled sewed together. Mazy had nearly torn her hair out before getting it right, but her stitches were so fine they could scarcely be seen.

Even though the effort left her shaky, Mazy pulled her white cotton stockings on by herself. Holding her foot aloft, she worked a wrinkle out of the toe. At least she was making progress; this was more than she could have done yesterday. Her head was much clearer since the doctor had not given her an injection this morning.

Cinnamon helped her up to sit in the chair while her bed was made. "Tell me about your family," Mazy said while Cinnamon spread linen and plumped pillows.

"It's just me and my pap. We live over on Juniper Street. You know of it?"

"No, I'm not from here. I live in the mountains. I'm here going to school."

"I know you live at Mrs. Pearl's. She's nice. She lets me pick whatever I want from her garden."

"I've never seen you there."

"I come late, after my day jobs and taking care of Pap. Mrs. Pearl doesn't mind."

"I agree Mrs. Pearl is a very nice lady. I like her a lot. Have you seen the kittens?"

"I saw that one girl set them out the other night."

Mazy's ears perked. "What girl?"

"The tall one with the auburn hair. I saw her open the door and scoot the mother cat out with the toe of her shoe. Then she pitched the kittens out behind her."

Eva. Mazy might have known. "That wasn't very nice. Why didn't you tell someone?"

"Lots of cats live outdoors," Cinnamon said. "I figured the big cat would take care of them."

"And she did," Mazy replied with a shake of her head. Why would Eva do such a thing? She decided she wouldn't say anything either, since the cats were all okay, but she would keep an eye on Eva.

After a lunch of more beef broth and four soda crackers, the doctor asked if Mazy was ready for a change of scenery. "The back garden is nice, and it's shady there," she said.

"I'm ready for a walk," Mazy said, standing beside the bed and cinching the tie of the robe that matched her gown.

"Not yet," the doctor said. "Loyal will carry you downstairs. He can sit with you for an hour or so." She turned her attention to Cinnamon. "Miss Spicer, we'll see you in the morning."

"Yes, ma'am. I'll be here." Cinnamon carried the heavy dictionary with her as she left.

"Miss Spicer certainly belies the old saying about the apple not falling far from the tree," Dr. Chambers said.

"She's very smart."

"Yes, maybe that will help her to escape her mother's fate." Dr. Chambers bent her head over the notes she was taking. "That father of hers . . ." She closed the chart with a snap. "Some people can't be helped."

Mazy didn't think the doctor expected a reply, so she kept quiet.

"Any questions?" the doctor asked.

Mazy screwed up her courage. The doctor seemed so approachable today, but before she could form a thought, she heard masculine footsteps on the stairs.

"Here's Loyal now. Ready?"

Mazy felt like a princess as Loyal carried her down the stairs. He was stronger than he looked, but then she was only used to Chanis, whose masculinity sometimes threatened to overwhelm her. Loyal, on the other hand, was not so overt. His tenderness was attractive to her.

They reached the garden, and he gently sat her on the side of a wicker chaise longue. When he lifted her ankles to swing them up onto the chaise, a thrill caused her to shiver. Attentively, he spread a mohair throw over her legs. The pink of the lightweight afghan matched the pink in the flowered cushions on the chaise, and both matched the lush gardenias and roses blooming in the garden. A waxed-linen patio umbrella shaded the sitting area.

This is exactly what heaven will look like, Mazy thought.

Loyal poured lemonade from a cut-glass pitcher into a stemmed goblet and handed it to her. "Mother said you could have some lemonade," he said as he sat in the folding chair he'd pulled up close. "She said the sugar would do you good."

Ice tinkled against the glass. Mazy took a sip. The drink was just right: not too sweet, but not too tart. "It's delectable," she said. *Just like everything else,* she thought.

Her eyes widened as Loyal leaned across her. With a twist of his wrist he plucked a rose.

"May I?" he asked.

She nodded.

He tucked the stem of the blossom behind her ear. She was ever so glad that Cinnamon had styled her hair into double Dutch braids that morning.

Sitting still as a mouse, she didn't pull away when his hand lingered just a touch too long at the curve of her neck.

"I may not be able to help myself," he said.

She swallowed. "Pardon?"

"I may have to kiss you."

Mazy rested the back of her hand against her lips. "You shouldn't," she said while hopelessly wishing that he would.

He leaned a little closer, his freshly shaved scent mingling with that of the roses. "Then stop looking so enticing."

"I'm only looking like myself," she said, chagrined.

"Therein lies the problem. It's the Garden

of Eden all over again."

"Adam ate the apple," she said.

"After Eve offered it," he replied.

From her sitting position, Mazy made a mock show of looking under the chaise. "Goodness, we must hope there are no serpents abiding in this garden."

Laughing, Loyal fell back against his seat. "Touché."

While his eyes were closed in laughter, Mazy studied him. He was stylishly dressed in beige corduroy knee breeches and a navy-blue serge suit coat. He wore camel-colored suede work boots with laces a shade darker. The socks covering his calves matched the color of his jacket. Oddly, the collar of his white shirt fell open. Mazy couldn't remember if she'd ever seen a grown man in an open collar. Even her father's nightshirts were buttoned all the way up to his Adam's apple.

She couldn't help but compare Loyal to Chanis — heavily starched, sharply creased, buttoned-up Sheriff Chanis Clay.

In the sudden flare of a match, Loyal lit a cigarette. "Do you mind?" he asked, blowing a stream of smoke over his left shoulder.

"I don't guess so," she said. Eva smoked; she said it was sophisticated, but all Mazy saw when Eva squinted her eyes and pursed her lips were wrinkles.

He shook another cigarette loose from the pack. "Want one?"

She shook her head.

"Ever tried?"

"No."

"Do you drink?"

"No!"

"Not even wine?"

"Drinking's drinking," Mazy said primly. "I wasn't raised that way."

"I've offended you. I'm sorry."

"You probably think I'm an old fuddy-duddy," she said.

"Want to know what I really think about you?"

"I guess."

"I think you're beautiful and sweet." He touched his left index finger to her bottom lip and then put it to his mouth. "Very, very sweet."

Mazy's heart fluttered. He might as well have kissed her; it seemed such an intimate gesture. From the heat of her face, she was sure she matched the pink of the flowers in the garden.

Loyal took a long drag on the cigarette and released it slowly, appraising her through the haze. "I just might have to marry you," he said, serious as a judge.

Too warm, Mazy folded the afghan to the foot of the chaise, then quickly pulled it back up to her waist. She felt like she was sinking in a pool of desire, in way over her head.

"My mother likes you, and she's impressed that your sister is also a doctor." Loyal tapped ashes onto the ground. "My mother is not easily impressed, believe you me," he said, narrowing his eyes.

Mazy felt the need to change the subject. "What do you do?"

"Do?"

"What keeps you busy? How do you earn your keep?"

"You mean like a job? I'm in real estate. I manage our properties. When my father died, he left me in charge of the work and Mother in charge of the money." He slouched in the chair, waving smoke away.

"That sounds interesting."

"Some of it is. We own a hotel on Broadway and government buildings on Short as well as half of the cheap houses in Cedar Bottoms. My plan is to turn the five hundred acres my father inherited from his father on Paris Pike into a first-class horse farm. If I could get my mother on board, I'd like to get into racing. I'd love to have a derby winner someday."

Mazy was impressed. She liked that he had big dreams. "What's the part you don't like?"

"The riffraff. You wouldn't believe the excuses some people come up with for not paying their rent. Some kid's always sick, or somebody's mother died and they had to use the rent money for a funeral. I'd like to torch every shack and shanty we own in the Bottoms and put up office buildings. Now that's the way to make some serious money."

"But where would those folks live?"

"I suppose they'd have to find somewhere else."

His head jerked toward the house when they heard his mother calling from the portico. "Loyal, bring our patient in now, please."

"Speak of the devil." After stubbing his smoke on the sole of his shoe, he flung the butt into the rosebush, then pinched a sprig of mint from a terra-cotta pot and popped it into his mouth. With a finger to his lips, he gave Mazy a don't-tell-on-me look before he swept her up into his arms. "Your chariot, my dear."

She couldn't help but laugh. He was so utterly charming.

CHAPTER 17

Mazy was so happy to see Ernestine and Polly after supper that she clapped her hands. She felt ever so much better since her time in the garden. Maybe it was the lemonade and fresh air, or maybe it was Loyal.

"I'm so glad to see you," Polly said, rushing across the room and hugging Mazy. "I was so scared when the doctor took you away. I thought you were going to die."

"There's nothing to worry about. I'm much better now, just very weak and awfully tired."

Ernestine joined Polly, both girls sitting on the side of the bed. "Dr. Chambers told Mrs. Pearl that you are doing well. She said you might come home in a day or two. The doctor thinks you have food poisoning from that tonic, which is bad enough, but at least you won't have to have surgery."

"But being poisoned is terrible," Polly said.

"It's pretty bad, but the good news is I'll get well."

"Don't you hate being alone?" Polly asked.

"Cinnamon has been keeping me company."

"Cinnamon?"

"She's that girl we keep seeing around town. She's very kind and smart."

"You're too good to be true, Mazy. You never say anything bad about anyone," Ernestine said.

"Except Eva," Polly said with a grin.

"Don't tease her, Polly," Ernestine said.

"That's okay," Mazy said. "I need to remember to be nice to Eva even when I don't want to be."

"Look what I brought you," Polly said as she took the lid from a shoe box and lifted a kitten from a mound of tissue paper.

"Oh, sweet little thing." Mazy took the kitten and stroked its head. "Oh, you pretty gray darling."

Polly lifted the corner of the cover on Mazy's bed. "You can keep him under here."

"Don't be silly," Ernestine said. "I'll take him back with me. Polly's staying the night. I came along for a visit."

"We've talked about nothing but your sheriff," Polly said. "He's simply gorgeous.

247

We're all wondering when he's coming back."

Mazy shrugged. Chanis seemed so far away. "I don't have a clue."

"But he's your beau, right?"

"I have to tell you what happened today," Mazy said, stroking the kitten's silky head. "I'm going to burst if I don't."

"Do tell, then. We don't need Mazy all over the room," Ernestine said.

"I had lemonade in the garden . . . with Loyal Chambers. You wouldn't believe how nice he is."

"I can't wait to tell Eva," Polly said.

"Don't stir the pot," Ernestine said, standing. "I'd better go."

Mazy nestled the kitten in the box. "Thank you. Everybody has been so good to me."

"That may end soon. Tomorrow night is Eva's turn."

"That will be interesting," Polly said.

"What about Clara?" Mazy asked.

"Gracious, we forgot to tell you. Clara's gone."

"But why? She was so glad to get this opportunity. She told me so."

"She went to see Mrs. Carpenter this morning and never came back."

"All her things were gone. Mrs. Pearl said she'd taken the train home. She wouldn't tell us anything else," Polly said.

"But she was ill," Mazy said. "She was throwing up too."

"I know," Ernestine said. "Every morning for a while."

Polly's eyes bugged out of her head. "You don't mean . . . ?"

"I don't mean anything," Ernestine said. "We shouldn't speculate."

"Poor Clara," Mazy said.

"Poor indeed," Ernestine said with a wave good-bye.

Mazy thought she knew what Ernestine was hinting at. If so, it was dreadful news for Clara. This could be what Clara meant when she hoped to finish the semester. It was not a thing that could be kept hidden for long.

While Polly put her toothbrush and toiletries in the bathroom, Mazy prayed for Clara, asking God to keep her safe. There was nothing else she could do.

Mazy couldn't help but feel privileged and perhaps a little spoiled, lying in bed being pampered and waited on. She had always known she was loved; she'd never gone hungry, never been denied anything she really needed. Her parents had expected her to do her share of household chores, study hard in school, and always be on her best behavior, but how hard was that when her life had been so blessed? Even her fear of serious illness was something conjured up from words in a dictionary, a silly girl's self-indulgence. If she were ever really challenged, would the easy faith of her childhood stand up to the test?

Polly had let down her hair and put on her nightclothes before she came out of the bathroom. "What am I supposed to do for you?" she asked. "I've never taken care of a sick person before."

"Just sit here and talk to me while I take down my hair. Tell me about your home. Do you have brothers and sisters?"

"It's just me. My mother says I'm the only jewel in her crown. She says she should have named me Ruby."

"And your father?"

"He died right after I was born. That's probably why I'm so close to my mother."

"I'm close to my mother too, but also to my sisters. They mean everything to me."

"Don't you miss them something awful?"

"When I first came here to school, I did. I wanted to turn around and go right back home, but it's better now."

Polly tucked her feet up under her in the chair. "What are you going to do when we graduate? Will you stay in Lexington?"

"Oh, Polly, I don't know. I thought I wanted to be a secretary, but now I'm not so sure. Everything is so confusing."

"You must know your sheriff loves you. He looks at you like you're the last dish of strawberry ice cream."

Mazy was suddenly tired and weak again. "But, Polly," she whispered against the tears that threatened to spill, "I don't want him to love me. It puts a burden on my heart."

"That doesn't seem much like a burden to me."

The dam broke. Mazy sobbed into her hands. She wept from relief that her illness hadn't been more serious and because she was confused about her feelings for Chanis, because the afternoon had been so beautiful and because she couldn't make Eva like her. She cried for Clara and for the kittens, who would have to find new homes, and because the girl, Cinnamon, didn't have a decent dress to wear.

"Please stop," Polly said, blotting Mazy's cheeks with a handkerchief. "I didn't mean to hurt your feelings. I know I talk too much, but I can't seem to help it. My mother says I was vaccinated with a phonograph needle."

"It's not you, Polly. I don't know why I'm so upset."

Dr. Chambers appeared in the doorway. She gave Polly a sharp look. "What's going on in here?"

Polly folded her hands and tucked her chin. Mazy couldn't hide her blotchy, tearstained face.

The doctor laid the back of her hand against Mazy's forehead. "You're feeling feverish. Open up."

The thermometer she stuck under Mazy's tongue tasted sharply of alcohol. The doctor tapped her shoe against the floor. Three minutes seemed weeks long to Mazy.

Finally with a sharp flick of her wrist, the doctor shook the thermometer down. "Are you in pain?"

"No, ma'am. I'm sorry to make a fuss. I was feeling a little overwhelmed, that's all."

"Are you having a visit from your friend?"

"Oh, sorry — Dr. Chambers, this is Polly. Polly, Dr. Chambers."

The doctor raised her perfectly arched eyebrows. "That isn't what I meant."

Mazy blushed and dropped her eyes. "No, it's not that."

The doctor snapped her fingers and pointed at Polly. "Run down to the kitchen and ask cook for a pot of tea and a serving of the rice pudding left over from supper."

"Is she gone?" Polly whispered when she came back with a serving tray.

Mazy nodded. "She said I need to start eating again."

Polly set the tray in front of Mazy and went to close the door. "She might have offered me a cup of pudding."

Mazy took a spoon from beside the teacup and handed it to Polly. "I'll share."

"This is tasty," Polly said, trying a tiny bite of pudding.

"She asked me all sorts of questions about my sister and my mother," Mazy said in a lowered voice. "She wanted to know how many children they have had and if my sister Lilly is as small as me." Mazy licked her spoon before putting it back on the tray. "And she asked if I was regular. Why would she ask me that?"

"Sounds like she's buying a cow," Polly said.

Mazy nearly snorted rice pudding out her nose. "Polly, you are so bad."

"Made you laugh, didn't I?"

" 'Laugh tonight and cry tomorrow,' my mother would say."

"Well, you've already done both, so I'd

253

say you're safe." Polly went to the window and looked out. "Let's sneak out. Nobody would see us if we take the back staircase."

"And then what would we do?"

"I don't know — go in the garden and eat worms? Honestly, Mazy, how do you stand just lying there? I'd go stir-crazy."

"It hasn't been too hard because I've felt so worn-out from not eating, but this afternoon in the garden with Loyal I wanted to dance."

"Good grief, Mazy," Polly said. "I mean, Loyal Chambers is nice-looking, but Sheriff Clay, oh, my word."

Mazy sighed dramatically. "It seems I have an abundance of blessings."

Polly giggled. "You sound like a Victorian maiden. Are you going to swoon now?"

Mazy joined in the giggling. "I've already done that, too."

"We'd better hush, else she'll come back in and make me go get you another cup of pudding. 'Go fetch, Polly.' I think she mistook me for a Labrador retriever."

Tears of laughter streamed down Mazy's cheeks. With her downturned eyes, Polly looked more like a basset hound. "Fetch my toothbrush and I'll give you a biscuit."

"I'd rather have Chanis," Polly said, stretching out her legs to rest her feet on the side of the bed. "Now he would be a real treat."

Moonlight shone through the window when Mazy woke. The clock on her bedside table said 3 a.m. Polly was no longer sitting in the chair beside the bed, and Mazy needed help. Nature was calling. Listening, she could hear her friend's rhythmic breathing. Polly was sleeping on the floor beside the bed, her head resting on her bent arm.

Mazy weighed whether to wake Polly or chance a trip to the bathroom by herself. Sliding out of bed, she stepped over Polly, testing the strength in her legs. It was wonderful to be standing on her own without anyone hovering about. Plentiful moonlight informed the room like a mercury lamp, but the bathroom was dark and unfamiliar. Still, it was easy to find her way around the small space. After using the water closet, she turned the faucet on the sink and washed her hands in a quiet trickle of water. Feeling around on the porcelain, she found a hairbrush and worked the tangles from her hair, then pulled it back with a ribbon hanging from the towel rack. It was tempting to switch on the light, but she didn't want to wake Polly. She'd like to have a glance in the mirror, but she probably looked a fright anyway. Untamed, her hair was always like a nimbus around her head.

She padded back across the bedroom to the window, which was raised. The soft night air toyed with the curtain sheers, blowing them out like a bellows. The opulent, enticing scent of gardenia blossoms tickled her nose and titillated her senses. The perfumed aroma must be coming from the yard in the back of the house. There were no gardenias in the front garden.

Like Eve in Eden, Mazy couldn't resist the serpent's call. Taking her robe from the end of the bed, she padded barefoot down the hall to the back staircase Polly had told her about. She trod lightly down the stairs, holding her breath and keeping her feet on the sides of the steps to avoid any squeaky middles. As she had hoped, the door was unlocked. She left it half-open and stepped out into the soft moonlit night.

Her feet followed her nose, leading her down a brick path to a garden hidden behind an evergreen screen. A splash of water lured her farther in. Moonlight bathed a rock-lined fish pond and turned the fish into silver streaks darting among saucer-size water lilies. The breeze picked up, rustling the swordlike blades of cattails, their dark-brown spikes bent over the water as if in benediction.

The brick path divided at the pond. Mazy walked around the left side. The bricks felt smooth and worn under her bare feet. A wooden church bench rested in the curve of the path. It was darker at this end of the pool, but Mazy knew she had found the gardenias by their sweet smell. Her mother kept a gardenia pot, along with other plants, on the windowsill in her room. The children were not allowed in their parents' bedroom unless invited or unless it was a very stormy night. But sometimes Mazy watered the plants in her mother's room. The gardenia liked a lot of water and did not mind sitting in a wet saucer.

As her eyes adjusted to the scant light, Mazy could see that the luscious plants were in containers. The doctor must take them in during the cold-weather months. Gardenias would not survive Kentucky's harsh winters if left outdoors. She cupped a blossom and brought it to her nose. The delicate, wildly fragrant flower fell apart in her hand, showering her feet with waxy-white petals. She caressed the glossy, leathery leaves before she let it go.

With her nightdress tucked beneath her, she sank down upon the bench and took deep breaths, relaxing more with each inhalation. When worry niggled at the corner of her mind, she pushed it away. Maybe she should be trying to figure what the future held in store, but not tonight. Tonight she would focus on the rippling water, the fragrance of flowers, and the full and beautiful moon. She could belong in this place.

The shadow deepened. Puffy gray clouds went scudding across the moon. Mazy stood with palms open, lifted overhead as if she held up the sky. Letting her arms fall, she retraced her steps, glad she had left the back door ajar. Above her a step squeaked. Was someone coming down or going up? Hand at her throat, she waited in silence before tiptoeing back to her room, glad for the comforting presence of Polly, who was still sleeping.

Mazy's sleep was deep and restful, and she didn't wake until Polly shook her shoulder. "Mazy, I'm leaving now. I hope you get to come home tomorrow."

"Thank you so much for staying with me last night, Polly. You're so much fun."

"I know when to have fun, but I also know how to keep a secret. Trust me, I'll keep yours."

Mazy was puzzled. "Do I have a secret?"

"Don't play coy with me, Mazy Pelfrey. I'm talking about you and Loyal Chambers."

"I'm sure I spoke out of turn about that," Mazy said, already regretting her indiscreet conversation with her girlfriends. "I spun a fantasy based on very little truth."

Polly laid her finger aside her nose and studied Mazy. "What is it about you? You're like a fairy princess spinning at a wheel — catching men unaware in your golden web."

"That's unfair, Polly. I don't mean to trap anyone."

"Of course you don't. That's why it works so well for you. Just you be careful that you don't snare a spider in that glittery web of yours."

"I need to think about that. I would never want to be that way."

"Don't be so serious, Mazy. I'm just jealous." Polly leaned in for a quick hug. "Friends?"

"Friends for sure," Mazy said. "Check on the kittens for me, would you?"

Polly finished packing her overnight kit, then headed for the door. "Don't forget I have dibs on your sheriff," she called back over her shoulder.

Mazy laughed. "You're a stitch, Polly."

"More likely a dropped stitch," Polly said and then was gone.

Mazy smiled. Polly would always have the last word. She leaned back against the pillows.

A tiny goldfinch landed on the ledge outside her window. It fluffed its wings, cocked its tiny head, and looked in at her through the screen. Wishing she had a palmful of corn bread crumbs, Mazy slowly approached the bird, surprised that it didn't fly away. "Little biddy," she cooed, pressing one fingertip against the screen. "Little biddy bird."

When the bird tapped at her finger with its beak, she felt ashamed. The tiny thing was hungry and here she was promising something she couldn't deliver. After a series of industrious pecks, the bird took off, winging toward a stand of clipped evergreen trees. Mazy caught her breath. She had dreamed last night of a secret garden hidden behind that screen. The dream was so real she could almost see a winding brick path, shimmery moonlight on water, flowers glowing whitely in the dark.

She'd always been a dreamer — sometimes even acting them out, sleepwalking toward a whisper, a promise. Her father had taken to locking the door to the well house. The sleepwalking ended when her mother traded her midwifery skill for a shaggy medium-size dog. Mazy and Molly had named her Dolly. They combed and braided the dog's hair, dressed her in their outgrown clothes, and wheeled her around in a pram. Dolly had slept at the foot of Mazy's bed for years, protecting her from herself.

Mazy wrapped her arms around her body and squeezed. "Don't start that again," she said to herself. "Folks here will think you are nuts."

When she heard footsteps in the hall, she slipped between the sheets and smoothed the coverlet.

"Good mornin', young lady," the maid she'd seen before said. "I thought you might be wanting your breakfast."

"Thank you; it looks delicious," Mazy said, taking in the sight of an egg cup and buttered toast.

"Hunger is the best sauce," the maid said. "I expect you are way past hungry by now."

Mazy's stomach growled. "I've been found out."

"Well, you enjoy. I expect Miss Cinnamon will be along shortly."

Tapping the egg's shell with the edge of a teaspoon, Mazy broke the white and scooped up the tasty yellow center. It melted in her mouth. There was enough honey in a small pot to both sweeten her tea and spread on the toast. Indeed, hunger *was* the best sauce.

She'd nearly finished eating before she noticed a length of blue ribbon, spooled as tightly as a measuring tape, tucked under the edge of the white doily beneath her plate.

Curious, she began to unfurl it and saw a word printed on the inside of the ribbon in navy-blue ink, then another and at the very end another. Holding it stretched between her hands, she read, *My sweet Eve.* Her heart thrummed like a hummingbird's as her mind whirled backward. The blue ribbon had been on the towel rack in the bathroom; she had tied it around her hair. She had gone down the staircase in the dark and across the yard to a hidden garden that was rife with perfumed flowers and melodious, darting fish. Testing herself, she looked at the bottoms of her feet and saw faint stains from grass.

She pressed a hand against her heart to slow its keyed-up beat. Somewhere along her mystical journey, she had lost the ribbon. Loyal had found it and written a message for her eyes alone. "Be still my heart," she murmured. The world she was entering was not a fantasy at all, but a place where dreams were made and wishes fulfilled.

She heard a *tap-tap*ping on the screen again. Taking the last bite of toast to the window, she prepared to remove the folding screen, but the goldfinch was not there. Instead, she saw Loyal pitching pebbles toward the window. His smile was warm as sunshine when he saw her watching.

"I'm glad to see you're up and about this morning," Mazy heard Dr. Chambers say behind her. "I expect you can go home tomorrow if you feel up to it."

Mazy spun around, suddenly feeling like a little bird about to leave its cozy nest. "I'm feeling much stronger. It will be good to get back to normal."

"Stay up and active as much as you like today — come downstairs if you wish, perhaps place a call to your sister in Skip Rock. But don't overdo — you have been very ill. I wouldn't like to see a relapse."

"Thank you for taking such good care of me."

"You're welcome," the doctor said with a bemused glance toward the window. "The pleasure was mine, I'm sure."

Chapter 18

Mazy rested most of the morning. The maid came up again and insisted on running her bath and sprinkling in bath salts. Mazy was delighted to sink into the lavender-scented water, which was just this side of too hot. She hadn't had an actual warm bath in a very long time. The bathwater at Mrs. Pearl's was always tepid. Most of the time, the girls washed their hair in the kitchen sink with water heated on the cookstove and took hurried pan baths in the upstairs bathroom. Spit baths, Polly dubbed them.

Rubbing steam from the bathroom mirror, Mazy studied her reflection. The hot water had caused her hair to kink like barbed wire. Three bears with bowls of porridge surely waited just beyond the door. She twisted and twirled her errant tresses into a semblance of order. She wished Cinnamon were here to work her magic again. The maid had wondered at her absence, it being unlike the girl, who often did odd jobs for the doctor.

"Poor girl child," the maid had said while she fluffed the pillows on Mazy's freshly made bed, "having to live hand to mouth like she does. Good thing she knows how to work."

"She lives with her father, right?" Mazy asked.

"Far as I know it's just the girl and her father, and him sick all the time. They live in Cedar Bottoms, same as me. My church takes food over there whenever we can. Times are hard, you know."

Mazy nodded. She was familiar with hard times: poverty, illness, little children with big eyes and stick-thin limbs. She'd been living in a coal camp, after all, and she had eyes, even though she didn't always acknowledge what she saw. Sad things overwhelmed her. She much preferred make-believe.

"Dr. Chambers said I could use the telephone when I come downstairs."

"If you come down the back way, it's on the wall right by the dining room. Poke your head in the kitchen if you need any help."

Mazy's strength waned as fast as the bathwater whirled down the drain. She poured a glass of water from the carafe on the bedside table and sat in the chair to drink it. After dressing in the clothes Ernestine had brought from Mrs. Pearl's, she felt a little better, although it felt funny to have on shoes again.

At ten o'clock she decided to call Lilly. Her sister would be at the office by now, and Mazy was anxious to hear how the twins were doing. Lilly's housekeeper lived right across the road from her and was always available to help out.

Finding the telephone, Mazy sat on the high stool beside it and lifted the receiver. She gave the operator her sister's number and waited. She loved the telephone; using it had been her favorite thing to do when she worked at the clinic for Lilly. It continued to amaze her that you could talk to a person many miles away and you didn't even have to raise your voice. Idly, she wondered how one became an operator.

"Hello?"

"Lilly?"

"Mazy?"

"Oh, Lilly, it's so good to hear your voice."

"How are you, sweetheart? Better?"

"So much better. The doctor let me get up today. I had food poisoning. I was as sick as you can get. But I've been worried about the babies."

"Praise the Lord they had mild cases of the measles. They are recovering and mean as striped snakes."

"Have you talked to Mama?"

"Yes. I didn't tell her you were ill. She and Daddy have had the flu, and I was afraid she would insist on coming to Lexington. I've been praying for you and am very glad you are under the care of Dr. Chambers."

"I'm glad Mama didn't come. I've had plenty of help."

"I hear Chanis paid a visit."

"Umm, yes," Mazy said, fiddling with the telephone, nearly disconnecting the call.

"I don't hear any excitement in your voice."

"Lilly, I've met someone. He's very nice. You would like him."

"I certainly want to hear more about it, but we mustn't tie up the doctor's line. Will you promise to take this very slowly?"

Butterflies had taken up residence in Mazy's stomach. She had thought Lilly would simply forbid her from even thinking of seeing anyone but Chanis.

"We've only just met," she said, and that was true — it wasn't her fault that her heart was full speed ahead. "Lilly, you know that box of clothing — the skirts and blouses that needed letting out? Could you send them to me?"

"Of course, but even if you've lost weight — which you should gain back as soon as you begin to eat — the skirts will still be too long."

"I know. They're not for me. I've met a girl who is nearly destitute. I thought she could use them."

"All right, sweetheart, I'll put them in the post today. Take care of yourself. I hope to see you soon. I love you."

"I love you too, Sister. Bye now."

"Good-bye."

The hallway was cool and dark, but Mazy had never felt so warm and full of light. Lilly had not said she shouldn't consider dating Loyal. Mazy knew once she met him, she would be charmed and give her full consent. Lilly probably thought it was a simple crush. But Mazy's heart knew differently. It was very exciting to be young and unencumbered by the expectations of others.

Mazy found the friendly maid chopping vegetables in the kitchen. "Do you need any help?" she asked.

"Oh no, miss. I'm supposed to be taking care of you, not the other way around. How about some chicken noodle soup for lunch? Dr. Chambers said you could have chicken noodle or beef barley. Chicken's better," she said with a dimpled smile.

"I'll have chicken." Mazy looked around the well-appointed kitchen. "Where is everybody?"

"This is the doctor's surgery day at the hospital and Mr. Loyal's rents day. Miss Cinnamon didn't show up, as you know. Doctor said for me to keep an eye on you, in case you felt bad again. She was put out with Miss Cinnamon, I could tell. I expect she's having to take care of her father."

"I'm fine, really. I don't want to be the cause of trouble."

The maid's knife sliced and diced. Green and red bell peppers piled up on the chopping block. "You're nothing of the sort, miss. You're to enjoy your day and rest. Dr. Chambers wouldn't be happy if you had a setback."

"Would it be okay if I sat in the front garden for a while? It looks so pretty out."

"Long as you feel up to it. I'll let you know when soup's on. Doctor said to make yourself at home. She said if you wanted something to read, I should show you the library."

Mazy truly had died and gone to heaven. Dr. Chambers's library was a whole room to itself. The walls were lined with shelves,

269

which were full of books. A ladder on a track of some sort leaned against one set of shelves.

The maid pointed out one low section under a window. "These here are the made-up stories. Pick whatever you like, but stay off that ladder. We don't need you to fall and conk your head. Doctor would have *my* head if that was to happen."

Mazy stared longingly at the shelves of fiction. She loved to read and hadn't had a chance since starting school. Running her finger along the spines, she stopped at a familiar orange cover. *Elsie Dinsmore* by the author Martha Finley jumped out at her. She'd read the adventures of Elsie two summers ago when she'd lived with Lilly. Feeling light as air, she took the book outside and settled down in the chair beside the chaise longue.

Flipping through the pages, she looked for her favorite passage and found it at the beginning of chapter 9:

"She is mine own;
And I as rich in having such a jewel
As twenty seas, if all their sand were pearl,
The water nectar, and the rocks pure gold."
SHAKESPEARE, Two Gentlemen of Verona

Mazy sighed with contentment. Nothing was quite as satisfying as a good book. She loved the first line of this chapter after the verse from Shakespeare: *"And now happy days had come to the little Elsie. Her father treated her with the tenderest affection . . ."* That would have been the perfect ending.

Dreading what was coming, she read on through the chapters to the last page and the saddest sentence she'd ever read: *"He longed to tell her that all her fears were groundless, and that none other could ever fill her place in his heart, but he did not like to wake her, and so, pressing another light kiss on her cheek, he left her to dream on, uncon-scious of his visit."*

She dashed tears from her cheeks. Why had Martha Finley left Elsie on such a gloomy note? If Mazy had written this book, she would have ended it differently. Perhaps Elsie at a birthday party or a piano recital. Something light and airy — anything but her poor little flushed cheeks and tear-swollen eyes.

Of course, the reader could suppose from the rest of the book that Elsie woke to happy days, but Mazy would have liked to read about it, not have to make it up in her own mind.

She considered going around to the back

of the house to see the secret garden but decided against it, afraid the daylight would break its lovely spell. It was so good to be outside and not lying abed.

Rays of sun twinkled between the leaves of the roses, enticing Mazy to move her folding chair to a patch of sunshine. Turning her face up to the warmth, she vowed to sun for just a moment; she didn't want to freckle.

She woke to a familiar voice.

"What a nice surprise."

Mazy raised her hand to shade her eyes and saw Loyal revealed in an aura of brilliant sunshine. He might have been an angel, he was so bigger than life and striking to her. Without a moment's hesitation, she reached out to him.

He took her hand and kissed it. "You are lovely," he said.

Shocked at her own boldness, she slowly pulled her hand away. "I've been reading."

Loyal picked up the fallen book from the grass. "Heavyweight entertainment," he said, handing it back to her.

"Oh, my, I've let your mother's book fall. I'm sorry."

"It's not damaged. The ground is dry."

Mazy looked the novel over and saw that

he was right. "Still, I shouldn't be so care-less."

"Should I serve lunch out here, Mr. Loyal?" the maid said, approaching them in the yard.

"Don't go to trouble for me, Beulah. I'm not staying. I only stopped in to get some files. Miss Pelfrey has had enough sun. She'll be in, in a moment."

"I will?" Mazy taunted flirtatiously after the maid had left. "What if I choose to sit right here?"

"Then I'll be forced to throw you over my shoulder and carry you in yet again."

Mazy thought she might like that. She knew she'd been too forward, though, and already regretted her actions. It was as though she became a braver, more outspoken person in his presence. Her face felt warm and tight, whether from embarrassment or the sun, she wasn't sure. Life would be easier and definitely more fun if she didn't have an angel on her shoulder constantly reminding her to mind her reputation — an angel who sounded suspiciously like her sister Lilly.

"You're right; I should be going in." She stood with the book.

He offered his arm and escorted her across the yard. When they reached the welcome shade of the wraparound porch, he stopped. "Wait here. I'll be right back."

He came back with a rose, presenting it with a deep bow. "My lady," he said. "Listen, we're having a get-together on Friday night to celebrate Independence Day. If you're feeling up to it, would you like to come?"

As much as she'd hoped for a moment such as this, Mazy was nonplussed. Was he asking her for a date or just inviting her to drop by? "Is it a big party? Is it formal?"

"Not so big — maybe fifty or sixty friends of my mother's and of mine." He stooped down to look her in the eye. "Say yes. I'll pick you up at seven. Come on; you'll have fun."

In a momentary panic, Mazy didn't feel so grown-up. She'd never actually been asked out by a man. Chanis was just always there and already approved of by her sister. And they'd never had a real date. Visiting family and going to Sunday school picnics with friends didn't count because they were never really unaccompanied and certainly not closed up in an automobile. Wouldn't that be the equivalent of being alone in a room together with no chaperones hovering close by? Having her fondest wish come true left her feeling unmoored. It was like she'd wished for a kitten and been given a cat.

Her hesitation seemed to make him even more aggressive. "There'll be fireworks. Bring your friends. What do you say?"

He won her over. She'd be above reproach if the other girls came along — even Lilly would agree with that. She was not going to allow any negative thoughts, any self-doubt, to intrude on what was surely a wonderful moment.

"I shouldn't speak for the others, but I think we would love to come."

His hand brushed hers as he reached to open the door. A feeling of great tenderness overtook her. Her hand trembled, and she nearly dropped the rose. She clutched it tighter. It would be pressed in her dictionary along with the two other blossoms he had given her. Perhaps, on some far-off day, she would carry them tucked into her wedding bouquet. A girl could always dream.

The chicken noodle soup was appetizing. Mazy had a small bowlful with saltine crackers and a side dish of canned peaches. Fearful of spilling something on the faded Oriental carpet under the massive dining room table, she spooned the soup in tiny bites and wiped her mouth with the merest edge of a heavily starched napkin. She could hear her own throat swallowing in the hushed and elegant room, crowded with antiquated furniture and fusty with an old-wood smell.

The table had eight leaves and sixteen harp-backed chairs cushioned with crewel-work pads. On the sideboard was a silver punch bowl (at least she thought it was a punch bowl) and graduated sizes of silver candlesticks spilling over with hardened beeswax. The bowl could have stood a good polishing. The mirror over the sideboard was patchy with age, the blacking showing through. The brass pendulum of a tall case clock bonged twelve times, the sound muffled by the heavy tapestries hanging on either side.

There were several gold-framed portraits on the walls. They looked faded, as if they had been in place for a very long time. Portraits of people she'd never met always made Mazy wonder about the stories behind the faces. One picture was of a lady. She had a long face and sad-looking eyes. Her hair was pulled back severely. It looked like she was dressed in black, but who could tell? There was an air of mystery about her. For some reason it made Mazy think of her own grandmother who had drowned when a buggy overturned in Troublesome Creek. It shamed her to think how, when she and Molly were girls, they would act out the buggy-in-the-creek story. In their reenactment, however, everyone was always saved. They were both too tender to entertain the thought of death.

Goose bumps pocked the flesh of her arms and she shivered. The downward turn of her spirits that had started with the Elsie book returned. If she were a writer, she'd pen happy novels — light and entertaining only. How hard could that be?

A light switched on in her mind. Why couldn't she be a writer? She already knew how to type.

While she carried her dishes to the kitchen, she tried to figure out how an author would start a book. The kitchen was empty, so she put her dishes in the sink, ran some water, and sprinkled in some washing powder she found on the windowsill. The mindless washing of dishes always stimulated her imagination.

Her nose tickled. She scratched it with the back of her wrist. Through the window over the sink, she could see the maid — Beulah, was it? — standing at the clothesline beating a rug with a large wire whisk. Clumps of dust dotted the grass. It was a homey scene contrasting sharply with the opulent garden just beyond the cedar screen.

A soap bubble floated upward and popped against the ceiling. Bubbles were light and airy and happy things. How could Mazy turn the feeling they caused in her into a book title? Lost in thought, she knit her brow, straining to come up with something — anything — that lifted her spirits and made her smile. Soap bubbles, kitten paws, spring sunshine, peacock feathers, puffy clouds, buttermilk . . . She shook more soap powder into the sink and stirred the bubbles. This was more difficult than she thought it would be. She could hardly name a book *Buttermilk.* That would be ridiculous.

What she needed to get her started was a yellow legal pad and a new ink pen. She could imagine sitting in the garden, words spilling from her pen, creating sunshine on the page. Even a married lady could be an author. Loyal would be proud of her. As soon as she could, she would visit the stationery shop and purchase supplies.

A stern voice from the kitchen door popped her bubble. "What have we here?" Dr. Chambers asked, peering over her half glasses with ice-blue eyes.

Despite herself, Mazy jumped, dropping

the spoon she was washing back into the sink. Somehow her dreams of a life with Loyal never included his mother. "I finished my lunch and thought . . ."

Dr. Chambers walked over to the sink. "Beulah!" she called through the window.

"Please don't be angry with her," Mazy stammered. "She didn't leave me to do this. I was bored, that's all."

"Sometimes she forgets her place," Dr. Chambers said.

Beulah hustled through the doorway. She looked from the doctor to Mazy and then to the sink. "I turn my back for a minute . . . Child, you don't need to be doing my work."

"Precisely," Dr. Chambers said.

Mazy hung her head. She'd never in a million years imagined she would need to apologize for doing dishes.

"We'll take tea in my office."

"Yes, ma'am. Would you be wanting some of that lemon cake I made this morning? It's got that coconut icing you like."

"Thin slices, and don't neglect rinsing the teapot with hot water before you steep the tea. I don't like it cold." Then Dr. Chambers turned to Mazy and said, "Come along."

Mazy followed behind. Looking back over

her shoulder, she mouthed, *"I'm sorry"* to Beulah.

Beulah shrugged in a never-mind sort of way. Mazy supposed she'd learned how to get along with Dr. Chambers. Maybe Mazy could too.

CHAPTER 19

Sitting at his desk in the sheriff's office, Chanis found it hard to concentrate on the ups and downs of crime and punishment in Skip Rock. All he could think about was Mazy. He tapped a pencil against the desktop, rapping out his edgy energy.

"What's eating you?" Tully asked as he took a ring of keys from a hook on the wall.

"Nothing. What are you fixing to do?"

"Thought I'd repair that bunk in cell two. Good time to get it done while the jail's empty."

"All right. Need some help?"

"Not unless you want to spruce it up a bit . . . maybe put up some wallpaper? Hang some curtains?"

Chanis tossed the pencil on the desk. It skittered across the surface and landed at Tully's feet. Tully tossed it back.

"Think I'll go to the clinic — check on Oney, see if he's ready to go home," Chanis said as he took his hat from the rack in the corner.

"You might stop by the store and pick out some linoleum to match the paper," Tully ribbed.

Chanis shook his head and closed the door behind him, careful not to slam it. He was never going to live down the wallpaper incident; might as well let Tully have his fun.

A nurse showed him into Doc Lilly's office and indicated for him to take a chair.

Doc closed the chart she was working on. "I was hoping to see you," she said. "I thought you'd want to know that Mazy has been ill."

"But I just saw her on Friday. She was fine."

"A bad reaction to a purgative her housemother gave her, poor darling. I've meant to come by and tell you, but between Mr. Evers and the twins . . ."

"Is she okay? I can get back to Lexington by evening."

"She's much improved after a few days of rest. She's going back to class tomorrow."

Chanis sensed a reserve in Doc Lilly's manner when she talked about Mazy. Was she telling him everything? "Are you sure she's okay?"

"Yes, I'm satisfied that the physician there made the proper diagnosis. It may take her a couple of days to regain her full strength, but Mrs. Pearl will watch out for her."

Chanis put his hand on his knee to stop its jiggling. He couldn't dismiss the thought that he was not hearing everything. "She didn't seem like her usual self when I visited. Maybe she was feeling poorly then."

Doc Lilly looked at him with a serious, level gaze. "Chanis, Mazy will have lots of new experiences there in the city. She'll soon be twenty, but a young twenty. Do you understand?"

He rubbed his jaw with his knuckles. "Not really."

"You don't understand or you don't want to understand?"

"Both," he said, drumming on the desk with his fingers.

Doc Lilly reached across the desk and put her hand on his. "She'll never be content unless she has the opportunity to explore her options, learn some lessons, and figure out what she needs to do to feel fulfilled."

"I want to be the one to make her happy. I can give her a home. I can keep her safe. Why is that not enough?"

Doc Lilly rested her elbows on the desktop and tented her fingers. "I'm not saying it isn't, Chanis. That's between you and Mazy. What I am saying is that you don't want to be the reason she doesn't figure that out for herself."

"What if she gets hurt in the meantime?"

The yellow songbird Doc Lilly had once rescued from the mines and now kept in her office hopped from the floor of its cage to its perch and began to preen its feathers. The doc filled the bird's tiny cup with seed from a box on her desk. "We can't keep her in a cage, much as we'd like to."

"Well, thanks for talking with me. I really came by to check on Oney Evers. Is he ready to go home?"

The doctor smiled. "You won't believe this, but his wife collected him last evening. She got her neighbor to bring her into town."

"Are you sure it was Miz Ina?"

Doc Lilly laughed. "I know. I never thought I'd see the day. Not only did she come, but she brought a three-layer chocolate cake with caramel icing. We had a long chat about that."

"Poor Oney. It's nothing but beans from here on out," Chanis said.

"A proper diet will buy him some time," she replied, standing to retrieve a package from a shelf. "I wonder if you'd mind taking this to the post office for me. Mazy asked if I'd send her some things, and with the children being ill and all, I'm having trouble finding the time."

Chanis stood. "Be glad to. You need anything else?"

"No, not at the moment," she said, smiling kindly at him. "It will all work out, Chanis. You'll see."

Chanis decided to pick up some lunch for himself and Tully before he went back to work. He could stand a baloney and cheese sandwich on Mrs. Rogers's homemade white bread. He'd have mayo; Tully liked mustard.

He was standing at the pickle barrels, trying to decide between dill and sweet, when Mrs. Rogers spied him.

"I've got good news," she said. "The extra paper you ordered came in this morning. Want me to have my boy put them in the truck?"

"That'd be good. Thanks."

"Now some of the paper is for your mother, right?"

"Yes. I'm hoping to surprise her."

Mrs. Rogers looked askance. "Are you hanging it by yourself? You know I'd be glad to help."

"I'm just surprising her with the paper. My sisters and I'll help her put it up."

The girl behind the counter wrapped his order in white butcher's paper. "You decide on the pickles?"

"Two of each, I reckon," he said.

Mrs. Rogers wrapped the juicy pickles in waxed paper and put them on the counter. The clerk pulled string from a holder and tied it around the sandwich packets. "Cookies?" she asked, inclining her head toward a glass display case.

"Sure." He fished two Dr. Peppers from the ice in the red cold case and popped one cap with the church key mounted on the wall. "Add these to my order, and this." He opened a sleeve of peanuts and poured them in his dope.

A boy pushed around him, chasing the bottle cap, which had rolled across the floor. "Can I have this? Me and Timmy's playing checkers."

With a nod to the clerk, Chanis took two more drinks from the cooler and handed them to the boy. "These are on me."

"Really? Wow. Thanks, Sheriff."

"Who's winning?" Chanis asked.

"Not me." His impish smile revealed two missing teeth. "Maybe these here will distract Timmy."

Chanis sat in the cab of the truck, drinking his Dr. Pepper and eating the salty peanuts from the bottom. He watched the boys playing checkers atop a barrel. He could hear them besting each other with loud belches. A hundred years ago, he and his brothers had done the same thing, albeit without the cola. What had happened to his youth?

He was beginning to bore himself with his woe-is-me attitude; time to put a lid on it.

Though out of the way, he swung by the house on his way to the jail. It was time to turn the tables on his buddy Tully.

After lunch, Chanis went back out to his truck and carried the wallpaper, a bucket of paste, the tray, and two pairs of scissors into the office.

Tully paused midpickle. "What you got there?"

"Thought we might as well get something done this afternoon." Chanis broke the seal on a roll of border. Lilacs spilled across the worn wooden floor. "Do you like this pattern?"

"Uh, I reckon, but you don't mean to . . ."

"I think it's right cheery. Plus it'll give the prisoners something to do — counting flowers on the wall. Give them a break. No pun

287

intended."

"You're the boss. So what do we have to do?"

Chanis slapped a pair of scissors in front of Tully. "We're going to cut this out."

"This here's awful narrow. Are you sure you bought the right thing?"

"Have you never helped the missus hang paper? This is the border. It goes on top of the paper."

"Why?"

"You got me there. I don't have a clue," Chanis said with an I-surrender gesture.

The steady *whisk, whisk* of the scissors in combination with his full stomach nearly lulled Chanis to sleep.

"I wish somebody would rob a bank or something," Tully said, examining his index finger. "I got a blister."

"There's tape and gauze in the first aid box."

"I think Rhoda would like this," Tully said as he went to get the box. "She's always favored lilacs — carried them down the aisle when we got married. Smelled so sweet."

Chanis watched spirals of paper gather around his feet. "Sounds real pretty," he said.

"She was — still is."

Chanis put his scissors down and

shrugged, trying to unkink the muscles in his shoulders. "You tell her that?"

"Not near often enough. You know, things changed once the kids came along." He scratched his beard with the tip of the scissors. "Think I'll stop by the store on my way home."

"You've got to measure the room first," Chanis said.

Tully wrapped his finger in a plaster. "You special ordered wallpaper for the jail?"

Chanis flung a swirl of scrap paper at him. "Got you," he said.

"Man, you really had me going," Tully said, brushing the paper from his head.

"Would you really have let me make a fool of myself — putting wallpaper in the cells?"

"Experience is the best teacher." Tully started rolling up the border he'd finished. "So is this for your house?"

"Nope, my mother's."

"Good deal. I don't mind getting blisters for your mom."

When the phone rang, they both jumped. "Hello," Tully said. "Yeah. . . . Yep, he's right here. Hold on."

"This is Sheriff Clay. . . . Is that right? . . . Sure, me and one deputy — we can find it. . . . Yeah, yeah, a truck — glad to be of help," he said before hanging up.

He looked around the office, which looked more like a parson's parlor than a jail. "Stick this stuff somewhere out of sight while I unlock the gun cabinet."

"Was that really — ?"

"Yep, the Feds. Looks like we're going on a whiskey raid."

"They say who they think's working the still?" Tully asked, sticking paper underneath the desk.

"They didn't name names, but supposedly an informant says it's up Jake Leg Creek near the old mill."

"Nasty," Tully said. "That place is mostly swamp since the dam broke. The family that ran the mill died out years ago."

"Which is why it appeals to bootleggers," Chanis said, loading bullets.

"This makes me uneasy," Tully said. "The locals won't take kindly to strangers. It would have been better if they let us take them down on our own."

"You think?"

"Your dad would have backed me on this. Busting stills was his specialty."

Chanis felt keyed-up as he slid into the truck. These things could go wrong in a hurry. "Did you go out with him a lot, Tully?"

"There was this one time . . ." Tully

started on one of his beat-around-the-bushes tales about his and Chanis's father's escapades.

Chanis half listened as he drove, using the time to make a plan, think out what they would do if they actually came upon a still. There were times he missed his father so much it made his teeth ache.

"Then all three of them moonshiners laid down their weapons," Tully wound up. "Your dad didn't even cuff them — just walked them into town, his shotgun pointed at the ground. Truth be told, we never had but one set of cuffs — that's how stingy the county was back in the day. Sheriff Clay was something else. Most respected man I ever knew. Hardly ever drew his weapon, used reasoning instead. He could've sold water to a drowning man."

About a mile from Jake Leg, Chanis turned up a logging trail and parked behind an unmarked black Model T with an Illinois license plate. *They might as well have a flag stuck to the hood,* Chanis thought.

He couldn't remember ever being in this part of the county. It wasn't exactly a Sunday stroll sort of place. After replacing his hat with a billed cap, he pulled waders from the back of the truck and handed a pair to Tully.

Four nattily dressed gentlemen stepped out of the car. Introductions were made, handshakes exchanged.

The lead agent, Ernest Adams, slapped at his ear. "Bloodsuckers — big as cats."

In a few words he explained what they wanted from Chanis and Tully. They were escorts only. They should leave their weapons behind. Chanis declined. He offered his waders to the officer, who pulled a face, looking like Chanis had offered him a stone instead of bread.

"My deputy knows this area best," Chanis said while tugging the olive-green hip boots on over his shoes.

The officer studied the thick brush and stunted cedars choking the hillside. "Do you have a machete?"

"Good way to announce unexpected company," Tully said, crossing his arms across his chest. "All that whacking and thrashing around. If you're aiming on surprise, it'd be better to wait until dark."

Adams fixed a glare on Tully. "Nobody asked you. This is my operation."

Mosquitoes whined in clouds of aggravation. Chanis willed himself not to react and waited for direction. He'd watch and learn.

One of the Feds stayed behind to watch the car. The other three followed Chanis, who followed Tully, who held back brambles and low tree limbs when necessary, allowing the others safe passage. Nobody spoke — who knew how close the still was.

About a mile in, they came upon a clearing marred by a slimy green drainage basin, the surface alive with threadlike horsehair worms. Dragonflies darted about, their iridescent wings reflecting the glare of the waning sun. A snapping turtle sunned on a rock midpond, and near the edge, a patch of sludge pulsed like a heartbeat.

With a stick, Tully peeled back the black muck, revealing a frog trapped underneath. Adams swatted the back of his neck. Checking the pond's depth with the stick, Tully waded in. Chanis forged along behind him, feeling the suck of mud against the soles of his rubber waders. Looking over his shoulder, he saw the agents kicking off their shiny shoes and rolling the cuffs of their suit pants.

On the other side of the foul-smelling pond, he and Tully waited while the agents hopped around, silently picking fat leeches from their ankles like a bunch of crazy mimes. There were things a fancy suit wouldn't protect you from. Pulling snowy white handkerchiefs from their pockets, they wiped silt from between their toes before they put their socks back on. Tully smiled and shook his head.

They trooped another half an hour before Tully stopped them with a warning hand. The still was so well hidden amid a blind of trees, they nearly stumbled right into the middle of the action. Just beyond the fire that fueled the operation, a man sat in the low, dark mouth of a cave, rolling a cigarette. A shotgun rested on his knees. Another filled a bucket from a spring that trickled down the rock face of the cave. A third, whose slouch hat hid his features, stirred the coals under the cauldron. The fire sputtered and spit and gave off only a thin ribbon of smoke. Chanis figured they hadn't been at it long today, probably just settling in for the night.

Adams made a motion, and they all crouched down among the bushes about twenty-five feet back. There were five of them against three of the whiskey makers. Good odds. But suddenly a fourth man appeared. He carried a hundred-pound sack of sugar across his shoulders. Huffing, he slid it off and dropped it onto the ground. Chanis watched Slouch Hat disappear into the cave. There was something vaguely familiar about the guy. He tried to catch Tully's eye to see if he had the same reaction, but Tully was stationed about forty feet back from the site. Not a good idea to Chanis's mind, but he was taking orders the same as Tully.

It was at least two hours until full dark; the best time to catch the criminals unaware was after they had settled in for the night.

Chanis lay flat on the ground, his nose inches away from the muck of leaves and twigs. The canopy of trees overhead was so thick, the ground probably never dried out. The smell of mold and decay was thick as cotton batting up his nose. An arm's length away an agent so young his five-o'clock shadow was little more than peach fuzz began to snore. Chanis poked him and he startled awake, a look of alarm on his face. He fumbled to retrieve his weapon. He'd foolishly gone to sleep with it lying under his armpit.

A line of black ants marched under Chanis's nose, industriously dragging a dead beetle backward through the debris. His ankle itched fiercely. Felt like chiggers — the bane of his existence, blight upon the earth, as bad as Pharaoh's plague of locusts. Sweat pooled under the waders that had been so welcome back at the pond. He wished he had thought to take them off after they'd left the water. Once he'd put them on, he was too intent on saving face. Now he could see how they might slow him down.

The insects had started their evening drone before the young agent screwed up his face and sneezed. It seemed as loud as the shot heard round the world. Doves startled from their nests. A deer bolted out of the woods, its white tail bobbing quickly out of sight.

Adams sprang up, sheltered behind a tree. He pointed his gun toward the men at the still. "Hands up! Drop your weapons! You're all under arrest!"

If the Feds had thought the moonshiners would meekly give up, they were sorely mistaken. They scattered like buckshot. A blast of gunfire lit up the night. Chanis's ears rang. The young agent caught the first round. Like a chicken with its head cut off, he ran back up the way they had come and collapsed at Tully's feet.

The moonshiners retreated, crashing through the woods. The two remaining agents followed in hot pursuit. Chanis tripped over his own feet but recovered quickly, running toward the route he'd seen Slouch Hat take. The ground was wet and springy underfoot. Just feet ahead, he could see the man he was pursuing dodge a rotten log. Chanis was gaining on him — a few more feet and he could take him down. He wouldn't shoot a man in the back no matter what.

Fueled by a burst of adrenaline, Chanis jumped the log and landed hard. Suddenly he was jerked upward. When his body stopped bobbing, he was hanging by one ankle ten feet off the ground. Now he knew why the runner had dodged the log. Unwittingly, Chanis had tripped a snare.

Chapter 20

Dr. Chambers decided Mazy was well enough to go home that evening but insisted on driving her so she could speak to Mrs. Pearl. They found her in the kitchen washing up after supper. "Well, look who's home," she said, drying her hands on the front of her apron. "Has she fully recovered then, Dr. Chambers?"

"I believe so, but it would be prudent to keep an eye on her and, of course, modify her diet for a while. I know I can count on you."

Goodness, Mazy thought, *I'm standing right here. I'm fully capable of speaking for myself.* But she didn't say a word. She was much too intimidated. Besides, she had strained her brain trying to come up with conversation during the car ride here. Mostly she answered the doctor's questions. Surely now Dr. Chambers knew as much about her family as she did. Really there wasn't much to tell — no cattle rustlers, bank robbers, or rumrunners in the bunch.

"Walk me to the car, dear," the doctor said as she took her leave.

Mazy could feel her eyes widen. *Dear?*

Dr. Chambers held the front door open for her. Shouldn't it be the other way around? Mazy needed a quick brushup on etiquette. Things were starting to feel very *Alice in Wonderland.* She could hardly wait to talk to Ernestine and Polly.

"I'll stop by during my rounds tomorrow, Mazy," the doctor said, slipping a business card from her pocketbook. She smiled a thin, tight-lipped smile that did not reach her eyes. "Call anytime."

"Yes, ma'am," Mazy said. "Thank you for taking such good care of me."

"There's something about you that I quite like," she said. "Did my son invite you to our little get-together on Friday?"

"Yes, ma'am," Mazy said, sounding like a trained parrot. *Yes, ma'am. Yes, ma'am. Yes, ma'am.* "I hope it's all right if I ask my friends to come also. Loyal said to, but . . ." She felt her cheeks warming with a dreaded blush. She was being too familiar.

"Are you speaking of the girls who visited with you while you were ill?"

"There's Ernestine and Polly and one

more you didn't meet, Eva. She was going to take a turn tonight if I'd stayed. I know she would have." Mazy felt like a babbling brook, trying to cover her discomfort with words.

"Of course they must come. The more the merrier."

Mazy waved as the car drove away. It seemed the proper thing to do.

"May I please dry the dishes for you?" she asked when she joined Mrs. Pearl in the kitchen. "I need to do something normal."

"Grab an apron. I'll be glad for the help."

"Where is everyone?"

"They walked down to the drugstore. Polly needed poster board for one of her projects."

Mazy dried a serving platter. "I'm so glad to be out of bed."

Mrs. Pearl handed her a fistful of forks. "Not as glad as I am to have you back. I've never been more upset. I was sure I'd killed you."

"But, Mrs. Pearl, at least I didn't get the flu."

Mrs. Pearl dropped the washrag into the sink and pulled Mazy into her arms. "Bless your sweet heart, honey. Promise you'll tell me if you feel the least bit bad."

Mazy wanted to sink right into the embrace. It was the closest to a hug from her mother that she could have — despite the wet handprints on her back.

They finished the dishes, laid out the plates and cups for breakfast, and put the pots and pans away. Mazy headed for the pantry. Three of the kittens were in the basket with their mother. Two sat on the floor with their tails curled around their feet. Mazy laughed. "How cute. They look so grown-up."

"The good news is they're spoken for. I'm keeping one of the boys for a mouser."

"But they're so little. They can't go yet. And what about the mother?"

"They won't go until they're weaned, and I'm keeping her for a house cat. She's grown on me."

"When I have a house, I'm going to have a dozen cats."

"Start with one and you'll have a dozen in no time. That's the way it works."

"Do you think our pets go to heaven?" Mazy said, sitting on the floor beside the basket. She stroked the back of the mother cat, procuring generous purrs.

"The Bible says the lion will lie down with the lamb. I reckon our dogs and cats won't be left out."

"What about pigs? I had one I fed from a

bottle. I called him Q because of his cute little tail. He followed me around like a dog."

"I won't ask what happened to Q," Mrs. Pearl said with a smile.

"Bacon. So sad. I was peeved at my daddy for the longest time."

"Some animals God gives us for companions and some He gives for nourishment," Mrs. Pearl said. "Gracious, listen to that thunder. This has been the rainiest summer. I hope the girls get home soon. They didn't even take an umbrella."

Mazy jumped up. "I'll take a couple and go meet them. They can't be far."

She was just turning the corner when the rain began to fall. Opening one umbrella, she stuck the other under her arm and hurried on, counting the seconds between the rumbles of thunder. The storm was coming fast.

"Hurry," she called when she saw her friends coming down the sidewalk.

Ernestine unfurled the extra umbrella and held it over herself and Eva. Polly clasped Mazy's arm, her awkward package bumping Mazy's hip. "When did you get home? It's so good to have you back."

Mrs. Pearl had ginger tea and iced cookies waiting for them. "Ginger's good for the digestion," she said.

Mazy took an experimental sip and found she liked it.

Polly put a poster board on the table and began to draw on it with colored pencils. "I'm supposed to make a poster encouraging conservation," she said. "I need extra credit."

"She wasted six sheets of carbon paper," Ernestine said. "Mrs. Carpenter was miffed."

"Yes, she was," Polly said. She wiggled her smudged fingertips. "This ink is impossible to wash off."

"Mrs. Carpenter is always miffed," Eva said, taking a mouse's nibble from the edge of a cookie. "I'll be so glad to graduate and get away from her."

"I like Mrs. Carpenter," Mazy said.

"You would," Eva said snippily.

Mazy stirred her tea and let the remark go. "You'll never guess where we're invited on Friday."

"We're going to High Bridge," Eva said. "We missed last week because of your supposed illness. The other girls didn't want to leave you behind."

"It's not written in stone, Eva. Stop being such a crab," Ernestine said. "Why don't you let Mazy finish, and we'll decide what

303

we want to do."

Mazy thought fast. She didn't want to further antagonize Eva. "Dr. Chambers has invited all of us to an Independence Day celebration. We can dress in red, white, and blue. Won't that be fun?"

Eva looked surprised. Mazy knew she wanted the chance to see Loyal, but she also wouldn't want to give up control.

"Oh, let's, Eva," Polly said. "I have the perfect hat to wear. It's a straw boater. I could decorate it with crepe-paper streamers. We can carry some of those little flags from the store."

Eva picked pink icing from the top of her cookie as if she couldn't care less. "Whatever you all decide I'll go along with."

Mazy was the first one up the stairs. It had been a long day and she was tuckered out. It made her heart ache to see Clara's bed tidily made up under the window beside hers. There was no robe draped across the foot, and the bedside table was free of clutter. Now Clara would never find her expensive prescription spectacles. Nobody had mentioned her all evening. It was as if she'd never existed.

Mazy put her overnight bag on her bed and emptied the contents. She hung her dress in the closet, put her dirty clothes in the hamper, and slipped her nightgown over her head. She sat on the side of her bed and stared at the empty space, wishing she had paid more attention to Clara. Rummaging in the narrow clothes closet, Mazy found the patent leather shoes that Clara had borrowed to wear to High Bridge. She arranged them under Clara's bed. It made her feel better to see the shiny toes peeking out from under the bedspread — like a memory marker that said, *You were here.* Kneeling by her bed, she said her prayers, careful to include Clara.

When she heard the others coming up the stairs, she turned down her covers and got into bed. Her pillow felt like a rock after the fluffy, luxurious one she had slept on the last few nights. Closing her eyes, she feigned sleep. She didn't want to talk anymore.

Sometime after midnight, she woke with a crick in her neck. She wondered if Lilly had already mailed the items she had asked for. If not, she could add Mazy's favorite feather pillow to the package. It was worth asking.

Aggravated, she punched the pillow and flipped it over. An envelope fell from the bed to the floor. Curious, she picked it up and took it down the hall to the bathroom. After closing the door quietly so she wouldn't disturb the others, she pulled the string to the overhead bulb and flooded the room with light. Blinking against the glare, she saw that the envelope was addressed to her.

She prized the flap open and took out a single sheet of paper, folded in the middle. Holding the letter up to the light, she read:

Dear Mazy,

I am sorry you are ill and sorry that I won't be able to come to sit with you. I trust this finds you well again. Of all the girls, you were the kindest to me. I don't know why because I was not always the same to you.

The truth is I am desperately throwing myself on your mercy. Mazy, I have shamed myself and I don't know what to do. I have to leave school. When you read this, I will be back in my father's house. I cannot bear the shame my condition is going to bring to my family. I am only glad my mother is not alive to see what a mess I have made of my life.

You are my only hope. You have often spoken of your mother, whom you have said is a midwife. Mazy, do you think she might take me in? I pray you will find it in your heart to ask her. I know it is far up in the mountains, and that is fine with me. I have saved enough money for train fare. Please tell her I will work for my keep.

I beg you to let me know as soon as possible at the address I have written below. It won't be long before I can't hide my shame. If you can't bring yourself to do this, I will understand. But only let me know. Please, let me know.

I remain your friend,
Clara

Rain tapped at the window, reminding Mazy of the bird that had pecked on the sill outside her sickroom. Mazy could hardly bear to imagine how scared Clara must be. Evidently Ernestine's suspicion was true. How had Clara let such a thing happen? She read the letter through again, then folded it and slipped it back inside the envelope. There was only one thing she could do. Feeling a sense of urgency, she headed for the stairs.

Mrs. Pearl kept stationery for the girls to use in one of the cabinets in the dining room. She only asked that they pay for their own stamps. Later, Mazy would put her pennies in the cracked cup that held the coins. Under the flickering light of the gas lamp, she began to write in her very best script:

Dearest Mama,

First off let me say that I am well. There, I didn't want you to worry. Lilly said that you and Daddy are recovering from the flu. GET BETTER SOON.

I'm going to get right to the point, Mama, as you so often have asked me to do (SMILE). I am enclosing a letter from a young woman who goes (I guess I should say went) to school with me. I know you will read between the lines.

Mama, the funniest thing happened. I PRAYED for her tonight and then found this note under my PILLOW!!! I feel like the Lord is speaking to me. You always say we are HIS EYES and HIS EARS here on earth. Now I know what that means.

The girl's name is CLARA GOOD-PASTOR. I will write to her and tell her she is more than welcome to come to you. So be expecting her soon. Daddy or one of the boys will need to pick her up from the train station.

Oh, Mama, I miss you so and love you

BUSHELS and BUSHELS.
                    Your loving daughter,
                               Mazy
                        XOXOXOXO

P.S. "HIS EYE IS ON THE SPAR-
ROW."
   (This is a new hymn I've just learned.
I'll sing it for you when next we meet!)

With a few quick strokes she drew a
diminutive bird in flight before applying
blotter paper. While she waited for the ink
to dry, she selected two envelopes from the
drawer. One she addressed to her mother
and one to Clara. She sealed the letters with
mucilage and put a tiny drop of the glue on
the stamps. She'd drop them in the mailbox
at the corner rather than leave them for the
postman to pick up. It was best if no one
questioned why she was writing to Clara.
The least she could do was keep her friend's
confidence.
   She took the first raincoat she came to
from the hall tree, pulled the hood up over
her head, and stepped out into a dark night
and a light rain. There was a sense of
freedom in daring to walk barefoot down
the sidewalk in the middle of the night.
Goodness, what might she do next? Throw

away her lightly boned corset? Chew gum? Deliberately fail to indent a paragraph on her next typing test? Oh, the glory of doing the unexpected. She pirouetted, dancing in the rain, when she reached the corner.

The door to the mailbox screeched like an owl after a mouse when she pulled on the handle and let the letters fall into the depths. She whisked her hands together. "There, mission accomplished." It was amazing to think of the power a person had to help bear another's burden if they chose to do so. For there was no doubt her mother would help Clara. No doubt at all. And Mazy had been the medium.

Back in her room she prayed again, this time with a light heart. When at last she put her head down, her pillow didn't feel nearly as hard.

CHAPTER 21

The blood pounded in Chanis's head, and each time he pulled on the noose that kept him suspended above the forest floor, the rope tightened around his ankle. With every effort he made, the branch of the tree that sagged under his weight bounced him up and down like a fish on a line. He couldn't yell for help just yet. He didn't want to interfere with the chase. Shots rang out. Men screamed. It sounded like war.

He felt like an idiot trussed up like a turkey. On the ground, not two feet from his yearning fingertips, was his trusty pocketknife — so near and yet so far. The knife had blades in three sizes, a flathead screwdriver, and a can opener. He sharpened the blades once a week right before he trimmed his nails. He'd never used the flathead, but the can opener had come in handy on numerous occasions. He also counted seventy-five cents in scattered coins and took note of his key chain. The one with the rabbit's foot. What kind of a fool trusted his luck to a rabbit? He guessed he knew what kind. And who knew where his gun had landed.

Think, he told himself. *Think.* Maybe he could get the branch to give enough for him to grab the knife. It was worth a try. He swung himself back and forth, gaining momentum with each swing. Even though it was hard to focus, he kept his eyes on the tree limb. The branch was strong, but with each swing, the rope slid down the branch, causing it to bend closer to the ground.

I could use a little help here, Lord, he prayed silently just before his fingers brushed against the knife. One more lunge and he had it.

It felt good to hold the knife; at least he'd accomplished something. But try as he might, he couldn't reach up far enough to cut the rope. He thought his head was going to explode. Then he felt himself slipping downward. He curled his torso up as far as he could in hope that his shoulders would take the brunt of the fall instead of his head.

With an inglorious thump, he landed. He lay still for a long moment, catching his breath and considering what he should do next. Sitting up, he examined his ankle, which was circled by an angry red welt. The rope had sliced clean through his hip boot and released the tension on the snare, which was why he was free and why his foot wasn't laid open to the bone.

Chanis heard a low rustle in the underbrush. He scrambled to his feet and ducked behind a bushy cedar. He could see a form appear in a break between the trees. Slouch Hat was circling back — probably to dispatch Chanis to his reward. But when the man appeared, he didn't have any weapon drawn but a knife. The fight would be even.

The man stood with his back to Chanis, looking up at the empty tree. He was a foot shorter but stout. It wouldn't be an easy takedown. But he put up no struggle when Chanis surprised him from behind with a forearm lock to the throat.

Chanis stuck the end of his knife case into the soft spot just behind Slouch Hat's ear. He hoped it felt like the barrel of a gun. The guy drooped down as if he'd gone soft in the knees.

"Please don't shoot me, Sheriff Clay. I was coming back to cut you down. I swear I was."

Feeling like he'd been punched in the gut, Chanis pulled off the slouch hat and released the boy, who fell to his knees and clasped his hands behind his head. Chanis shoved him and he fell over. "What are you doing here, Junior?"

Tully Jr. burst out crying. His face was white as a sheet. "They're all shot," he said, his eyes pleading. "Ever' one of them is dead."

"Who's been shot, Junior? Which ones?"

"Joe and Turtle and Rooster — all of them." He breathed a ragged breath. "They didn't give them a chance. Shouldn't they have had a chance? It's not like they ever killed anybody."

Chanis knew that low-down bunch of petty thieves. "What were you thinking, hooking up with them?"

"I don't know. I thought I'd make a little money — have some fun. Please don't tell Daddy."

"You're in big trouble, Junior. One of the lawmen was shot. He might be dead for all I know."

"But I didn't do nothing! This is the first time I've been up here. I swear! I didn't even have a gun. Daddy keeps mine locked up."

From a few dozen feet away, they could hear the sound of something heavy being dragged through the woods. They hunched down and watched one of the Feds tugging

314

what was left of Rooster toward the site of the still. It was enough to make a grown man chuck up, never mind the fifteen-year-old boy who had turned as green as the slime in the drainage pond.

Chanis knew how the need for revenge could settle in a body's soul, taking over all rational thought. He'd plotted a dozen ways to kill the man who'd killed his father. Thankfully, he never got to carry any one of them out, for the man was found dead with a rambling letter of remorse and apology in his breast pocket. He liked to think he was above that now. It was best to let the law exact vengeance the legal way.

Junior continued to bawl. He wiped snot from his nose on the sleeve of his shirt.

Chanis made a slashing motion across his throat as random gunshots rent the air. It sounded like the Feds were firing at anything that moved — bloodlust. The kid was going to get himself shot — maybe get both of them shot — if Chanis didn't let it be known they were there. He didn't want to think what would happen to the boy once they arrested him. Life in prison was likely — if he lasted that long.

Making a split-second decision, he grabbed the front of Junior's shirt and dragged him to his feet. "You get the heck away from here," he said in a low voice. He shoved the slouch hat in the boy's face. "And get rid of this."

Whoops of victory emanated from the area of the still. Chanis's blood ran cold.

Junior collapsed against Chanis's chest, sniveling like a two-year-old. Chanis shook him until his teeth rattled. "Leave — now! Don't make any noise, and stay away from the road! Don't say a word to anyone about this! You got it?"

Junior nodded. "I've wet myself," he said.

"You'll dry. Now get!"

Junior turned and ran off into the dusky evening, surprisingly light on his feet for such a hefty boy. Chanis gave him five minutes to get safely away before he gathered up his scattered belongings and found his gun behind the log. He limped back to the others, where he found the bootleggers' bodies stacked in the mouth of the cave like so much cordwood. Somebody had dumped the sack of sugar over them.

"There was no call for this," he said, nearly grinding his teeth.

"One of them shot Johnson," Adams said. "It calls for whatever I say it does. Bunch of backwoods yahoos got what they deserved."

The young Fed, Johnson, stood supported by Tully at the edge of the site. He was bare-chested except for what looked like a pressure dressing made from an undershirt wrapped around his torso. The bandage was stained with blood. Tully had probably kept him from hemorrhaging to death.

"Did you shoot them in the back?"

"What's it to you? I see you didn't bring the other one in."

"He got away." Chanis crossed his arms. "Tully and I will track him down. You can bet on that."

Adams stood with his hands on his hips. "Got away? Just slipped through your fingers? Likely story." He jutted his chin. "I'm not leaving until he's draped across the hood of my car."

Chanis wanted to coldcock him. Drop him like a boat anchor. "Want some advice?"

Adams pushed his regulation hat back off his regulation forehead. His regulation badge glowed in the light from the fire. "Does it look like I need it?"

Night fell like a heavy curtain. Frogs croaked, coyotes yipped, and from somewhere on the ridge behind them a panther yowled. It sounded like a woman's scream. Adams rubbed his arms and swallowed hard.

Chanis fixed him with a stare. "Go back to wherever you came from. Leave the rest to us." He walked to the bodies, crouched down, and began to dust the sugar off. "When their families hear how you left them, they'll string you up and gut you like a deer."

Adams kicked a rock, skipping it into the fire. Sparks shot up. "You're crazy if you think I'm going to let you get away with this."

Chanis continued what he was doing, acting like what Adams said didn't matter a whit to him. Sugar swirled around like a spit of fine, cold snow. "Here's the thing," he said. "None of them shot your man. He shot himself. Check his weapon. I might have to file a report to the bureau myself."

It was after midnight before Chanis and Tully got back to Skip Rock. They didn't even have to pound on the undertaker's door to wake him up. He opened it before Tully raised the knocker. Chanis thought he must sleep fully dressed — always prepared for death. What a job.

Out of respect for the dead, he and Tully hadn't talked during the ride to town. Chanis wished he didn't ever have to talk about what had happened. It went round and round in his mind. Legally, he should have given Junior up. Rules were rules for a reason, and he had sworn to uphold the law. Morally, he thought he'd done the right thing. It would be better all around for Junior's fate to be handled through the local system. A few months in jail beat being shot in the back every time.

"Man, what a night," Tully said when they got to the office. "Reckon I'll head on home."

"Come in for a minute," Chanis said, unlocking the door. "I'll put some coffee on. We need to talk."

CHAPTER 22

Clothes were scattered all over the room. The girls took turns at the dressing table, except for Eva, who didn't have to share. She hadn't left her room all afternoon.

"I wonder what the queen is wearing," Polly said, holding up her arms so Mazy could help her into her blue poplin dress.

"This has a million buttons," Mazy said.

Polly sidestepped to the mirror as Mazy fastened the pearl buttons. "But do you like it? That's what's important." Polly stuck a hat pin into her hat to secure it. Red, white, and blue crepe paper streamed down over the brim.

Mazy bent to fasten a sparkly red brooch to a white sateen ribbon around Polly's waist. "You will be the most patriotic, I'm sure. Ouch! Hold still. You've made me stick myself."

"You two," Ernestine said. "It's just a Fourth of July party, not a fancy dress ball."

Polly's eyes bugged out. "Where did you get that dress? I should be wearing that. It goes with my hat."

Ernestine primped in front of the mirror. Her outfit was red cotton gabardine. She popped a matching parasol.

"Seven years of bad luck!" Polly squawked. "Don't you know not to open an umbrella in the house?"

"Seven years is if you break a mirror," Ernestine said, twirling the parasol coquettishly.

Mazy giggled. It was fun to see earnest Ernestine preening. "You look wonderful," she said. "But really — where did you get a red dress?"

"I got it at Suzanne's."

"I thought she just made hats," Mazy said.

"She had this dress on display in the window. I bought it right off the mannequin."

"And it fit?"

"Mostly," Ernestine said, tugging at the skirt. "It might be a tad short."

Mazy stood back and looked her friend over. "I can see your ankles, but that's fashionable now. Your stockings are black, so it's hardly noticeable. Red becomes you, and your parasol — so clever."

A knock at the downstairs door went

unanswered. "I'll go," Ernestine said.

"Furl that parasol first," Polly said. "Bad luck is bad luck however long it lasts. You'll make it rain for sure."

Mazy slipped her own dress over her head, careful not to disturb her hair, which she'd kept casual, simply pulling it back from her face with a ribbon — the robin's-egg-blue ribbon. She hoped Loyal noticed. Her dress was blue dotted swiss muslin with an overskirt and a blouse waist. It looked more Sunday school picnic than Independence Day, but it was what she had.

When Eva swept regally into the room, Polly and Mazy gasped. Her dress was red — Ernestine's red — the starkness of the bold color softened by a scarf of white crepe de chine. It fit her perfectly. Her hat sported a daring cockade of red ribbon and gold-and-white feathers. Eva knew how to dress up an outfit. All eyes were sure to turn her way.

Mazy and Polly locked eyes. They could hear Ernestine coming up the steps. It was like watching two trains on the same track. There was going to be a collision.

"Delivery for Miss Mazy Pelfrey," Ernestine sang as she came in the door.

"My dress," Ernestine said, pointing at

Eva. Polly caught the vase before it hit the floor.

"You'll have to change," Eva said haughtily.

"No, I won't," Ernestine said with a shake of her head. "We'll go as mirror images."

"You are so tiresome, Ernestine," Eva huffed. "Come and help me, Polly. I have a lovely royal blue that will go well with my scarf. The scarf is the best part of my ensemble anyway."

"Just a second," Polly replied while pulling a tiny envelope from the vase of roses. "Ooh, they're from the Flower Shoppe."

The vase was white milk glass and the roses pink. Mazy didn't have to open the envelope to know who had sent them.

"Mazy's got a boyfriend. Mazy's got a boyfriend," Polly teased. "Hmm, are these from the handsome sheriff or from the smitten man-about-town, Mr. Loyal Chambers?"

Eva's face was redder than her dress. Mazy wished Loyal had not been so bold. It was not as much fun to best Eva as she had imagined it would be.

"I'm sure these are meant to be shared," she said.

"Hurry up if you're going to change, Eva," Ernestine said. "You're going to make us miss the trolley."

The house on North Broadway was festive with luminarias spaced evenly along the walk. Flag buntings were hung like valances all along the wide porch. People stood in small groups, chatting and laughing. On the left lawn a band struck up a Sousa march. Everything was so different, so light and festive, Mazy felt like a stranger.

Polly grabbed Mazy's hand. "This is magical," she said. "Ooh, look, a butler. Fancy."

The man stood blocking the door, greeting people as they came up the porch stairs. He asked their names and checked them against a printed list. "Drinks are being served in the back garden," he said, indicating a graveled path.

"Can't we go inside?" Polly asked as gravel crunched beneath their feet.

"The hosts may still be getting dressed," Ernestine said. "They probably don't want people wandering around the house until dinner is served."

"I hope there's food," Polly said. "I'm starving."

"Don't be a bore," Eva said. "They wouldn't have a party at this time of day if they didn't have a spread of some sort. Look, there's a tent. Let's peek inside."

Round tables were placed around the perimeter of a dance floor. Each dressed table held a red, white, and blue floral arrangement. The chairs were slipcovered with white linen, secured with big bows across the backs. Candlelight flickered from oversize lanterns suspended from the tent's roof supports.

"Ooh la la," Polly said. "But where are the drinks?"

"I don't see a garden," Ernestine said.

"It's just behind the evergreens," Mazy said, leading the way.

Just the other side of the screen, they found the drinks station. Mazy got pink lemonade and drifted away from the group. She was hoping to find Loyal and thank him for the roses. Sipping her drink, she wandered around the garden, curious to see it all again. It had not lost its magic even with other people strolling around. Under the gardenia bower, a couple sat close together on the bench. The man leaned close and whispered something in his companion's ear. Laughing, she playfully pushed him away. Mazy didn't realize she was staring until the fellow looked up at her.

"Hello," he said. "Are you looking for someone?"

"No, no," she stammered. "I was just

admiring the gardenias."

"Lovely, aren't they?" the woman said.

The man stood and introduced himself and his date. Mazy exchanged pleasantries before she walked on, sorry to have interrupted them. She wondered if they were friends of Loyal's.

Before leaving the garden, she noticed her friends had joined a group of other young people milling about the goldfish pond. Her feeling of loneliness intensified. Maybe Loyal was out front enjoying the band. She paused at the graveled path. Several people were coming. She'd walk around the other side of the house.

As she passed by the slightly raised window of the doctor's home office, she heard familiar voices — lowered voices. Oh, dear, she shouldn't have come this way.

"You look very handsome, Son," she heard Dr. Chambers say. "Where have you been all day? The workers could have used some help setting up the tent."

Mazy turned to go back the way she had come but couldn't resist staying for a moment when she heard Loyal's voice.

"I spent the day trying to get people to cough up the rent they've neglected to pay. It's like they think they can live there for free. It's very aggravating."

"It's business, Son, only business. How did it go?"

"Only two didn't pay up. One girl paid half, and so I gave her until next week."

Mazy heard a loud huffing sound and then the doctor spoke. "Is that our problem? You give too many warnings, Loyal. Think what your father would have done."

"I'll take care of it."

"I trust you will. Now, are you ready to greet our guests?"

"One in particular," he said.

"Did you send the flowers?"

"Of course."

Then Mazy heard a soft sound like a pat on a cheek.

Mazy didn't dare to breathe. She stayed rooted to the spot.

"She is perfect for us, Loyal. Sweet and obedient and not unintelligent."

The band struck up another tune. Mazy strained to hear the conversation.

"Give it a rest, Mother."

"There's not much time, Son. You know the terms of the will as well as I do. You cannot inherit until you are married."

"Father controlling even from the grave," Loyal said.

"Yes, well, perhaps we'll have the last word for once. It's really up to you."

Mazy tried to look casual as she walked back the way she had come. She strolled to the garden and up the path to the bench, which was now empty. Her mind was awhirl with what she had heard.

The ice in her lemonade had melted. She had forgotten she even held it. Careful not to splash her dress, she poured it out in the gardenia bed and set the glass on the small table that already held several other empties. She sat there for several minutes, going over each word. Were they speaking of her? Were Loyal's affections truly given or was he only trying to please his mother? She felt as if she'd been doused with cold water.

"I thought I might find you here," Loyal said. "You're shivering. Do you want my jacket?"

"No, I'm fine, thank you. I'm enjoying the flowers and the music," Mazy said as the strains of a song mingled with the exotic scent of the gardenias and the soft, warm breeze of the day turned to night.

Loyal extended a hand and pulled Mazy to her feet. She didn't resist. Maybe she was overthinking things as usual, and for sure she shouldn't have been eavesdropping. It didn't seem fair to spoil the night. "I'd best go find my friends. They'll wonder where I am."

"All right," he said. "I'm going to find Mother. I'll see you later."

Mazy easily slipped into the midst of people lining up to enter the dining tent. Standing on tiptoe, she scanned the crowd for her girlfriends. Ernestine's red dress was easy to spot, plus she was doing the same thing Mazy was. She waved for Mazy to join them at the front of the line. Everyone was in a festive mood and nobody protested when Mazy cut in just behind Ernestine.

"Where have you been?" Ernestine said. "We've been looking all over."

"Isn't this grand?" Polly interrupted, keeping Mazy from having to answer Ernestine's question.

With her lifted chin and perfect features, Eva looked to the manor born in her regal royal-blue gown. Mazy wondered how she kept the white scarf from slipping off her shoulders. If she had tried to wear such a garment, it would have fallen off a dozen times.

Polly spotted their name tags on a table on the left side of the tent. Everyone stood behind their chairs and watched as the band members reassembled on a slightly raised platform. They remained standing, waiting for their host and hostess to enter.

People started clapping when the musicians played the first lines of "Oh! Susanna." Applause swelled when Dr. Chambers, in white linen, entered on the arm of her son. The duo took a turn around the dance floor as the song continued, before Loyal seated his mother.

"That seems a funny song to introduce them," Ernestine said.

"The doctor's name is Suzanna," Eva explained. "They do this every year."

"You've attended before?" Ernestine asked. "I didn't know you knew the Chamberses."

"Dr. Chambers's husband and my father were business associates."

"I didn't know her name was Suzanna," Mazy said.

The lone man at their table scurried around behind them, pulling out their chairs.

"There are many things you don't know," Eva said haughtily.

"I'm sure," Mazy conceded, not rising to the bait.

The first course was served.

Polly turned up her nose. "What is this?"

"Oysters on the half shell," Ernestine said, selecting a utensil.

"But I'm hungry," Polly said.

Mazy felt the same, but she picked the

330

morsel loose from the shell with a tiny sharp fork, daintily hiding the slimy-looking oyster under a toast point.

"I thought there'd be wieners and popped corn," Polly lamented.

"For heaven's sake, Polly," Eva snapped.

The man who had seated them smiled broadly. "I'm sure there'll be something you'll enjoy." He tipped a whole oyster into his mouth and swallowed. "It's an acquired taste."

Mazy barely suppressed a shudder. She was glad to see the oysters go when the salad course was served.

Loyal proved to be the perfect host, dancing with each of Mazy's friends, saving Mazy herself for the last waltz. She found herself enjoying his company despite her earlier misgivings. He deserved the benefit of the doubt, and really, had he said anything so terrible? Surely she hadn't misjudged Loyal's character so badly. Sometimes you had to trust your heart.

As the festivities wound down, people began to wander up the street to a local park from which they would watch fireworks.

"Ladies," Loyal said as he approached the girls. "May I accompany you?"

Polly took one of his arms and Eva stepped in front of Mazy to take the other. Mazy and Ernestine followed a few feet behind.

"She still doesn't get the message," Ernestine said.

"I don't mind," Mazy said. "He's such a gentleman."

When they got to the park, Loyal spread a blanket on the ground. "Ladies," he said, "make yourselves comfortable. I'll be just a minute."

He came back with several small hand-held flags he'd purchased from a vendor, giving one to each girl and keeping one for himself. "A memento for this beautiful evening," he said as he sat on the edge of the blanket next to Mazy.

Ernestine gently elbowed Mazy's arm.

Mazy hid a smile behind the Stars and Stripes.

CHAPTER 23

Chanis rolled into Lexington well before dark. He'd booked a room in a local hotel and stopped there to freshen up before he went to see Mazy. He left the package he was to deliver in the truck and carried his valise into the lobby of Park Place.

Fancy, he thought as he followed a bellhop to the elevator. He didn't need such a lofty accommodation — he could have slept in the truck, but he hoped to make a reservation for tomorrow evening in the dining room here. He meant to have some time alone to talk to Mazy, and for that he needed an appropriate place. You couldn't take a lady just anywhere. He could ask her to take a walk with him, of course, but he had the feeling that would involve all the girls at the boardinghouse. It was hard to separate one chick from a flock.

The bellhop set his valise on a bench before opening the drapes. "Will that be all,

Mr. Clay?"

Chanis tipped him a quarter, feeling magnanimous. *What a job,* he thought as the guy closed the door to the long hallway, *getting paid to open curtains.*

He was a little jarred at being called *mister,* but he wasn't traveling in an official position and wasn't dressed in uniform. It felt odd, though. He wasn't sure he even recognized himself when he looked in the mirror.

After a quick shave, he sat on the side of the bed and looked through the complimentary copy of the Lexington newspaper. Someone stole his neighbor's push mower; the sheriff was hailed for breaking up a game of chance; Mrs. Henrietta White had startled a Peeping Tom. No shoot-outs, no stacked bodies, no busted moonshine stills. Of course, more than likely, it was probably just a slow day for news. There was not a place on earth that didn't have its share of crime — especially in these hard times.

On the front page was a banner wishing everyone a happy Fourth of July and an announcement about a fireworks display. He'd look into that — Mazy might enjoy an outing.

On his way out of the building, he passed a shoeshine stand. "Shine your shoes, sir," a boy said. Chanis hesitated. He wasn't one to let someone do for him what he could readily do for himself, but there was something about the day. He felt a sense of freedom that he hadn't felt in a very long time.

The boy sat on a stool at his feet, dabbing black polish on Chanis's shoes with his bare fingers before slapping a rag over the leather, bringing out a high shine. Chanis tipped him twice what he'd given the bellhop. If he stayed in the city long, he'd have to get a second job.

He'd promised himself he wouldn't give even a minute of his time away to thoughts about work, but it seemed an impossible promise to keep. Second-guessing himself had kept him entertained all the way from Skip Rock to Lexington. Granted, what went down with the Feds and Rooster's gang of misfits and then Junior getting caught up in the disaster needed some serious contemplation.

Before he left Skip Rock and after he'd fueled the truck, he stopped by Tully's house to speak to Junior's mother. He knew she would have doubts and questions. She asked him in and offered breakfast, which he declined.

Rhoda's eyes were red-rimmed, and tears slipped down her cheeks unchecked the whole time he was there. It seemed he needed to be blunt with her — to not sugarcoat Junior's involvement. Mothers had a way, he knew, of coddling their sons and refusing to acknowledge what was so plainly true. But coddling was far from what Junior needed. And so he told her exactly what he had witnessed, being sure she knew where Tully was while everything was happening so that she wouldn't blame her husband or think he could have prevented it in some way.

Her fears jelled and focused on whether her boy would spend time in jail, not on what he'd so foolishly done. Chanis told her truthfully that he didn't know. "So we just live with this uncertainty?" she'd said. "I don't think I can bear it."

"Could you look at it in a different way?" he'd asked as she walked out onto the porch with him. "Might God use this to pull Junior up short? To remind him of the path he needs to be on?"

Like a candle flickering in the dark, hope returned to her eyes. "I need to get my Bible out and study on this," she'd said. "Maybe it's me God is calling up short."

Unexpectedly, she'd hugged him briefly and thanked him sincerely.

He had no idea how he'd come up with

the words that had given her comfort, but she'd given him something important also. His Bible was in the glove box. He needed to pay it more attention.

After a couple of wrong turns — how did people survive this traffic? — he parked in front of the boardinghouse. Before he opened the door, he straightened the collar on his new cotton shirt. He wasn't sure he liked it, but the Sears catalog said the turned-down collar was the latest in men's fashion — which was also what it said about his stiff black dress shoes and the cuff on his gray flannel trousers. He'd ordered the whole shebang weeks ago in anticipation of visiting Mazy at some point, but this was the first time he'd worn it. He was hoping she would see him as a regular guy.

There was no answer when he knocked on the door, so he walked around back of the house. The kitchen door was closed, but a window was open. A string mop hung drying over the porch railing. If he were in sheriff mode, he'd look in the window, but he wasn't. The tabby cat jumped up in the window and pressed against the screen.

"Where is everybody?" he asked, tapping on the screen.

The cat sat down on the sill and began to wash its face. He heard a rustling in the garden. Maybe Mrs. Pearl was working there.

"Hello?" he called, stepping off the porch. "Mrs. Pearl?"

A skinny girl in a shabby dress stepped out from between two rows of corn and set a basket on the ground. "She's gone to the show at the park."

"The fireworks show?"

The girl dusted her hands on her apron. "Yeah. It will start soon as it's full dark."

"Thank you," he said. "Would you happen to know if Mazy Pelfrey went with her?"

"Everybody goes."

"How about you?"

"I've got stuff to do," she said, "but me and Pap can see most of the colors from our yard."

He offered his hand. "I'm Chanis Clay, by the way."

"Cinnamon Spicer," she replied. "It's good to meet you."

"I wonder if you could tell me where the park is."

She gave him directions and then picked up her basket. "Mrs. Pearl gave me permission," she said when she caught him eyeing the basket.

"Goodness," he said, "I'm not questioning. I just thought it looks heavy."

"Are you a friend of Mazy's?" she asked, resting the wicker basket on one hip.

"Yes."

"Me too. . . . Well, supper won't get cooked if I don't cook it."

"Do you live near the park? I could give you a lift."

"You have a car?"

"Better than that, I have a truck." He showed her and set the produce basket in the truck bed. "Those green beans look good."

"I could ride back here," she said.

"No, ma'am," he said. "You ride up front with me."

The house he pulled up to was little more than a shotgun shack of weathered gray wood. A rickety porch, the roof held up by two posts leaning in the same direction, looked like one puff could blow it over. "Home sweet home," he said without thinking.

"It suits us," Cinnamon said with no hint of irony. "This door is broken," she added when she tried to get out of the truck.

Chanis hopped out, went around, and opened the door for her. "Sorry; I keep meaning to get it fixed."

"Pap could fix it for you if he was feeling better. He's real handy."

"I have a mechanic at home who is going to fix it. I hope your father feels better soon," he said, lifting the basket out for her.

"Me too. Thanks for the ride," she said and headed toward the house.

As he drove away, he was surprised to see so many poor-looking houses all crowded together. He thought folks would live better in a city such as Lexington. There was no figuring out why it had to be that way in a place of such obvious wealth.

Miss Spicer had given excellent directions, but he could have found it anyway — just by following the music and all the people heading the same way.

He hadn't thought it would be so crowded, but he found a parking place fairly easily. He was feeling nervous. He wiped his moist palms on the front of his pants. What if Mazy wasn't glad to see him? Maybe he shouldn't have been so impulsive.

Dodging kids and dogs and vendors hawking peanuts and popcorn, he found the broad, perfectly groomed lawn where folks were milling about spreading quilts or woolen blankets over the grass. Women opened baskets full of picnic fare. He wondered how many chickens had given their lives for this day. On a temporary, unroofed bandstand, the band was playing a catchy tune. People waved small flags to the beat of the tune and sang along: " 'Daisy, Daisy, give me your answer, do. I'm half-crazy all for the love of you.' "

Exchange *Mazy* for *Daisy* and that could be Chanis's theme song.

There seemed to be an order of sorts to the evening. Elder folks sat in folding chairs directly in front, their ground-sitting days long over. Parents corralled their offspring to the left side, and younger people congregated on the right. Boys wove in and around the clusters of people, yelling and chasing one another as boys will do. One lit a string of firecrackers and flung it up into a tree, making doves rise from the branches in a frightened, cooing mass. The boy's mother grabbed the back of his shirt and smacked his behind.

Chanis was glad he had seen what happened, else the sound of the explosions might have dropped him to the ground. He skirted the crowd, deciding to approach the younger section from the rear. He didn't want to wander through the group calling attention like he was lost.

The night darkened. A shy little girl offered him a minute flag from the bunch she clutched in her hand. He gave her a nickel and she ran with it back to the souvenir stand. The band struck up the last song of the evening and everyone stood. A robust man stepped to the front of the podium. Chanis rubbed goose bumps from his arms as the powerful "Battle Hymn of the Republic" tolled out clear as a bell. An elderly man dressed in his Confederate uniform saluted the flag with its forty-eight stars and thirteen stripes. Grown men dashed tears from their eyes. Even the little boys stood quietly, some with their hands over their hearts.

A minister prayed, thanking God for the United States of America and asking for continuing peace in all the land and for prosperity for all. Then, *kaboom,* the night sky came alive with color. Chanis craned his neck, enjoying the splendor and wondering how he might bring about such an event for the folks in Skip Rock. He'd make it a priority to find out. It would be spectacular to hear and see such a spectacle bouncing off the mountains.

The crowd shifted, people laughing and admitting a troupe of latecomers into their midst. A guy and four girls joined another group. The guy seemed to know everyone and obviously commanded attention from the ladies. Oddly, he wore white slacks with a dark-colored sweater draped over his shoulders, the arms looped around his neck.

Chanis couldn't imagine such. It was a style he was sure would never be seen in Skip Rock. But it took all kinds, he reckoned.

He scanned the crowd, then settled on the girl sitting by the man in white. The man whispered in her ear and she turned her face to him. Chanis's heart dropped like an elevator cage. The girl was Mazy and she looked smitten. Fireworks boomed, releasing red and blue and white bursts across the night sky. Amid oohs and aahs, the fellow took her hand. Mazy pulled her hand away, but she smiled as she did so and stayed by his side.

Chanis felt like he'd been sucker punched. There was his girl — his Mazy — snuggling up to a fellow who acted like he deserved her. How long had this been going on? Was this why she'd seemed so distant last time he saw her?

A boy made his way through the crowd hawking syrup ices in paper cones. The fellow bought several, sharing with the others in his circle. He held one, teasing Mazy with it — allowing her tiny nips of the sugary treat. The intimate act made Chanis ill. He had to turn away.

The sounds and colors of the celebration merged in one great stabbing pain. The crowd faded away. He was a man alone in a sea of strangers, suddenly unmoored. He nearly fell to his knees.

Somehow he made it back to the truck. He put his hands on the steering wheel, anchoring himself. What a colossal fool he was — a straw man, of no consequence whatsoever. He plucked an errant piece of wallpaper from the dash. A sprig of lilac mocked him. While he'd been in Skip Rock preparing a home for the love of his life, she'd been here pining after another. Evidently absence didn't make the heart grow fonder after all.

He pondered what to do. The one thing he couldn't face right now was his house in Skip Rock. It was a good thing he had a few days off. What he wanted to do was punch someone — a certain dandy who'd stolen his girl. He felt like an ape in the jungle beating his chest and challenging his rivals.

Back at the hotel, he stopped by the desk for his key, then walked up three flights of stairs and let himself into his room. The bed was turned down and a carafe of ice water sat on the bedside table. So this was how the other half lived — petted and pampered while people like Cinnamon Spicer lived in tumbledown shacks and folks like that dandy-pants wooed innocent girls like Mazy.

He pulled a chair over by the window and

sat. Maybe he should go into politics. If he were president, he'd empty all the banks, shake up the money, and divide it fairly. He'd probably get two votes running on that platform, and one of them would be his.

Life would never be fair; he might as well get over it. Besides, what sin was uglier than envy? He had to admit that was what he was feeling right now. Envy and, well, plain old anger, and it certainly was not righteous.

It was hot and stuffy in the room, so he raised the window. The last of the fireworks mocked him. He doubted he would sleep, but he stretched out on the bed anyway.

Chanis woke up eight hours later determined to make the day count for something — minus Mazy. He wouldn't put her through a confrontation she didn't deserve. She didn't even have to know that he was in town. More than what he wanted for himself, he wanted happiness for her. He should have paid more attention to Doc Lilly. She had warned him in a way, but he didn't want to acknowledge her truth.

Using the hotel iron and board he'd found conveniently in the closet — he had to admit this kind of living did have its perks — he pressed the uniform he'd hung in the closet yesterday. After packing up, he car-

345

ried his valise down the stairs, then went to the desk to pay his bill and cancel his dinner reservation.

Slinging his bag into the back of the truck, he noticed the package. He'd forgotten all about it. With an exaggerated sigh, he hefted it out and went to find the bellhop.

He stopped at a diner for breakfast, surprised at how good it was. Funny, though, they served toasted bread with the bacon and eggs. Biscuits weren't even on the daily board. But the hot, flavorful coffee revived him.

When he went to pay, the man behind the counter refused his money. "It's on the house," he said. "We don't charge officers of the law, even if you're from out of town."

They exchanged a few words, the usual "where are you from?" sort of talk. Chanis was surprised at how friendly the man was. Actually, he had to admit everyone he'd met had been very nice. Maybe he'd have to revise his opinion of the city. He was beginning to feel like a hypocrite.

He pulled up to the jail, where a couple of deputies stood around outside having a smoke. The one he recognized from his previous trip here approached as he parked. "Man," he said, "this is only the second vehicle like this I've seen. You rework it yourself?"

"Yeah," Chanis said, "my deputy and I. We wanted to be able to haul things around."

The deputy walked around the truck. "Good idea. Henry Ford couldn't have done a better job. Say, what happened to the door?"

"You remember that guy I brought in a couple of weeks back? The big one?"

"Yeah, Frank Cheney. He do this?"

"Yeah. Like a fool, I left him handcuffed to the frame. He jerked the panel off, then drove away — left me standing in the dust."

The other deputy joined them, laughing. They joked around for a few minutes, swapping stories, before Chanis went inside. He had decided to see if he'd be allowed a visit with Cheney. He remembered their conversation about northern Kentucky. Chanis had always wanted to see more of the state, and now was the perfect time. Besides satisfying his curiosity, he might find a little peace. The terrible incident at the still and what felt like Mazy's betrayal had his gut roiling and his heart sore as a bruise.

The Fayette County sheriff met him with a hearty handshake. "You here for Cheney?" he asked.

"I thought I might have a visit with him, if that's all right."

"Visit?" the sheriff said in a booming voice. "You can have him. Take him off my hands for a while."

"What are you talking about? Surely he hasn't been released."

"His sister bonded him out. He's free until the trial."

"A bank robber bonded out? How's that work?"

"Who can figure what's going to happen next in this business? I'm just doing my job."

"If she bonded him out, why's he still here?" Chanis asked.

"Paperwork. Dotting i's, crossing t's. The sister has no means of transportation, so things have been done through the sheriff's office in Mason County, where she resides. She sent a train ticket. He's got no restrictions except to stay in the state and out of banks." The sheriff gave another who-can-figure? shrug. "Maybe you can drop him off at the depot?"

Chanis followed him down a long, dark hallway to a row of cells. Frank Cheney was in the next-to-last one. He jumped up like a kid when he saw Chanis. "Buddy!" he yelled like he and Chanis had been best friends since grade school.

"Frank," Chanis acknowledged, "I hear you need a ride."

CHAPTER 24

Mazy didn't know you could be so tired from having fun. But when Mrs. Pearl announced breakfast on Monday morning, she could barely drag herself from bed. On Saturday they'd all gone back to the Chambers house for an afternoon of croquet, and yesterday, after church service, there had been a Sunday school picnic. She and Polly and Ernestine and even Eva had enjoyed a grand time together. Loyal had been attentive to all of them, but not overly so to Mazy. She was glad because that took some pressure off and reminded her that he truly was a gentleman.

But now it was Monday morning — time to pay the piper. A cup of tea would surely perk her up. While the bathroom was occupied, she went downstairs to help Mrs. Pearl lay the table.

"You're a good girl, Mazy Pelfrey," Mrs. Pearl said as she ladled oatmeal into individual bowls. "What makes your eyes sparkle so this morning?"

"I'm so glad to be feeling well, Mrs. Pearl; even oatmeal looks good this morning."

A glop of cereal slid down the side of a bowl. Mrs. Pearl wiped it off with a dishrag. "Would you fill the sugar bowl?"

Mazy got the bowl from the table. "Brown or white?"

"I like brown with oatmeal."

Mazy took the lid from the canister. "I do too."

"Mazy, I have to ask you something. Are you seeing someone? Polly said something about a boyfriend."

"Oh, Mrs. Pearl," she whispered, "Loyal Chambers seems to really like me, and I think I like him."

Mrs. Pearl shook her head. "Chambers, you say? What about the sheriff?"

Mazy took glasses from the cupboard. "It makes me so confused to think about Chanis Clay that I try not to. He's so steady and good, but he's also stubborn and set in his ways. There's just a spark about Loyal that Chanis doesn't have. I need to talk to him, but it's hard when he's so far away, and I'm not going to write a letter about something that might hurt his feelings."

Mrs. Pearl straightened a napkin beside a

bowl. "Did you ever build a fire, Mazy?"

"Once in a while, if the fire went out in our Warm Morning stove and Daddy was not at home. It's not an easy job."

"A spark can kindle a flame, Mazy, but a spark won't keep you warm for long. It takes a good supply of fuel to keep a real fire going."

Footsteps announced someone was coming. Mazy hurried to put the sugar bowl on the table before going to the pantry for cream. The tabby arched her back and purred when Mazy bent to pet her head. Eva being mean to the kittens was another thing she didn't want to think about.

"Kitty cat," she said while she scratched behind its ears, "I sure have a lot to think about. Maybe I'll talk to you later. You could help me sort things out. I'm sure you would be a good listener, and I wouldn't have to wonder what in the world you are trying to tell me."

None of them was up to snuff on the typing drill Mrs. Carpenter surprised them with. Mazy's word count was below average. She was disappointed; she thought she had figured it out. Mrs. Carpenter called for three students to stay after classes were dismissed. Mazy was the only one in her group to be detained. How disappointing.

Mrs. Carpenter tapped her desk with the pointer. "Ladies, you know there are only two days of classes this week. Don't get lazy. You must make every effort to stay on task." She set the timer. "Now, fifteen minutes without stopping."

Mazy let her fingers fly, but her mind was far away from her typewriter. During Saturday's croquet match, Loyal had mentioned a group trip to High Bridge. Several of his friends would be taking a train excursion there on Friday. He invited all of them to come along. Of course, they had all jumped at the chance.

She turned the page of her exercise book, keeping her eye on the print. It reminded her of the lady who played the piano at church. She could flip a sheet of her music with one practiced hand while not missing a note with the other. It always looked so elegant. But the page Mazy was turning flipped back, costing her precious seconds.

Pay attention! Pay attention! she reminded herself while clacking away. She squinted at the book. What was that line? Why hadn't she chosen a familiar drill? This was all *Q*s and *V*s and lots of punctuation. It didn't make sense.

What would she wear on the train? Everyone had already seen all her outfits. It would be fun to have something new. Since there would be time for shopping, maybe she'd see what Suzanne's had in the window, but mightn't that set Eva off?

Finally the dinger sounded. Mazy let her hands relax while studying her work. The drill was so odd, she couldn't really tell how she had performed. Saying a little prayer, she pulled her paper from the machine, dusted the keys, and covered it. She felt like a slacker and hoped that she had not disappointed Mrs. Carpenter. For sure, she'd find red marks all over the test tomorrow. There was nothing to do now but turn it in.

She didn't tarry to commiserate with her classmates as she might have done on another day. She wanted to find the other girls and then get back to her room and look through her things. Surely she could come up with something different to wear.

Mazy headed toward the library to catch up with her friends. Nobody was in the mood for their studies since this was a half week, but it was a good place to assemble. They often looked at magazines or the newspaper. Mazy hurried up the wide stone steps and entered the hushed, cool building.

Polly waved her over to the table they had

commandeered. "Look," she said, pointing to a spread in the local paper. "There are pictures from the Fourth of July celebration. Guess who's featured with Loyal Chambers?"

Mazy's hand went to her throat at the thought of suddenly being the center of attention. She could feel herself coloring, but what fun.

It was a very good picture of Loyal . . . and Eva. She was the embodiment of sophistication, even in the grainy black-and-white. Standing, Loyal leaned over her shoulder in the photograph while, sitting, Eva looked directly into the lens as if she'd had her likeness captured a thousand times before. If Mazy hadn't known better, she would have thought they were the perfect couple.

"And look, Mazy," Polly said, pointing to another frame. "Here's one of us, but you're sort of hidden."

Indeed, there they were — Polly and Mazy, who had a cone of blueberry ice stuck in her face. Her tongue had been purple for hours after that treat.

"You look like a clown," Eva said.

"I do sort of," Mazy said, pretending she wasn't stung. "It would have been better if I had been wearing the cone on my head."

"We had fun, didn't we?" Polly said.

"Thankfully, when I saw the camera lens pointing at us, I had the good sense to hide behind my parasol," Ernestine said.

"You should have put it in front of Mazy," Eva said.

"Meow," Polly said.

"It would have been a kindness," Mazy replied. She would not let Eva best her. It was understandable that Eva would be a little jealous because Loyal had picked Mazy. She would surely get over it in time. Mazy would have to be extra kind until then.

When they got back to the house, Mazy went right upstairs to her room. She buried her nose in the vase of fragrant pink roses. Taking the blue ribbon from her pocket, she let it slip through her fingers, calmed by the silky feel of it. When she was little, she'd had a small quilt made of silk squares. Each square was decorated with an embroidered heart. She had rubbed it raw. Molly had one also, but hers remained pristine in Mama's blanket chest. Mama said Mazy always loved everything to pieces.

She had picked up the vase to take it to the bathroom for fresh water when she noticed the box on the dressing table bench. It was a square pasteboard carton addressed to her. The return address was Lilly's, but oddly there was no postmark. She finished with the flowers, then untied the string on the box and pried up the flaps. It held the clothes she had asked Lilly to send. There were several dresses and even underthings as well as cotton stockings. Thoughtful as ever, Lilly had included a darling straw bonnet. Mazy could hardly wait to see Cinnamon's face when she saw the things that were just for her.

After supper, she showed Mrs. Pearl the clothes and asked when she thought Cinnamon might come by again.

"It was left on the porch this morning. It's really good of you to get those things for Cinnamon, Mazy. Poor little thing sure needs them."

Mazy held up a dress. "Do you think this will fit?"

"I expect so. We'll make them work. I'm a good hand with a needle and thread."

"Look, Mrs. Pearl. Won't she look pretty in this hat?"

"How do you know Cinnamon Spicer, Mazy?"

Mazy told her housemother about the girl's visits with her at Dr. Chambers's house.

Mrs. Pearl tied a bow in the bonnet's

strings. "I didn't know she worked there. But that's typical of the doctor — gives with one hand and takes away with the other."

Mazy wasn't sure what Mrs. Pearl meant, but she'd rather not ask. "Cinnamon's very smart," she said instead.

"Yes, maybe too smart for her situation. I've given her numerous things, but I think she sells them."

"To take care of her father?"

"I suspect so. I know he's fallen on hard times."

"That's so sad," Mazy said, nearly moved to tears.

"Sometimes life is sad," Mrs. Pearl said.

"That's why we have to look out for one another."

Tuesday was rain, rain, rain — great cloud-bursts that came in with rolls of thunder and cracking lightning. Wednesday was more of the same — puddles everywhere and gutters overflowing.

"It better be nice tomorrow," Polly said as the girls came in from their half day of class.

Mazy furled her umbrella and stuck it into the metal-lined tray that was part of the hall tree. "Rain, rain, go away, come again another day."

"Wouldn't you think," Ernestine said,

"that someone could figure out a way to manipulate the weather?"

"No showers, no flowers," Mazy said.

"That's for April," Polly said. "This is July."

"Why are we standing here in a wet knot?" Ernestine said. "Let's go plan our excursion."

"I have a better idea," Mazy said. "Let's go to the train station and purchase our tickets."

"There's no need to go ahead of time like a bunch of local yokels," Eva said. "They'll still have tickets on Friday."

Mazy bit her tongue. She had prayed for patience and love, but it wasn't coming easily, mostly because Eva insisted on trying the patience Mazy had so fervently asked for.

It was late afternoon on Thursday before Mazy had a chance to hop the trolley and go to Cedar Bottoms to deliver her package to Cinnamon. Mrs. Pearl had drawn a little map on the back of a used envelope, and Mazy kept it close at hand. The trolley line didn't go that far out, so Mazy would need to walk part of the way. She remembered that Cinnamon lived on Juniper Street. It shouldn't be too hard to find. She was ever so glad it wasn't raining.

The box got heavy during the first mile and heavier still during the second, but the map was true and she found the clutch of dwellings easily enough. She looked for street markers. There were none, just one muddy street jutting off another muddy street. She kept to the grass along the side of the road.

A woman sweeping her porch nodded a friendly hello Mazy's way.

"Could you help me, please?" Mazy said. "I'm looking for Juniper Street."

The lady pointed with the handle of her broom. "You're almost there. See the store? Make a left there."

Mazy rested the box on her hip. "Thank you so much."

"You looking for the Spicers?"

"Why, yes. How did you know?"

"Just hoping," the lady said, returning to her task.

Mazy soon saw why, for as she turned on the street just beyond the store, she saw a man sitting on an overturned milk crate in a muddy yard. Cinnamon was running in and out of a broken-down house with bits and pieces of household goods, piling them up in the yard.

Two men jammed a chest of drawers

through the open front door. Cinnamon struck one of them on the head with a ladle. "Be careful with that," she cried. "That belonged to my mother."

The man didn't react, just kept on pulling until the piece of furniture squeaked through; then he and the other man carried it down the porch steps and set it alongside a kitchen table and two narrow bedsteads. A ruptured mattress spilled feathers onto the grass.

"That it?" one man asked.

Cinnamon dragged a humpbacked trunk out the door and across the porch. It screeched like sled runners against rock.

The man reached to take a handle. "Let me help you with that."

"You've done enough!" she said, smacking his hand away. "I only needed five more dollars. I can't believe you'd do this over five dollars."

The man pushed his hat back on his head. "Not my choice, ma'am. Sheriff's orders." He tacked a yellow notice beside the door. Mazy could read the big black letters from the road. *EVICTION NOTICE.*

"I need the key," the man said.

"I never had a key." Cinnamon ran over to the man sitting on the crate. "Pap, do you have a key?"

With effort, her father fished a door key
from the breast pocket of the rusty-looking
suit coat he wore. Cinnamon slapped it into
the man's hand. "You're not going to make
me cry," she said.

"That is not my intent, ma'am," he said,
turning the key in the lock. "Sorry about
this. I'm just doing my job."

"Lousy way to make a living — off the
backs of others," Cinnamon said.

"Sometimes," he said, following the other
man down the steps.

"Wait," Mazy said, surprising everyone.
"Can't you move Mr. Spicer under the
shade tree while we figure out what to do?
It's terribly hot out here."

The men dragged one of the bed frames
under the oak tree in the side yard and
covered the springs with an Army blanket.
Gently, they carried the ill gentleman and
helped him lie down. "Thank you," he said
as if they had done him a great kindness.

One of the men took a coin from his pants
pocket and tucked it in Mr. Spicer's hand.
"God bless you," Mr. Spicer wheezed, obviously fighting for breath. The man took him
under the arms and helped him sit up, resting against the headboard like a rag doll.

Mazy hadn't realized she was still holding
the box until it cut into her arms. "Oh,

Cinnamon," she said. "What are you going to do?"

"The deacons and the preacher are coming," she said. "They'll help us. What are you doing here, Miss Mazy?"

"It feels silly now, but I brought you some things. I can see it's not nearly enough."

"Can I look?" Cinnamon asked.

Mazy unfolded the box flaps. "It's just some dresses and things. I was thinking you might like to have them. You make such good use of old things."

Cinnamon fingered the bow on the bonnet. "It's real pretty. You should go now, Miss Mazy. It'll be dark soon."

"I can't leave you like this. Please let me help."

Cinnamon unfolded each dress, each muslin slip and pair of cotton hose. "The house the church ladies are fixing up for us is much nicer than this one. Right, Pap?" she called out to her father. "It's over on Aspen. We can stay there until I find us a different place." She set the bonnet on her head and gave Mazy a crooked grin. "Now I really look like you, Miss Mazy."

Mazy could see right through the confident face Cinnamon was putting on. She was sure Cinnamon was trying to make things easier for her father. It was the bravest thing Mazy had ever seen. "I could help you more, Cinnamon. I have a little money."

Cinnamon shook her head. "Mrs. Pearl is giving me a job doing laundry, so we'll catch up. I start tomorrow and it's not even Monday. She says she can sign me up with lots of ladies, and once I prove myself, I can move on up to cleaning houses."

"What about your father?"

"Pap just needs his easing medicine and he'll be right as rain. This is not the first time he's had a spell."

Mazy hoped she was right.

A horse pulled a wagon up the road. Mud flew up from the wheels when they stopped. Several men and boys hopped off the side and began to move things, making short work of it. They lifted Mr. Spicer, bed and all, and loaded him on the wagon before fastening the tailgate. "We're ready if you are, Miss Spicer," the driver said.

A boy took the pasteboard box. Cinnamon climbed into the wagon. She waved until the horse turned the corner.

CHAPTER 25

The trip to High Bridge was not nearly as much fun as Mazy thought it would be. Loyal sat two seats behind her with some fellows he knew. They were loud and rambunctious, causing some of the other passengers to cast disparaging looks that way. *It will be better,* she thought, *when we get to the park.* The girls had packed a picnic basket full to overflowing. Last evening they'd baked a chocolate cake. Polly carried it separately in an old hatbox of Mrs. Pearl's. Mazy hoped it would get there in one piece.

The good thing was that she had found a dress she had never, ever worn, though she didn't know why she'd even brought it to Lexington. The floral organdy frock had lace trim and made her look like a twelve-year-old. She'd cinched the waist with a white patent belt she'd borrowed from Ernestine, which helped a little. Nothing would help her eyes, however. She'd cried so much after leaving Cinnamon that she'd wakened this morning with eyes that were red and puffy.

She leaned her head against the window and let the rhythmic clack of the train wheels soothe her. Polly had moved up to crowd in with Ernestine and Eva. They seemed to be having a good time without her.

Behind her, Loyal was regaling the guys with a story about some of his tenants. That's what he called them: *tenants.* Mazy guessed that meant renters. He didn't sound as if he cared about them at all.

"You wouldn't believe what I put up with," he said. "Seems like you should be able to pitch them out without a question, but you have to go through the sheriff's office. Why they give deadbeats rights, I don't know. It's my property, after all."

"Right," one of the guys said. "Next time call us. We'll help you bust them up." They chuckled, all bravado. Mazy doubted Loyal needed their help. He would keep everything on the up-and-up.

"Anyway," Loyal continued, "they got put out last night. I wash my hands of them. Good riddance to bad rubbish."

Mazy's heart squeezed tight. Was he speaking of the Spicers? When he had told her about his business, she imagined he was talking about criminals and layabouts, not folks like Cinnamon and her father. Suddenly she wished she were anywhere but here.

The path to the park that had been so pretty only weeks before was pocked with oily puddles. Swarms of mosquitoes darted about, and the sun beat down, enveloping them in humid, stifling heat.

At the end of the path, a gate was closed and padlocked. "That beats all," one of the fellows said. "What do we do for fun now?"

"Let's go to the railroad trestle," another suggested. "That's always good for a laugh."

Ernestine had the picnic basket. "I'm not going up there," she said.

"Me either," Polly said, slapping at her ear.

"You fellows go ahead," Loyal said. "I'll catch up." He took the basket. "Ladies, follow me. I know the perfect spot to eat." He escorted them along a winding, tree-lined trail that led down to the river and to wooden tables with attached benches. Two of the tables were already occupied. "This is better anyway — no mosquitoes and plenty of shade. And there is still a table available."

"I hope the cake hasn't melted," Polly said.

"Mazy, take a walk with me?" Loyal asked.

She followed him even closer to the river, gathering her thoughts, knowing she had to confront him.

Other people walked along the bank commenting on the wildness of the river. One mother grabbed her son by the arm and pulled him away when he ventured too close.

"Beautiful, isn't it?" Loyal said. "Would you believe this is a popular spot for swimming? There's usually a nice wide beach. We can come back when the river's down — try it again."

He bent down, trying to look into her eyes. She turned her head. Fresh tears clouded her vision — tears of disappointment this time.

"Mazy, look at me. What's wrong?"

"I need to ask you something, Loyal," she said, keeping her voice low so others couldn't hear.

"Ask me anything," he said.

"I overheard a conversation between you and your mother at the Fourth of July party. I was eavesdropping and I shouldn't have been, but I need to know —"

"I'm sure I can explain," he said, cutting

367

her off. "What exactly did you hear?"

"Something about a girl being perfect for you and something about a will and how you had to marry before you could inherit." Her voice fell to a whisper. "It made me feel as if you are only pretending to like me. It feels like I am part of a bigger plan hatched by you and your mother."

"I'm so sorry you heard that, Mazy. But listen, my feelings for you are true. I've never felt this way before. I promise you."

"So what does it mean, then? About a will and an inheritance?"

He closed his eyes and took a deep breath before he looked at her again. "It's about business, Mazy, and money — it's always money. My father's will is written in such a way that I can't own any of the property until I'm married — which to my father meant grown-up and responsible. My mother wants everything settled. She's worried that I won't get what's coming to me if something should happen to her. She only meant you are good for me — that she hopes you are the one."

Dirty water frothed and tumbled down the riverbed, churning like Mazy's emotions. She couldn't imagine it ever being calm enough for swimming. The sound was like low thunder but oddly soothing, mesmerizing. She took a step closer.

"Be careful," he said. "The bank is slick."

She couldn't look at him. "Did you put the Spicers out of their house?"

"Yes, I did. I had to."

"How could you do such a thing?"

"But I told you about it," he said, his voice perplexed. "It's just business. They didn't pay their rent."

"I'm so disappointed in you," she said, "and in myself."

"Surely we can get past this," he pleaded. "I know you have feelings for me too."

"I've been so foolish," she said. "We're too different. I don't know why I didn't see that from the start."

He put his hands on her shoulders. "Come on, Mazy. Don't be so stubborn. You're my girl. I love you."

She shrugged him off . . . and slipped on the wet grass . . . and fell backward down the steep bank and into the rushing, tumbling river.

"Mazy! Mazy!" she heard Loyal screaming from the riverbank. "Somebody help!"

Like a leaf caught in an eddy, she floated on the surface, buoyed by her organdy dress. She watched people gathering on the bank and saw Polly running. As her father had instructed when he taught her to swim,

369

Mazy raised her arm to signal distress. She tried to swim, but the eddy turned into a whirlpool that twirled her around like a tornado, disorienting her, clouding her senses, and she went under. She felt the river bottom against her back, but as fast as the vortex had taken her down, it twirled her back up again. She gulped air and kicked hard against the sucking current before she went back down. The whirlpool released its death grip and sent her sliding along the bottom of the river. Rough rock scoured her back and tore into her legs. She feared her lungs would explode just before she bobbed to the surface, gobbling air and dirty water.

There were angels on the bank — her mother and Molly, Lilly and Mrs. Pearl with a basket of kittens. Mazy struggled to release them from fear and worry — to tell them she was okay and ready to meet her Lord. She was washed clean and forgiven — sailing along on grace. Heaven was so near. She tried to lift her head so she wouldn't lose sight of her dear ones, but it was too heavy. The water felt soft and comforting, lapping at her with kind fingers, calling her into its deep. She relaxed and let the river take her.

CHAPTER 26

Funny how things work out, Chanis thought as he drove through the pretty little town of Mount Olivet in Robertson County on his way back to Lexington. With its rolling hills and green meadows, the area reminded him of home, minus the mountains and the coal smoke. He was in no hurry to speak to Mazy, so he'd taken a detour after dropping Frank Cheney off at his sister's in Maysville along the Ohio River. He wanted to see as much as possible of this part of Kentucky.

Talking to Frank during the trip had cleared his head. He knew Frank could talk — man, did he have a story for everything — but he hadn't known that the man could also listen. Neither had he known how desperately he'd needed another set of ears. He'd kept his own fears and frustrations so close to the vest since his father died that they threatened to crush him.

As the miles accrued, against all suitability

and common sense, Chanis had found himself spilling his guts to Frank Cheney, a known criminal. He was sure he'd broken all kinds of official sheriff codes of conduct by doing such, but once he started, it was no holds barred.

They'd stopped at a fruit and vegetable stand along the road, where Chanis purchased a bag of summer apples. It was one of those honor system stands where you left your money in a coffee can. He'd seen Cheney eyeing the rusty bank — easy money.

"That's just plain stupid," Frank said. "They're asking folks to pick them off."

In the distance was a white farmhouse with green shutters. The barn was red and looked freshly painted. There was a weather vane in the shape of a horse on the peaked roof. Good, salt-of-the earth farm people lived here.

"They trust you, Frank."

Frank shoved his hands in his pockets. "Hmm."

They rolled on. Chanis told him about the killings at the still and about his own hesitation when it came to Junior — how he could not let the boy's fate rest in the hands of the keyed-up federal agents that night, but how he couldn't just let him go scot-free. His stomach still churned when he thought of it.

Frank grew quiet. "I wonder how my life might have been different if there'd been one man that talked to me, that cared for me as much as you cared for that boy," he said, plucking a piece of fruit from the bag on the floorboard of the truck. "You probably don't know, but you've made me want to be a better man."

Chanis laughed. "What about that fruit stand, Frank?"

Frank juggled the apple between his beefy palms. "Thinking ain't the same as doing, Sheriff. If that was so, there's not a man alive who wouldn't be incarcerated."

"True enough," Chanis allowed.

Frank ate the apple in three bites and tossed the core out of the moving truck. "I'm just like Johnny Appleseed," he said. "You know that story?"

"I do."

"I'll bet you didn't know he was a missionary as well as a conservationist."

"I think I had heard that somewhere — church based out of Sweden, right?"

"Well, I bet you didn't know that he actually planted his trees in gardens, not flung willy-nilly along the road."

"I knew that too," Chanis said.

"Did you know his apples were favored

for making applejack?"

Chanis gave up. "I didn't know that. Doesn't sound very tasty."

"Drinking's not about the taste, Sheriff. Anybody tells you that, they're pulling your leg."

It had been dusk before they passed a wooden road sign: *Twenty miles to Maysville.* "Mind if I give the rest of these to my sister?" Frank asked, nudging the bag of apples at his feet.

"Help yourself. Say, Frank, I've been wondering about your sister. You told me she didn't know where you were — that you didn't want to embarrass her — yet you're going to her house."

Frank linked his fingers and cracked his knuckles. "I don't know how she found me, but I'm glad she did. Man, I'll tell you what; it's bleak sitting in the hoosegow without a friend in the world. Drives men crazy; makes them mean."

His words struck a chord with Chanis. Suddenly he knew what he was meant to do. "That makes good sense. Hey, flip open the glove box. There's something in there that I want you to have."

Frank took out the Bible. "No, now, Sheriff, you don't want to be giving your Bible away."

"Take it, Frank. It's freely given, just like the blood of the Lamb. If you have the Word, you'll always have a friend."

There was a light in the window of Frank's sister's house. Frank hefted the sack of apples like it was gold bullion. "Thanks for this," he said, then raised the Bible and added, "and for this. I will treasure it." He shoved the truck door open with his massive shoulder. "Take care of yourself."

"Send me a word now and then," Chanis said. "I'd like to know how you're doing."

Frank leaned in through the open window and punched Chanis in the arm. "Will do, buddy. Thanks again."

Chanis had spent the first night in a hotel right on the river; after that he'd let the road lead him wherever it would for a couple of days. He bought a fishing pole and other supplies at a general store. "Fish ain't biting. Creek's too high and the river's muddy," the storekeep had warned, but he didn't care, for what he wanted was time to sit on the bank and think. When the sun shone, he fished (the storekeep's prediction proved true) and hiked, and on the one day it rained hard, he sat in the truck and enjoyed the sound of the rain thrumming against the roof. He was thankful he had

had the time for prayer and reflection.

After his drive through Robertson County, feeling refreshed in body and soul, he'd stopped for the night at an inn in Paris. It was just a short drive from Lexington, and he had things to do there before he headed back to the mountains. Most importantly, Mazy deserved to know he understood that she cared for someone else. She deserved a decent good-bye. He had jumped the gun in their relationship — she had never promised to be more than friends. Regardless of how sad it made him, it was her right to be with whoever made her happy, even if it was a sappy dude in white pants.

After he saw Mazy, he'd swing by the seminary, where he hoped to be enrolled next year. He'd done well in school, but he wasn't sure what was required to become a chaplain in the prison system. It might take years, but he was determined. He could rent his place and use the income to defray his expenses. That wouldn't be enough, he knew, but he could work nights and weekends. Finally everything he'd been through made perfect sense. He was grateful.

Following the smell of woodsmoke, Chanis found Mrs. Pearl in the backyard of the boardinghouse. She and the Spicer girl appeared to be cleaning out the old shed — the one Mazy had found the kittens under. "Hey," he called, hoping not to startle them.

Mrs. Pearl beamed when she saw him. "Goodness, Sheriff Clay, what brings you here?"

"Morning, Mrs. Pearl, Miss Spicer. What are you up to?"

Mrs. Pearl pitched a battered hamper onto a trash fire. "We're fixing up the shed to start a laundry service. I think the girls planned a picnic just to get out of helping," she laughed.

"Mazy's gone to High Bridge," Cinnamon said in her direct manner.

"I've heard of it," he said. "Tallest span of railroad bridge in the world."

"I didn't want them to go," Mrs. Pearl said, rubbing her arms. "The river's way up, what with all the rain we've had. I've had a bad feeling all morning."

"Maybe I'll drive up there," Chanis said. "I've always wanted to see the bridge, and I really need to have a word with Mazy."

"I wish you would," Mrs. Pearl said. "You know where it is? It's kind of hard to find if you're not familiar."

"No, but I'm sure I could find it."

"I could show you," Cinnamon said. "We used to live near the bridge. Pap liked to fish in it."

"That's a great idea," Mrs. Pearl agreed. "That would put my mind at ease."

"Let me get my bonnet," Cinnamon said.

Chanis sure hadn't planned on taking anyone along, but how could he say no? He had intended to come back to town anyway. What could it hurt to let her come with? He noticed she didn't look as rough today — it was her clothing. He guessed Mrs. Pearl must be taking Miss Spicer under her wing. That was good.

The girl hung on to her bonnet all the way to High Bridge, but she didn't want Chanis to slow down. He was glad she had come along, for she told him shortcuts — more than likely shaving an hour from the trip.

Chanis could tell something had happened from the moment he parked the truck on the side of the road behind some other vehicles. There was a commotion from beyond the trees that lined the parking area, which was blocked off due to standing water. What had they been thinking when they put the parking lot so close to the river?

"Wonder what's going on," he said to Cinnamon as he opened the truck door for her.

"Folks come here to view the river when it's high. You can see the most interesting things going by."

Suddenly a high-pitched scream rent the air.

"Come on," Chanis said as he took off toward the river.

Polly saw him before he saw her. She flew toward him, screaming and waving her arms.

"She's in the river! Mazy's in the river! She drowned!"

"Mazy?" Chanis said, unbelieving. "When?"

"Just now, minutes ago. Hurry!"

People milled around on the bank. One guy was lugging a branch down to the water. Another waded in but turned back when the current nearly swept him off his feet.

The muddy river roiled angrily down the bed. Chanis unbuckled his gun belt and kicked off his boots. "Where is she?" he yelled. "Where'd she go in?"

The guy who'd nearly lost his footing scrambled up the embankment. "We were right here. She was right here when she fell." He sank to his knees in the grass. "It's so cold," he sobbed. "I didn't know it would be so cold."

Chanis had unbuttoned his shirt, and Polly tugged it from his arms. He scanned the water before he began to jog along the river. The current was swift and menacing, and the water filled with debris. Maybe she'd been swept up on the shore downstream. He knew she could swim, but what match would a body be against this monster?

"Sheriff, here! Here! Sheriff, here!" He heard Cinnamon screaming before he saw her. A dead tree had fallen from the bank into the river. Cinnamon was crawling across the trunk, only feet above the raging flood.

"Lord, help us," Chanis prayed as he plunged feetfirst into the water. Keeping one hand on the trunk for balance, he treaded water and inched toward Mazy. She was wedged between two branches. He dove under the water and came up just beneath her body. With one arm around her waist, he tugged as hard as he could but couldn't budge her. She was held fast in the arms of the tree.

He came up beside her, heaving for air.

Cinnamon was just above him on the trunk. "You need to reach around her," she said. "See? Her belt is caught. I could see it when you moved her."

Cinnamon was right. The belt had snagged on a branch and kept Mazy from being swept away. Such a small thing, but it made the difference between life and death.

Once he freed Mazy, Chanis took one second to cradle her face in his hands. Her eyes pleaded with him as her lips moved silently.

"Shh, sweetheart," he said. "You're safe."

Other hands helped him get her to shore, where a blanket was spread upon the grass. When he gently laid her down, someone covered her tattered dress with a jacket. There must have been twenty people on the bank and not a dry eye in the crowd. One woman was singing, and another shouting, "Praise the Lord!"

Careful to keep Mazy covered, Chanis turned her on her side. Cinnamon knelt beside them and held Mazy's head while she spewed a bucketful of dirty water. Chanis had never seen a more beautiful sight.

Mazy struggled to sit up, and Chanis gathered her in his arms. Her lips trembled with effort, and he bent his head in order to hear.

"Take me home," she said. "Oh, Chanis, take me home."

CHAPTER 27

Mazy woke to the sound of her sister's voice. Her throat was so raw even a whisper hurt her. Instead she waved her hand.

Lilly handed a chart to a nurse and hurried to Mazy's side. "Call Dr. Chambers," she said. "Tell her Miss Pelfrey is awake."

She took Mazy's hand. "Well, hello, sweetheart. How are you feeling?"

Mazy raised her eyebrows and mouthed, *"Where am I?"*

"You're in the Lexington hospital. You've been very ill with pneumonia. But you're going to be fine."

Mazy shuddered. "I drowned, Lilly," she whispered hoarsely.

"Almost — you almost did, but you were too strong for that old muddy river." She lifted Mazy's head and held a glass to her lips. "Take a sip, even if it hurts. We need to get some fluids in you."

Mazy sipped and swallowed. Surely there

were shards of glass in her throat. "The twins?"

"They're fine. Their spots are almost gone. Thankfully, when Chanis called with the news, Tern had just returned from a trip. It's the first time he has had Julia and Simon on his own. Do you think he'll survive?"

Mazy wiggled her hand in a maybe-yes-maybe-no gesture before managing to ask, "Chanis?"

"He didn't leave your side for two days, Mazy, except when one or another of the nurses chased him out; then he sat in a chair right outside the door. He's just left to get some rest." Lilly settled a stethoscope against Mazy's chest. "Deep breaths. In . . . out . . . in . . . out. Good," she said with a smile. "Much better."

"So many flowers. So pretty," Mazy said.

"Do you want me to read the cards to you?"

Mazy nodded.

"These lilies are from your classmates and Mrs. Carpenter." Lilly tugged another card from a tiny envelope. "This mixed arrangement is from Dr. Chambers and her son, Loyal — very nice. Chanis brought the daisies. And this little wildflower bouquet is from Cinnamon Spicer. I was here when she brought them. Chanis said she helped to rescue you."

Mazy covered her eyes with her hands. She could feel tears leaking out. "Cinnamon's life is so hard."

Lilly smoothed the hair back from Mazy's forehead. "You're not to worry about anything right now, Mazy. Mrs. Pearl has taken the girl under her wing and will see that she learns a trade. We'll keep in touch about the situation. After we had a consult, Dr. Chambers went to check on her father. He's actually here — just down the hall in the men's ward. We were fortunate to get a private room for you. I believe Dr. Chambers pulled some strings."

Mazy caught her sister's hand. "I need to tell you something, Lilly."

Lilly pulled a chair up close to the bed. "I want you to rest your voice, Mazy."

"But I'll pop if I don't tell you. I can only whisper anyway."

"I've talked to Chanis and your friends Polly and Ernestine, so I believe I already know the gist of the story."

"I've been really stupid."

"No, not stupid, just young and a little naive. You're not to blame yourself for any of this."

Mazy adjusted the sheet that covered her.

It smelled faintly of bleach and starch — not an unpleasant odor. "I fell for a handsome face and a pretty line, Lilly. I thought Loyal Chambers was the one."

"I'm sure he can be charming, Mazy. He is very sorry about disappointing you. However, I did see a boot print on his backside."

Mazy's eyes widened.

"I'm teasing, sweetheart. Chanis handled him like the gentleman he is." She scooted her chair even closer and dropped her voice. "Mazy, listen to me. You don't owe your affections to anyone — not even Chanis Clay. You need time not only to recover from two serious illnesses in a very short period, but also to find yourself. It is time for all of us to step back and stop putting our expectations on you."

Mazy turned toward her sister. "Lilly, I need you to expect things from me — else I'm like a feather in the wind, blowing here and there with no place to alight."

"Rest awhile, Mazy, and then we'll fix you up a bit before visiting hours. Your friends are dying to see you."

"I want to go home, but I hate to miss my classes. I was just getting the hang of typing."

"We're leaving by train in the morning.

You can practice your skills on my type-writer while you are recuperating. You'll need something to keep you from being bored."

"Lilly, I don't think I will ever be bored again."

The train station was bustling with folks coming and going, saying tearful farewells or welcoming hellos. The air seemed charged with anticipation. A big chalkboard announced departures and arrivals as clerks slipped tickets across counters and porters hauled trunks and suitcases around on flat-bed trolleys. Mazy was sure she stuck out like a sore thumb with her head wrapped in gauze and a lap blanket tucked around her legs. Lilly said she had twenty stitches in the back of her head and many more on the backs of her legs from being dragged along the riverbed. It would be a while before she could wear stockings again.

It seemed like everyone she'd ever met in Lexington had turned out to see her off at the depot. Many of the girls from school had come, even though she didn't know them well, along with the minister from the church she had attended and even the pharmacist from the drugstore and the lady from behind the counter who had so often made her lunch. She didn't know whether to be sad that she was leaving them behind or happy that she'd made some true friends.

Mrs. Carpenter gave her a totally unexpected kiss on the cheek and a manila folder full of typing exercises. "Don't neglect your studies," she said. "You were coming along beautifully."

Mazy stood up from her wheeled chair and hugged Mrs. Carpenter's neck. "You were always so patient with me. Thank you."

When Mrs. Carpenter stepped away, Polly and Ernestine hurried up.

"You'll come back, won't you, Mazy? As soon as you're feeling better?" Polly asked. "We'll have absolutely no fun without you."

"We'll see," Mazy said, which was what Lilly had said to her when she asked how long her recovery would take.

Ernestine took her hand and squeezed it gently. "I'll miss you, Mazy Pelfrey."

"And I you, dear Ernestine," Mazy said, suddenly bereft at the thought of losing touch with these dear friends. "You must both write to me. Promise you will."

"Of course," Polly said. "We'll do round-robins and be pen pals. Fun!"

Mazy's eyes scanned the crowd. Loyal had come by the hospital during visiting hours last evening. They had made amends and said good-byes, so she didn't expect him to see her off, but she'd hoped Eva would come. They hadn't spoken, though Ernestine had told Mazy that Eva was very shaken up by what happened at the river.

"We must go, Mazy," Lilly said while signaling another porter to push the wheelchair.

Mazy was holding back tears when Mrs. Pearl and Cinnamon Spicer hurried up.

"Dear me," Mrs. Pearl lamented. "We nearly missed you. We had a time trying to find Albert."

"Albert?" Mazy said.

Cinnamon placed a picnic hamper in Mazy's lap. "That's his name," she said, lifting one side of the hinged lid to reveal one of the tabby's kittens. "He's a prince, Prince Albert." The tiny cat looked like a dab of marmalade cuddled in a nest of toweling. "If he has an accident, just peel a layer away and toss it," she demonstrated. "And here's a half pint of milk and a saucer. He already knows how to lap it up."

Mazy took Mrs. Pearl's hand and held it to her cheek. "You are both so dear to me," she said. "I'll take good care of Albert."

"I have no doubt," Mrs. Pearl said. "And I'll take good care of Cinnamon."

"We'll take care of each other," Cinnamon

said. "Good-bye, Mazy. Good-bye."

Chanis Clay followed the train like a tin can on a string until the tracks veered away from the road. It was very hard to let Mazy out of his sight, so strong was his need to protect her. Their time together since the incident, what little of it had been spent alone, filled him with hope. Her eyes lit up whenever he walked into her hospital room. But he wouldn't push. She was still as fragile as a butterfly in cupped hands. If he wanted her to be truly his, he had to let her go.

He made a right turn toward Wilmore. The highway was well marked, and finally he felt as if he was on the straight and narrow path to fulfilling his destiny. He had an appointment with the president of Asbury College. It would be several months before he could enroll in the diploma course for nontraditional students, but he wanted to get the process started. Meanwhile, he'd give the folks of Skip Rock plenty of time to elect a new sheriff — Tully was next in line and so deserving — while he decided what to do with his house. He really hoped the city council would let him buy the truck. Old Ray had become his right arm.

In his shirt pocket he had a letter of

recommendation from the sheriff of Fayette County, who just happened to be Mrs. Pearl's brother-in-law. Hopefully he could get a part-time position with the law in Wilmore, or if not there, then maybe night shift at the jail in Lexington. *If worse comes to worst,* he thought wryly, *I could always get a job as a paper hanger.*

He trusted the Lord would help him work it out.

EPILOGUE

Mazy thought the secret garden had never looked more beautiful, and it smelled divine. Huge baskets of yellow tulips and purple irises filled in whatever bare spots there might have been among the roses and gardenias. The fish pond had been extended and now sported a fountain. Luminarias lit the brick path leading to the back of the garden. It was a lovely setting for an evening wedding.

She hadn't realized how deep the garden was. There was plenty of space for the dozens of chairs provided for guests. Dr. Chambers had asked her to sit with the family, so she took a chair on the front row. Her arms felt empty, they were so used to holding Clementine. She knew her little girl would be well cared for by her sitter, but still Mazy missed her.

Someone nudged her elbow. One of the

flower girls — a pretty-as-a-picture six-year-old Mazy had met at last night's rehearsal dinner — shyly offered a book.

"Would you sign my book for me, Miss Mazy? My mommy said I could ask."

"Do you like *A Basket Full of Kittens*?" Mazy asked, fishing in her handbag for a pen.

"Oh yes, ma'am. I like the pictures best, but the words are good too."

Mazy doodled a kitten's face before she signed, *To Elizabeth, With Love, Mazy Pelfrey Clay.* Her first book — she couldn't help but be a little bit proud of the work she'd done while she was recuperating from her illness. She handed the book back to the girl. "You look very pretty, Elizabeth."

"Will you draw me another book, Miss Mazy?"

Smiling, Mazy retied the pink ribbon sash that belted the girl's embroidered eyelet cotton batiste frock. "I'm working on one right now."

"Okay," Elizabeth said and sauntered back up the aisle. After a few steps she turned and waved.

Mazy waved back. She surely hoped Clementine would have such good manners one day. Right now she was all about blowing bubbles with her peach or pear purees. She was a good, contented baby and easily pleased. As she often did, Mazy sent a silent prayer of gratitude heavenward. And as she always did when she thanked the Lord for Clementine, she asked Him to watch over Clara — wherever she might be.

The chairs began to fill. A string quartet made up of two men and two women strolled around the garden, and a harpist seated herself at her instrument and began to pluck the strings.

Mazy had always imagined herself being married in just such a setting — as pretty as a fairy tale. She and Chanis had set a date and picked a church. She had even designed a dress of white satin with lace trim and a floor-length veil, but then she had decided — felt compelled, actually — to attend Clementine's birth at Mama's house on Troublesome Creek.

Poor Clara, dear Clara, had turned her face away from the baby. A week after the birth, she was gone, leaving only a note:

Mazy, it's not that I don't love her. It's that I do. She has no chance with me. Her name is Clementine, after my mother. I know you'll find a good home for her. I'm sorry. Please pray for me.

When Clara left, Mama retained a wet nurse for the baby so she wouldn't have to be bottle-fed for the first few weeks, but Mazy took care of all her other needs. Every night she rocked the baby to sleep before tucking her in the cradle. Clementine would snuggle her tiny face against Mazy's neck and sigh in contentment. The feeling this stirred in Mazy's heart was ten times what she'd ever felt for her pets even though she loved them dearly.

She had fallen in love with the baby in much the same way she had fallen in love with Chanis — naturally, completely, joyfully. It was as if she had finally stepped out of her own way and let things develop as they would.

During one of Chanis's many visits to Troublesome Creek, she had broached the subject of raising Clementine with him. "A ready-made family," he said while rocking the baby girl in his arms. "What more could a fellow want?"

"A cat?" Mazy said as she lifted Prince Albert from the cradle for the hundredth time.

"Might as well get a dog too," he said in a hopeful way.

"Perfect," Mazy had said, stooping to kiss his cheek. "Prince Albert loves dogs."

The note from Clara was tucked in Mazy's Bible. Someday she'd share it with Clementine.

And so she'd worn a long purple cape of silk ottoman over her tailor-made wool suit and married Chanis in her mother's house with Lilly and Molly as attendants. February 14, 1914, had been a cold winter's day, but Daddy had had to bank the fire in the Warm Morning stove, so determined was she to wear that regal cape at her wedding.

Mazy placed her purse in her lap. She didn't really show yet, but there was the slightest strain tugging at the waist of her dress.

Dr. Chambers slipped into the chair beside Mazy.

"Everything is lovely," Mazy said.

"Yes," the doctor said. "I'm quite pleased. It has been a whirlwind. Mrs. Pearl and Cinnamon put the final crystal bead on the bride's gown last evening. Their business is doing quite well."

"They've done some alterations for me, too — wonderful attention to detail. I've heard they are so busy that they don't take in laundry anymore," Mazy said.

"More's the pity. It's hard to find a good laundress these days."

Mazy craned her neck to see who else had

arrived. Polly and her beau were seated three rows behind her. She suspected theirs would be the next wedding. Polly had snagged a job as a secretary at Asbury, and her beau took some of the same classes as Chanis. Polly rented a room just doors down from Mazy and Chanis's bungalow in the small college town of Wilmore. She often came to supper and was a great comfort to Mazy when Chanis was working late.

Dr. Chambers fanned her face with one of the pasteboard fans placed on each linen-covered chair. "We wouldn't have been so rushed, but Loyal is set on joining the Army right now! He acts as if that dreadful war in Europe is going to need American intervention any day."

The doctor's words caused a seed of unrest to burrow into Mazy's heart. "Chanis talks of joining too. He says it would be good training for a chaplain. I say there are plenty of people right here who could use his help."

Speaking of her handsome husband, Chanis stepped in front of the congregation. His eyes sought hers as they always did when they had been apart for any length of time, be it minutes or hours.

Loyal took his place beside Chanis. He

fiddled with his tie and then with the red rose on the lapel of his jacket.

"Dear boy, he's so nervous," Dr. Chambers said.

Chanis said something behind his hand. Loyal smiled. Mazy smiled too. It was an amazing blessing that the two had become friends. Chanis had led Loyal to Christ and had immersed him in Christian baptism just weeks ago.

The harpist struck a chord. Everyone stood and looked down the aisle.

"Oh, Ernestine makes a beautiful bride," Mazy said, admiring her friend dressed in white satin and Brussels lace. Her tulle veil covered her face, but as she passed by on the arm of her father, Mazy could feel her radiance.

"Yes," Dr. Chambers said. "She has grown on me."

Chanis caught Mazy's eye. "Dearly beloved . . ."

DISCUSSION QUESTIONS

1. Cinnamon describes picking garbage at the dump as "earning a living — such as it was," dismissing the perceived shame of her job. Is there any task — either in your life or someone's else — that you consider shameful? Do you think this feeling is justified?

2. Mazy says nothing when her secretarial school friends make fun of Cinnamon because she collects stuff from the garbage dump. Have you ever kept quiet when you should've spoken up? Did you regret your decision later? If you could relive that moment, what would you say?

3. Mazy isn't sure her secretarial school cohorts are her friends. Do any of the girls behave as true friends to her? What are the traits of a good friend? And how are such friends made?

4. Clara wants to run away from her past and do something different. Have you ever

wanted to do the same? How did you act on that desire?

5. Chanis Clay grows fond of the prisoner Frank Cheney. Do you find that some troubled people are endearing? Why do you think Chanis had compassion for Frank?

6. Frank tells Chanis, "I wonder how my life might have been different if there'd been one man that talked to me, that cared for me as much as you cared for that boy. . . . You probably don't know, but you've made me want to be a better man." Have you ever had the privilege of influencing someone in this way? Who in your own life has made you want to be a better person?

7. When Cinnamon prepares to bathe Mazy during her recovery, Mazy feels embarrassed about her own silly fretting, knowing this young woman has so little and never asks for anything for herself. Describe someone who has had that kind of clarifying effect on your life.

8. Loyal Chambers doesn't like the riffraff in his town and desires to tear down their homes and put up office buildings. What does this plan say about his personality and character? Do you think he's wrong in his thinking?

9. Mazy worries whether "the easy faith of her childhood" would stand up to deep trials in life. Do you believe your faith is able to stand up to life's great struggles? How do we build that kind of faith?

10. Chanis encourages Junior's mother by saying that maybe God will use the current bad scenario in Junior's life to "remind him of the path he needs to be on." Can you think of bad patches in your life or in the life of someone you love that might be used by God to find the right path?

11. Mazy takes a long time to realize who Loyal is at heart. How is your own discernment when it comes to relationships and as a judge of character? What are some ways you can develop this trait?

12. Over the course of this story, Chanis and Mazy have to figure out God's direction for them — both individually and in their relationship with each other. What did you think about where they ended up? When have you struggled to determine God's plan for your life, and what was the result?

ABOUT THE AUTHOR

A former registered nurse, award-winning author **Jan Watson** lives in Lexington, Kentucky, near her three sons and daughter-in-law.

Buttermilk Sky follows *Tattler's Branch, Skip Rock Shallows, Still House Pond, Sweetwater Run,* and the Troublesome Creek series, which includes *Troublesome Creek, Willow Springs,* and *Torrent Falls.* Chosen Best Kentucky Author of 2012 by *Kentucky Living* magazine, Jan also won the 2004 Christian Writers Guild Operation First Novel contest and took second place in the 2006 Inspirational Reader's Choice Award contest sponsored by the Faith, Hope, and Love Chapter of the Romance Writers of America. *Troublesome Creek* was also a nominee for the Kentucky Literary Awards in 2006. *Willow Springs* was selected for *Library Journal*'s Best Genre Fiction category in 2007.

Besides writing historical fiction, Jan keeps busy entertaining her Jack Russell terrier, Maggie.

Please visit Jan's website at www.janwatson.net. You can contact her through e-mail at author@janwatson.net.

The employees of Thorndike Press hope you have enjoyed this Large Print book. All our Thorndike, Wheeler, and Kennebec Large Print titles are designed for easy reading, and all our books are made to last. Other Thorndike Press Large Print books are available at your library, through selected bookstores, or directly from us.

For information about titles, please call:
  (800) 223-1244

or visit our Web site at:
  http://gale.cengage.com/thorndike

To share your comments, please write:
Publisher
Thorndike Press
10 Water St., Suite 310
Waterville, ME 04901